RACE
to
TRUTH

Book Two
of the
RUN FOR YOUR LIFE
Adventure Trilogy

This is a work of fiction. Although Bellingham, Washington, is a real town, Quarrel Tayson Laboratories is a fictional company. Names, characters, places, and incidents are products of the author's imagination or are used fictitiously and are not to be construed as real. Any semblance to actual events, locales, organizations, or persons, living or dead, is entirely coincidental.

WILDWING PRESS
3301 Brandywine Court
Bellingham, Washington 98226

One

The two bodies on the floor are not moving. At first I think my parents are playing an elaborate Halloween joke, punishing me for sneaking out my bedroom window to be with my friends, but then I realize the darkness surrounding them is blood, not shadow. As my brother is dragged from his bedroom by two ninjas in black clothing and facemasks, his scream shocks me out of my paralysis.

"Tana? Tana!"

I snap back to the present, and then I have to swallow hard to recover my wits. I'm at the zoo where I work, behind the tigers' enclosure, pushing the door open to exit with my cart of feline doo-doo and my cage cleaning equipment. The head cat keeper, Nathan Ransek, just smacked his own cart into mine. His contains a gory load, hacked-up body parts from what used to be a deer, judging from a cloven hoof protruding over the edge.

Post Traumatic Stress Disorder is like a warp jump. One second I am transported to another time and place, the next second, I'm back to normal. Well, as normal as I ever get.

Ransek quirks an eyebrow at me, his forehead creased

beneath his graying hair. "You okay, Tana?"

"Of course." I take a breath. "You just surprised me. And, well...ugh." I point at the bloody mess in his cart.

"Animal pickup dropped it off this morning, still warm from the highway." He tilts his head in the direction of the low grunts and growls coming from the other side of the wall, where our two tigers are pacing, eager to be let out into their habitat area. "Big score for our tabbies."

"Bad news for the deer, though," I comment.

"Life is harsh when you are prey." He grabs the handle of his cart with both hands and wheels it out of my way.

I push my equipment through the exit, careful to keep my eyes away from the puddle of red in the bottom of Ransek's cart. *Disarticulate* is the word that runs through my brain. *To separate bones at the joints, or to pull apart an argument.* That vocabulary lesson from my Wordage app this morning, along with the sloshing blood in Ransek's cart, has triggered my flashback. Now that I think about it, though, my worry started with the disturbing email message I received an hour ago:

> *Tana, here's another one from that mysterious*
> *p.a.patterson@qqq.net. IP address is from Kigali,*
> *Rwanda. Msg for Tanzania Grey: Where is Amy?*

The other messages I've received from this P.A. Patterson track back to various parts of Africa, most often Johannesburg. This is both more and less creepy than you might think. My mom grew up in Zimbabwe, and because the nitwit sportscasters insist on calling me "the African American Princess of Endurance Racing," I get fan mail from Africans who aspire to become athletes. Everything gets routed through my website, set up and maintained by my sponsors at Dark Horse Networks. I never give out my personal contact information to the public. You never know who you're dealing with on the internet.

This P.A. Patterson is more than a fan. Once, during a race, he sent me a necklace identical to the one belonging to my murdered mother, and now he's telling me that he knows her name, too. Somehow he suspects the truth that I need to hide, that four years ago I was Amelia Robinson.

The burning question: Is Patterson one of my parents' killers? Are they still hunting for me? I've worked so hard for the last four years to cover my tracks.

I've never responded to any of Patterson's messages. It haunts me that he keeps sending them. What does he want?

I wheel my cart toward the compost area to empty the mix of dirty bedding straw, leftover bones from last night's predator feedings, and animal excrement. On the way there I stop to tease Skye, the baby giraffe, holding out my hand as if I have a treat for her. I love to see her extend her eighteen-inch-long tongue. When she figures out that I have tricked her again, she snorts in disgust, jerks her head back inside the fence, and gallops to her mother.

My cell chirps like a cricket. When I pull it from my pocket and thumb it to life, the screen delivers a second message:

> *2 Tanzania Grey:*
>
> *Way2Go Extreme Team requires endurance champ*
>
> *4 mtn run, road bike, canoe. C U in Bellingham 4*
>
> *Ski2Sea? -JJ*

My first reaction: *Wahoo!*

I grew up with Ski to Sea. I've always wanted to be part of

that amazing relay race. This year, for the first time, the Ski to Sea Contest is going to include ten extreme teams of three along with the traditional eight-person teams. And this JJ—whoever *he* is—is flattering me by recognizing that I am a champion endurance racer.

My second reaction: *Oh, hell no!*

Go back to Bellingham, where my family was murdered four years ago? Where thugs in a black SUV chased me through the streets, intent on adding me to the death count?

I look a lot different now and I've reinvented myself, but I still can't risk going back there.

The word *COWARD* flashes on in my brain like a neon sign. In all caps, making it impossible to ignore.

I can't let the killers get away forever with erasing my family. I don't know who those ninjas are or why they murdered my parents. I don't know if my little brother survived.

I scan the message again. Sometimes opportunity knocks. Sometimes, like this, it whacks you up the side of your head. Maybe this is the opportunity I've been waiting for.

I'm not that fourteen-year-old kid anymore. I can't hide out forever. I take a deep breath, drag the keyboard onto the screen, and reply to JJ.

More info, pls.

-Tanzania Grey

If there are clues to follow, the trail will begin in Bellingham. The problem: the trail could end there, too.

So could my life.

Two

Some days I'm more of a chameleon than a girl. Whenever I travel by bus or train to a place where I might meet someone from my past, I like to take on different personalities to throw off any stranger who might be tracking me.

Today, a month after I accepted JJ's invitation, I am Sunita Brown. At least that's what I tell the Amtrak agent when I hand him the cash for my ticket. He barely glimpses at my fake student ID from the University of Washington.

I am dressed in a turquoise-patterned salwar kameez that sets off my bronze skin. The uber-comfy tunic and pants, with matching shawl draped over my black hair, instantly transform me into a young Asian woman. I even pasted a maroon velvet bindi with a silver diamond between my dark eyebrows. Traditional Hindu women wear red powder circle bindis, but nowadays you can get all colors and shapes in peel-off sticker packs. Quite attractive, if I do say so myself. It's crazy, how good I have become at disappearing into someone else.

Maybe I did too good a job today, because the Sikh guy sitting a few rows behind me says something to me in Hindi or

Urdu when I pass him in the aisle.

I smile and duck my head and pull my scarf closer to my face. With luck, he will think I'm shy or don't speak whatever language that was. I will stay glued to my seat until one of us gets off the train.

I hunch over my tablet computer to write an email to Emilio Santos, my soldier boyfriend. I tell him about the animal antics at home and at the zoo. It might be a while before he reads this, but whenever he gets a chance to log on to the camp computers or use his cell, he'll be happy to see a long message waiting for him. It's hard to schedule regular videochats when I'm on the west coast and he's halfway around the world. I know it's important for soldiers to connect with home, so I try to stack up messages for him when I can.

When the speaker in my train car announces Bellingham as the next stop, I realize I'm out of time and I haven't even told Emilio my big news. I quickly type *On my way 2 Bellingham 2 race in Ski2Sea day aftr 2morrow. Wish me luck, Shadow!*

I call him that because he's quiet and dark and always looks like he needs a shave. As the train slows, I click Send and then put away my tablet. I wait a few seconds for passengers to clear out, but a glance over my shoulder proves the Sikh guy hasn't moved. His destination must be Canada. Vancouver, British Columbia, is the next stop.

Shouldering my backpack, I pull out my phone so I'll look busy. I try to study all sorts of subjects whenever I can so I won't feel quite so ignorant when I'm with my friends who are lucky enough to go to college.

Wordage coughs up *Sashay—to move easily and confidently.*

As I pass the Sikh's seat, our eyes meet briefly, and then I'm out onto the platform and that encounter is over, thank heavens.

I stick my phone in my roomy salwar pocket, where it hangs heavily in the silky fabric, slapping my thigh with each step, making it difficult to *sashay*. This outfit clearly needs updating for the electronic world.

A middle-aged couple step out of the train ahead of me. I stare at their joined hands, one black, one white.

Dad. Mom.

It's a good thing that hallucination vaporizes before I reach out to them, because of course, there's no way these two could be my parents.

A flapping noise draws my attention to the banner above the station door that advertises the Ski to Sea Festival. My parents always made a big deal out of the annual relay, volunteering as support staff for local teams and cheering on their favorite racers.

Here's how the race traditionally goes: When the starter horn sounds near Mount Baker, thousands of cross-country skiers stampede away to pass their timing chips to their teammates on downhill skis or snowboards, who zoom down steep slopes until they reach the runners.

The runners switchback down the mountain highway and hand off to road bikers, who ride for forty-two miles before they tag their canoe teams on the Nooksack River. The canoeists paddle like mad to meet up with mountain bikers, who ride to the harbor. Then, in the final leg of this ninety-four mile relay, kayakers navigate windy Bellingham Bay, getting slapped around by waves of cold saltwater.

The first kayaker to land at Marine Park, run up the hill, and ring the bell wins the race for the team.

Rules for the traditional Ski to Sea teams: Each team consists of eight people: two to paddle the canoe section and one for each of the other six legs of the relay. Each team member can compete in only one leg.

As a little kid, I dreamed I would be the first to ring that bell at the end of the race. Never mind that I wasn't a kayaker back then. Heck, I also dreamed I'd be an astronaut and travel to distant planets.

Now I know I can't be an astronaut. I can't be that bell ringer, either, because I'm not yet a kayaker. But I still hope that I will be on the winning team.

Ski to Sea should get worldwide attention, but most people have never heard of it. That's probably because the course is stretched out across mountains and rivers and fields, so the race is hard to film. But even more likely, it's because no company has ever found a way to make major bucks from Ski to Sea.

There's no big money prize for the winners. Sometimes local companies donate prizes like gift certificates for pizza or sports merchandise, but so far it remains a race where athletes compete for fun, not for cash. Depending on the results this year, all of that may change.

One of my hometown heroes, Alexander Armand, has tried for the last decade to convince the Ski to Sea organizers to allow solo athletes to do all seven legs of the race. Armand is Bellingham's only Olympian (marathon and hurdles). He has skied, run, biked, and paddled the whole course by himself four and three-quarters times. He didn't get to finish his fifth attempt last year because he dropped dead of a brain aneurism in the mountain bike section.

I shrieked at that news. It was like hearing that Superman crashed into a skyscraper on his way to save humanity.

But even heroes die. I should know.

Anyhow, this year, as homage to Armand, the Ski to Sea Committee is allowing ten extreme teams to participate. The committee couldn't quite bring themselves to allow solo competitors like Armand wanted, but I think he'd still be proud.

Rules for the extreme Ski to Sea teams: Each team will consist of three athletes, who can divide up the seven legs any way they want, except that no athlete can compete in more than three legs.

Everyone is eager to see if the extremes will make better time or if they'll drop dead along the way like Armand.

Drones from two broadcast companies are going to film the whole race for the very first time. Which is probably the reason my sponsors agreed to pay for my train ticket and loaned me an uber-fancy racing bike.

It hardly snowed at all this winter in the Cascades. So the cross-country ski leg has been replaced by a parkour course where the competitors have to navigate all kinds of obstacles to get up a hill. The downhill ski/snowboard leg will be much shorter than in years past, too. To make up for that, the normally quick road-running leg has been replaced by a longer mountain run. That's where I come in.

I've never met this JJ who invited me, but he obviously knows my reputation. Sort of like archers and surfers, we endurance racers never end up in the spotlight unless we die in some spectacular way. But we have our small contingents of loyal fans.

Endurance races usually last several days. Runners pick their routes from one checkpoint to the next. The races are typically held in remote places with all sorts of challenges, including unpredictable weather and dangerous wildlife.

Extreme racing is my passion. In the last year, I won the Women's Division of the Patagonia Marathon and placed second in the Grand Canyon Challenge. And before that was the Verde Island Race, which I don't think any participant will ever forget.

So, the mountain run—I can do that in my sleep. As for the road bike section, when my housemate Sabrina and I don't carpool, I ride my bicycle the thirty-eight miles from my house to my job at the zoo. My legs are ready.

Canoeing is new to me. I've only been on a river three times, but with all the shoveling I do at work, my arms are plenty strong and my partner will probably have more experience. If this JJ believes I'm up for canoeing, then I believe it, too.

I watch to be sure the Amtrak crew unloads the box containing my loaner bike from Dark Horse Networks. It's an eye-catcher, with fancy rainbow-colored carbon wheels and the company name emblazoned across the solid material.

I'm not eager to ride this flash bike around town; it's pretty memorable. Not to mention, it's an expensive piece of equipment. I hope it's well insured.

After I watch the handlers shove the box into the luggage room for safekeeping, I use the station restroom to change from my salwar kameez into tights, pullover, and running shoes, pushing everything else into my pack. I peel off my bindi—goodbye, Sunita Brown—and shove my hair up into a ponytail under a black baseball cap. Hello, Tanzania Grey. Then I sling my pack onto my back and head out the door.

Amelia Robinson vanished from Bellingham at the age of fourteen. Since then, I have aged four years, grown nearly five inches, gained thirty pounds, and created a totally new persona. My previously short curly hair is now long enough to hang in waves down my back.

With luck, I won't look familiar to anyone.

I'm excited to be back in my home town. I've missed it terribly.

But I'm also vibrating with anxiety.

My race invitation could be a setup. JJ could be luring me into a trap.

Three

The race takes place on the Sunday before Memorial Day. It's only Thursday, but the whole town is gearing up for the holiday weekend. Red, white, and blue everywhere. A lot of houses display American flags, and Ski to Sea banners flap from many of the buildings near the train station. This evening, I've agreed to meet my teammates at an extreme team launch party near Zuanich Park, only five miles away, a quick jog along the waterfront.

Bellingham is threaded with trails for walkers, runners, and bikers. I really miss all those nice paths. It took me weeks to hack out a trail around the border of my sixty acres just to have a decent place to practice my runs.

The house I grew up in is not far away from the Amtrak station. The thought of seeing my old home again pulls me like a magnet. I have a brief debate with my cautious self about whether it might be dangerous to go there. My daredevil self argues that I have time, and my neighbors, if they remember me at all, would remember a little kid, not me.

Besides, it would be mortifying to be the first person to arrive at the extreme team party.

Instead of strolling down the sidewalks that line the streets, I cross the off-leash dog park and then slip down an alley between backyards and garages, my running shoes crunching on the gravel. The potholes seem deeper than ever. Judging by the bikes chained to trees and the spare parts lying around, it looks like Mr. Johansen still runs his bicycle fix-it shop back here.

The big oak marks the border of what was my backyard. The tree is right on the property line, so my mom and dad built this really cool fence out of interwoven branches that hug the trunk tightly on both sides. Mom told us that was a typical fence in Zimbabwe. The evergreen clematis climbing on it is lush with honey-scented white flowers that drip over the top of the fence, hanging down nearly to the ground.

The limbs of the oak extend out over the alley. I jump for the lowest one, grab on, and pull myself up. I did this hundreds of times when I was little. It's a lot easier now that I'm taller and stronger. As I settle myself next to the trunk, a Douglas squirrel chirps in alarm above my head, sounding more like an angry bird than a territorial rodent.

And there it is—our house with the big picture window overlooking the backyard. The color of the trim around the windows is now a boring white instead of the stand-out chartreuse my mom chose, but the siding and the roof are the same dull slate gray color that I remember.

The heavenly perfume of the clematis takes me back to my childhood in that backyard. My whole family used to play volleyball back here. At age twelve, I developed a dynamite overhand serve that was hard to return. Mom, Dad, and even Aaron wanted me to play on their team.

I remember one time my Dad tried to step back to hit my serve but ended up falling on his butt as the ball sailed over his head.

"Amelia," he told me, "That was a killer serve. You were born to be an athlete."

Aaron was only seven then. He jumped indignantly up and down, shouting, "Me too, me too! I have a killer serve!"

"Not yet you don't, buddy." Dad grabbed him and tickled him. "But I'm sure you can learn how to do it, too. When you're bigger, Amelia will help you."

I was peeved that my parents wouldn't allow me to keep my killer serve to myself; I didn't want to help my pesky little brother learn that or anything else I did well.

Aaron was a klutz at that age. The next time he smacked the volleyball, he bounced it off the picture window.

I stare at the reflection in that window now, remembering when I stood outside in the rain after midnight, peering in to see if it was safe to sneak back to my bedroom.

My heart clogs my throat, threatening to choke me. Blood pounds in my ears. I am fourteen-year-old Amelia Robinson again, staring at Mom and Dad lying in pools of blood on the living room carpet. As the two intruders drag my brother into the kitchen beyond, the light from the stove hood reveals a mark on one attacker's neck. Between the black turtleneck and the ski mask that covers the guy's face, there's a V-shaped tattoo, like the silhouette of a flying bird.

My brother screams. Maybe I do, too, because then the ninjas spot me and I have to run for my life.

A movement behind the picture window shatters my vision, making me gasp. But it's only a little boy in a blue sweatshirt standing there, waving.

Before I can unwrap my legs from the limb I'm sitting on, he scampers out of the house and runs across the lawn. Flattening his hands against the tree trunk, he looks up. "Watcha doin'?"

Shit. I don't need anyone reporting my presence.

"My name ith Charlie," he lisps. His front teeth are missing. "What'th yourth?"

"Edna," I manufacture on the fly.

Edna? Where does my brain come up with these names?

"Watcha doin' in our tree?"

"I thought my friend lived here."

"I live here." He points to his chest, beaming like this is an accomplishment.

"I see that." I slide to the ground on the alley side of the fence and peer at his freckled face through a hole between intertwined branches. "Well, bye."

His mouth turns down at the corners. "Doncha wanna play?"

"Sorry, no time." I turn to walk away, when I hear a woman call out from the house.

"Charlie! Who are you talking to?" She strides in our direction.

Crapola. My firefly tattoos heat up on my back, which is what happens when I feel a strong emotion, which in this case is panic. I contemplate slinking away, but that might make me look like a potential child molester or something, so I stay put as Charlie tells his mom about me thitting in their tree.

The woman squints at me. We're about the same height, a few inches taller than the top of the fence. The perfume from the clematis between us is nearly overwhelming.

"Sorry, ma'am," I say. "I thought maybe this was the house that my friend Miranda Lewis lived in, but I wasn't sure enough to knock on the door."

She tosses me a skeptical look. "We've lived here for four years now. I've never heard of anyone named Miranda."

"Oh. Well, my family moved away nine years ago. Maybe she lived here before you did?"

The woman considers this for a couple of seconds. "I suppose it's possible there were some Lewises before us, but we bought the house from SCI."

"Esseeaye?" What kind of a last name could that be? Greek, maybe?

She translates for me. "Specialty Containers Incorporated, you know, one of the Quarrel Tayson companies. My husband works for them, so they sold us this house when we got transferred from Ohio."

I can't think of anything intelligent to say about that, so I ask, "How do you like it here?"

I mean Bellingham, but she thinks I'm asking about the house, because she says, "The place could use some updates. And the yard, too. For one thing, we've got to replace this ugly fence."

She curls her fingers around one of the branches that make up the intricately woven barrier between us and deliberately snaps off a twig. Several clematis blossoms shimmy to the ground. I clench my jaw to keep my mouth from popping open in dismay.

"Did Miranda's parents work at SCI?" She's decided to be helpful. "Maybe they got transferred somewhere else."

"Maybe," I echo, still bruised by the 'ugly fence' comment. "Anyway, thanks. Sorry to bother you." I give her a stupid little wave and back up a couple of steps.

"Bye-bye, Edna!" the kid chirps.

"Bye, Charlie." I walk away down the alley, feeling like a dunce. How did SCI get our house? Or did they always own it?

In the last year, I've learned something about property ownership. My current home is owned by WildRun, Inc., a company the guys at Dark Horse Networks helped me set up after I won major money. They said it's safer for a corporation to own property than for a teenage girl to have her name on the deed.

You'd have to research WildRun, Inc. to find out that the company consists only of me, Tanzania Grey. Most people never make the connection. I like that. The more layers of obscure info, the safer I feel.

It's surreal to be back on my home turf. I almost welcome flashbacks like the one I just had in the tree. I don't have graves to visit or urns of ashes on a fireplace mantel. These memories are all I have to remind myself that my parents are truly dead.

I never saw what happened to my nine-year-old brother, Aaron.

The morning after the murders, I watched a moving van cart off every scrap of our existence from our house, even the carpets and padding. Alex and Amy and Aaron Robinson simply vanished from my world.

There was no police report. I used pay phones to call the schools and the neighbors. Everyone had been told my whole family moved with no explanation. I was reported as a runaway. When I tried to tell police what happened, they treated it like a joke. Various authorities hunted for me. I can't imagine what would have happened if they'd caught me.

My memories seem like scenes from a cheesy horror movie. Some days I even doubt my own sanity.

A plaintive mew stops me halfway down the alley. The stray cat with the ragged ear is still here. I squat down to pet him. He's battle-scarred, and his fur is rough, but no ribs are showing. Either the mouse hunting is good, or some kind neighbor is feeding him. I used to slip him food whenever I could.

"I'm glad to see you're still alive, Buddy." I pull some of the stick-tight seeds from the fur behind his ears.

He rubs against my legs, purring. After a minute, I stand up. "Don't tell anyone you saw me, okay? Stay safe."

He parks himself on his hind legs and stares at me with curious amber eyes, switching his striped tail as I walk away.

I'm going to be late to the party if I don't get a move on. I jog out of my old neighborhood through a woodland and pass onto the sidewalk that borders Village Green. As I run down the gravel path to the north and onto the waterfront trail, I am relieved that I don't see a single familiar person. After clattering down the ramp of Taylor Dock to the boardwalk over the bay, I slalom around dogs tethered to their people with stretchy leashes. Moms and dads and even toddlers push baby strollers along the wooden planks.

This scene hasn't changed in the last four years. The boardwalk is always crowded. Even bikers use it, although I always used the streets nearby so I didn't have to thread my way through all the slow pedestrians and gawking tourists.

I'm a gawker myself today, peering over the railing as I jog. Beneath the boardwalk, two kayakers paddle between the pilings, flashing in and out from one side to the other. I've only been in a kayak a couple of times, but man oh man, I wish I was down there with them now, smelling the saltwater, listening to the waves slapping the rocky shore, admiring the orange and purple starfish glued to the rocks like ocean wildflowers.

And then—whump!—I smack into a big black dog, nearly taking a header over his bulk.

He's dragging a leash behind him. He whines and raises a paw. I quickly kneel and put a hand on his sleek head. "Did I step on your foot, big guy?"

My heart does a double backflip. I'm looking into the soulful eyes of Joker, my family's black Lab. His muzzle is flecked with white hairs now. His tongue flashes out and lays a wet stripe on my cheek.

We stare at each other for a long second. I never thought I'd see my canine buddy again.

I can change my clothes and my hair and my name every hour, but I can't hide my true identity from my old dog. I wrap my arms around him. I want to pick him up and take him home. I want him to sleep beside my bed again. I want him to lay his head in my lap whenever I'm feeling sad.

"Hi, Joke." My throat feels raw as I whisper into his neck. "I'm so glad to see you. But you need to pretend you don't know me."

His tongue washes my face again, warm and sticky and familiar. When I release him, he whimpers and puts his paw on my knee. I brush his ear with my hand.

"Joker! Bad dog!" The leash attached to his collar jerks him away from me.

The voice belongs to Mrs. Talston, our former next-door neighbor. My teary nostalgia flames into fright. I quickly duck my head to hide my face under the bill of my ball cap.

"Sorry," she says. "He got away from me."

I bend to pretend-tie my shoe, murmuring in a slightly southern accent, "No problem, ma'am."

What the hell will I say if she recognizes me? I focus on my shoelaces as I try to send a telepathic message to her. *I am not Amelia Robinson. I never lived next door to you. I've never seen this dog before in my life.*

Next she shouts, "Linnie! Linnie, come here! Right now!"

I raise my chin enough to see a curly-haired little girl running away from Mrs. Talston, laughing as she dashes down the boardwalk. Mrs. Talston tugs Joker along behind her as she pursues the runaway kid. My dog looks back at me over his shoulder, his soft brown eyes clouded with confusion and hurt.

I let out the breath I was holding, but my chest continues to ache. My tears threaten to spill over. How can running into my dog be so damned painful?

I turn to face the bay, curl my hands around the railing, and do some stretches while I wait for my eyes to clear. I suck in ten slow breaths as I remind myself that I am Tanzania Grey, Ski to Sea contestant, visitor. Just another jogger on this boardwalk.

The kayakers have paddled further out into Bellingham Bay now. They are black silhouettes against the setting sun glancing off the water. In front of their boats, I see the rounded head of a harbor seal pop up from beneath the waves.

The overwhelming familiarity of every detail of this place fills me with such longing that I feel lightheaded and nauseous. Is this what they mean by homesick?

When I can compose my face again, I jog on down the boardwalk, keeping my chin down and cautiously examining each approaching person from beneath my cap.

Amelia Robinson no longer exists. I can't afford to have any more close calls like running into Joker and Mrs. Talston.

The boardwalk empties into Boulevard Park, where parents grill hot dogs and burgers while their kids run barefoot in and out of the seawater lapping at the small beach. Littler kids climb on the pirate ship structure. I remember my brother standing in the bow, pretending to be captain, and me jerking him down so I could take his place.

Clouds scuttle across the horizon over the bay. The end of May is not quite summer in the Pacific Northwest. Grandparents and visitors from warmer climes sit hunched in fleece and windbreakers, as close to the charcoal grills as they can get without catching on fire.

A newer boardwalk on the north side of Boulevard Park connects with yet another waterfront park near downtown Bellingham.

If my family hadn't been murdered, I would be graduating from high school in a couple of weeks and right now I'd be planning to party hard.

But then I would never have found my foster mother Marisela or her nephew Emilio. I would never have become an endurance racer, so I wouldn't have traveled to exotic places. I would never have met my best friend Bash. I wouldn't have my own house. I wouldn't have Bailey.

I trot across the waterfront railroad tracks and dash on down the sidewalks toward the city center.

Most of downtown Bellingham looks the same as it did when I left. A lot of historic crumbling buildings on my right. On my left, the newer waterfront developments, built after all the old mills and fish processing plants were torn down. The glass and steel QTL headquarters, where my mom worked, still the tallest building in Bellingham at twenty stories, gleams blue and silver against the sunset.

Maritime Heritage Park, with Whatcom Creek spilling down its stairstep greens, is still home to loitering bums. One guy who desperately needs a shave and a laundromat salutes me with his paper-bagged bottle. His ragged friend whistles through a gap in his teeth and then yells, "Baby, baby!"

Ugh. Are they are the same losers that lived there when I was a kid? I know these guys are more sad than scary, but they add a major dash of ugly to such a pretty park.

I slow to a walk along the marina pathway to cool off as I near my destination—a harborside café where the extreme teams are meeting.

The door is propped open onto the sidewalk. The lights are on inside. I peer through the windows, but they are so plastered over with paper that I can see the crowd only in narrow strips between posters. A roar of noise drifts out.

My muscles knot with anxiety. I chew my lip uncertainly. There's nobody standing outside. I don't see any suspicious characters loitering in the few cars I can see from here. Is it a trap, or just a party?

I pull off my cap, slick back my sweaty hair, and then cram the cap into my pack.

Am I stepping into a crowd of friends, or is a net about to drop over me? If I see any faces that zero in on mine; if I see any thuggish types walking in my direction, I will bolt.

I shake out my shoulders to try and relax, do my best to wipe the fear from my face. Then I step into the hubbub.

Four

Standing just inside the doorway, I quickly scan the crowd. Instead of the thirty competitors I expected, there must be over a hundred people in this room. Everyone is busy eating, drinking, and talking. Only a couple of faces turn toward the door. The young black man quickly looks away, but a woman with a pixie haircut gazes at me for a long minute. My skin prickles. She looks vaguely familiar. Did I go to middle school with her?

Then she turns to the man next to her and laughs at something he says, so I guess she's decided I'm not anyone worth noticing.

The noise level makes the air seem thick. A muscular man brushes my shoulder as he passes, making me flinch.

"Sorry, mate," he murmurs. Australian.

A small group of Japanese, dressed identically in blue and white track suits, cluster together in the far corner. Apparently the extreme teams include at least two from other countries.

The crowd is mixed, men and women, all shades of skin and hair colors, even a few gray heads. Many look like athletes, but some have rolls of flab hanging over their waistbands.

I have no clue what JJ might look or sound like; we've only swapped email messages. He said he knew me, so I'm counting on him to step forward. But that's not happening. Now what am I going to do—shout out his name?

Then I spy someone I know, a tall blond woman standing alongside a table. She has a beer in one hand and a slice of pizza in the other. Catie Cole, the golden girl of endurance racing. The two of us have competed in many events around the globe, but I didn't expect to find her here. This rowdy scene doesn't seem like her kind of event at all.

Catie's the ultimate pro endurance racer. Plus, she's a model. I see her in magazines and internet ads for athletic clothes and skin care products. I can't imagine her vast array of sponsors wanting her to risk injury in a stampede like Ski to Sea. But this year there will be drone vids, so maybe that's why she's here.

Having Catie as a competitor lessens my chances of winning, but still, I'm glad to see a familiar face. I wait until she pushes the last bite of pizza into her mouth before I walk over and tap her on the shoulder.

She turns, still chewing, but her face lights up and she flicks up a manicured finger to make me wait. She swallows, takes a sip of beer, and then sets the glass down on the table.

"Tana!" She pulls me into a hug. Of course she even smells good—some light, lemony scent—while I am damp and odiferous, bathed in nervous perspiration.

"I never expected to find you here," I say when she releases me.

She lives in California. Normally, her used-to-be Olympian father-trainer is glued to her side. "Where's your dad?"

"He thinks I'm visiting my aunt in Seattle." She winks at me, and then takes another sip of her beer.

She has a fleck of tomato sauce in the corner of her mouth. I point to the area on my own mouth and she wipes hers with a paper towel and then smiles and shrugs.

It's nice to see Catie so...loose. She's usually immaculate, pristine and camera-ready. She's not a plastic doll, though. This girl can run. She and I have always been fierce competitors.

Leaning close so she'll hear above the roar of conversation, I tell her, "Bailey is alive and well."

"Bailey?" Even the slight frown looks pretty on Catie.

"My friend, the one whose life you saved."

She waves a hand in the air. "I stumbled. You won. End of story."

"If you say so." I don't believe her for a minute, but I love her for the pretense.

"How'd you hear about Ski to Sea?" she asks in a loud voice.

"I've always known about Ski to Sea."

"Really?" Her left eyebrow lifts. "Hardly anyone I know has heard of it."

Oops. I quickly backpedal. "My grandma had a friend who was one of the organizers. I always wanted to get on a team."

"I'm with an all-female team." She points to two other young women a few yards away. "Tiff's on the Olympic kayaking team and Jenn's a parkour and mountain biking champ."

Yeesh. Her two teammates measure lemon-colored T-shirts against their shapely torsos. The shirts feature big black letters proclaiming *Femmes Fatales Extreme Team.*

"There's the biggest competition." Catie tilts her head toward three muscular men wearing identical clingy gray tees and black pants. Like the Japanese, they are a matched set, but these guys are older, polished, and very proud of themselves.

When one of the men turns away, I see the back of his shirt says *Iron Men Extreme Team.*

I groan.

"Yeah," she confirms. "They are all winners of the Iron Man competition in Hawaii."

"At least there's no swimming in *this* race," I point out.

She laughs. "I feel *so* much better now. Good luck, Tana."

She glides back to the other Femmes Fatales. I'm pretty sure *that's* a sashay.

I'd like to hate Catie, but it's hard to loathe a competitor who shares her flowers and gifts with those of us who don't have dozens of sponsors and thousands of admirers. She's so annoyingly nice, it's embarrassing for the rest of us. And I will always owe her for what she did for me last year. If anyone is going to beat me, I hope it will be Catie.

"Zany!" A shout behind me precedes a slap on my upper arm.

Zany is the stupid name the sportscasters tagged me with years ago, their cutesy nickname for Tanzania.

"Tana," I automatically correct as I turn in that direction.

In front of me is a face I never expected to see again. I whoop and wrap myself around the guy in an ecstatic hug.

"Uh..." he grunts in my ear.

Then I remember that really, I barely know the guy. In fact, I've only seen him this close once before, and given the circumstances then, he might not even remember that. I drop my arms and step back, my cheeks flaming. "Sorry, Jason. I don't know what got into me."

It's just that I'm so glad to see him alive.

"I know exactly what got into you." A grin creases his face. "You were *there*."

He lifts his left foot from the floor and pulls up the leg of his jeans. Above his high-tops, his black ankle is decorated in a multicolored star pattern. Fireworks exploding in the night sky. He raps his knuckles against the hard plastic. "Check it out."

The last time I saw Jason, he didn't have a foot on that leg.

"Party foot." He puts it back on the ground. "I also have a dress foot to match my tuxedo, a Techblade 5000 for sprinting, and a super sick mountain biking foot. I'm thinking of getting a pogo stick foot just to freak people out."

I find my tongue again. "Cool."

"You need a drink." Jason steps over to the closest table, pours beer from a pitcher into a glass, and hands it to me. At eighteen, I'm still underage, but I'm not about to remind him of that. Plus, after my run, I'm thirsty.

The beer is good, some kind of dark, rich microbrew. Glass pitchers holding different shades of liquid from pale gold to molasses brown are scattered across the top of the table.

Ah, home. Bellingham has more coffeehouses and breweries per capita than anywhere else I know of. I learned to appreciate a variety of brews before I was even thirteen.

"There's pizza, too." Jason points to a second table littered with open grease-stained boxes.

I help myself to a slice of pineapple and Canadian bacon and bring it back to his side.

"Did you see Catie?" I ask between bites. "I can't believe there are three of us here from Verde Island. You *are* competing, right?"

He fixes his blue-gray gaze on my face for a second, and I'm afraid I've insulted him. "Well, duh, yeah, Za—er, Tana. Canoeing, kayaking."

He flexes his arms so I can see the muscles he's built up there. I appreciatively murmur, "Whoa!"

I never noticed how hot Jason is. It's great to see him vertical. Standing on two legs again, even if one isn't all flesh and blood.

And then—wham!—my brain is treated to a technicolor snapshot of Jason's former race partner, Madelyn Hatt.

I can see in his eyes that he's experiencing the same flash of memory.

Neither of us wants to prolong our time travel back to that nightmare, so we both avert our eyes and take big gulps of beer from our glasses.

After Jason swallows, he wipes his mouth with the back of his hand. "I'm doing the mountain bike leg, too; using that sick biking foot."

He pulls his cell out of his pocket, taps a few spots on the screen, then shoves the phone in front of my face.

I watch a short vid of him careening down a steep hill on a mountain bike. His special foot is a metal contraption that fits into the pedal cage. Just before the end of the vid, his bike hits a curved ramp and he does a loop in the air.

"I'm impressed." At the same time, I'm glad Jason is not my teammate. The whole designer foot thing seems a little sketchy, not to mention a wee bit creepy.

I would really like to win. This year, Alaska Airlines is donating plane tickets to the winning team. All my previous prize money paid for my farm and Bailey's rescue, so although I am technically a land baroness, I still scrape by day to day to meet expenses. If I had a winning plane ticket, I could meet my sort-of-boyfriend Emilio or my excellent just-friend Bash somewhere.

"Sadly, no aerials in this race," Jason laments.

"Yeah," I reply. "And I have to run on a *trail.*"

Only someone who has raced across the wilderness like Jason and I have can appreciate how different that is from running on a road or a groomed path.

"Yeah, that would be a drag, but it's not precisely true."

I raise an eyebrow.

"You have to stay between markers on both sides of the section, but you can choose your own course—they announced that change late yesterday."

"Excellent!" As an experienced endurance racer, being able to choose my own route could give me an advantage. Of course, it will help Catie, too.

"Yeah, I thought you'd like that." As he shoves his phone into his hip pocket, his expression turns somber.

I am an inconsiderate dweeb. How could I grumble about running on any course? Even with his designer blade, Jason will probably never compete in an endurance race again. Should I say sorry, or would that make things even worse?

Jason is studying the partiers around the room, so I do, too. So many people. "I thought this was supposed to be a party for just the extremes."

"Support staff, too," Jason tells me. "They help with

driving, equipment, food, stuff like that."

That explains the flabby types.

"Do you know anyone here?" I ask. "I'm on the Way2Go Extreme Team. I'm supposed to meet two guys named JJ and X."

He grins. Then he takes a sip of his beer and waits, staring into my eyes.

At least thirty seconds tick slowly past between us until I clue in.

Duh.

Jason Jones. JJ.

I'm so mortified that I make a very unladylike snorting sound, which embarrasses me even more. I want to press my beer glass against my burning cheeks to cool them off. Instead, I take another sip before I say, "Good one, JJ."

"And where's our other teammate, the ugly one?" He scans the room, focuses on a cluster of youngish guys. Putting a hand to his mouth, he bellows, "X!"

A slender boy looks our way.

"Over here," Jason yells.

X follows Jason's arm curl like he's being reeled in on a fishing line.

"Tanzania Grey—mountain run, road bike, canoe," Jason introduces me. "Meet my brother, Xavier Jones—parkour and snowboard."

Like Jason, his brother has sandy hair and blue eyes, but he's put product in his hair, forcing it up into little blue-tipped spikes. Freckles spatter his nose. Xavier looks a few years younger than Jason, about my age.

"X." I hold out my right hand for a shake.

He slaps his hand into mine and then yanks it back,

wiggling his fingers like touching me gave him an electric shock. "Zany!"

"Don't call me that, else I'll have to strangle you." I poke a fingertip into his chest. "I go by Tana."

He makes a face. "Tana, then," he says, a smirk playing across his lips. "Although wrestling you could be interesting."

Jason—JJ—rolls his eyes. "Yeesh. Get a room, you two."

X and I both blush with embarrassment, and then we simultaneously take sips of our beers like we rehearsed the move, which makes us laugh at each other again.

To X, I say, "Jason and I met before, you know."

"I heard," X says. "You were *there*. What happened to that friend you wanted to save?"

His brother must have told him why I needed the million-dollar prize from Verde Island.

"My friend's happy and healthy." I smile at the thought of Bailey patrolling the perimeter of my property at home, but I don't provide details. Too many people know about him already, and I can't be too safe.

On the far side of the room, a woman raises a beer mug and shouts, "Anarchy!"

So then every other team has to pick up their mugs and yell, too.

"Way2Go!" Jason, Xavier, and I bellow in unison as we knock our mugs together, sloshing beer onto the floor.

Our team shirts are green, one of my favorite colors, with *Way2Go!* in giant white letters across the front, *Extreme Team* on the back. The race patches are orange, so *Way2Go* will look like the Irish flag in this contest.

Jason hands me two team shirts, one short-sleeved, one

long-sleeved, and another Ski to Sea tee. This seems overly generous. "Thanks, Jason, I mean, JJ. And thanks so much for inviting me to join your team."

He dismisses my gratitude with a flap of his hand. "We need a champion runner. And everyone gets a Ski to Sea shirt."

We both look around again. There's a lot of competition in this room.

"I think we'll do okay," he says.

His tone is wistful. Like me, Jason has trophies from endurance races around the world. I hope one day he can win a sprinting challenge, or maybe a mountain biking contest; he looks pretty good at that, judging by his video. But here and now, since he has only one good leg, and his brother's a newbie and we are competing against Catie Cole and Iron Man marathon winners, I think we both realize that we're not likely to win.

That's okay, I tell myself. Ski to Sea is all about fun. I'm happy to be part of it. I'm really happy to know my invitation wasn't a trap. I feel safe with JJ and X and these other extremes.

And then I remember that the race is only part of the reason I'm back in Bellingham.

Five

The volume in the room goes up as fast as the beer goes down.

I have to yell into Jason's ear. "How many contestants are there this year?"

"Nearly two hundred in the regular classes," he yells back.

"Wow." I envision the riot so many competitors will create. Was the race always that big when I was a kid?

"Teams," he clarifies. "A hundred teams in the Competitive Class. And then there are the ten Extreme Class teams, and probably at least a hundred more teams in the Recreational Class."

I do a quick calculation. Sixteen hundred racers participating. Plus thirty extreme team racers.

The first competitor on every team starts at the same time. Two hundred and ten racers launched into a parkour course by the starter horn? It'll be a miracle if fifty percent of them aren't trampled into the mud right off the bat.

I tug on X's sleeve to get his attention. When he leans over, I shout, "I'm glad *I'm* not in first position."

He makes a dismissive face. "No sweat. I can deal."

I've never run in a crowd that large, and I haven't biked with anyone except three guys from a local club. Maybe the trampling would be a good thing, because I sure hope the stampeding herd has thinned out by the time X tags me.

"There are team lists on the wall." Jason points to papers tacked up on the wall. A few people are gathered around them. "The final rules are there, too."

I nod and then push my way through the crowd to look at the lists. The lighting is dim in the café, but fortunately someone was wise enough to post the paperwork under a light. The Extreme Class is the shortest list, with only one page in alphabetic order by team name. Yep, *Way2Go—Tanzania Grey, Jason Jones, Xavier Jones* is last on the list. Seeing my name in print makes me proud. I'm truly, finally, part of Ski to Sea.

The other lists are intimidating. There are twelve divisions in the Competitive Class alone, and as many as twelve teams in a few of those divisions. Mixed teams, all female teams, family teams. There's even a high school division. I'm going to feel like one miniscule caribou in a vast herd sweeping across the state. But now that I think about it, the numbers could work to my advantage in one way: the girl who used to be Amelia Robinson will not be noticeable in a pack of hundreds.

The corporate division has its own separate list on the wall. I run my finger down the names of teams on those pages. Sure enough, there's a team from Quarrel Tayson Laboratories, the big pharma company my mother worked for. With luck, I'll have a chance to talk to a couple of the competitors on that team and maybe get a clue or two to help solve the mystery of my parents' deaths.

There's no team listed for World Cargo West, an import-export company my dad often worked for. I want to find out more about what he did at that company.

All signs of the existence of Amy and Alex Robinson were so swiftly and thoroughly erased that it had to be the work of experts. I have to find out why. I see my little brother in every dark-skinned nine-year-old boy I run across. I have to know what happened to Aaron.

"About tomorrow," a loud voice says in my ear, dragging me back to the present.

I let the pages of contestants fall back into place as I turn to face Xavier and Jason.

"You're staying with the Fitzgeralds?" Jason asks.

"Yes." It's the name of a family who offered free housing to Sea to Ski competitors. I'm pretty sure my family never knew any Fitzgeralds when we lived here, so they seemed safe.

Their address is in Fairhaven, not so far from the Amtrak station. I can go back and get my bike before I ride to the Fitzgeralds' house.

"Pick you up at ten to go check out the course and practice?"

Some teams think it's too risky to practice the course only two days before the race, but the three of us have never seen any of the route before, and besides, we are extremes. Our bodies are used to multiple days of stress.

"Sounds good," I tell Jason, "But can we meet here? I have an errand to do first thing in the morning."

It's not exactly an errand. It's more like a gamble. A really scary gamble. But I have to try.

His expression is curious, but when I don't volunteer

anything more, he doesn't ask. Instead, he lays out the itinerary. "It'll take us more than an hour to drive up to the starting point. We'll look that over. X will do his thing. Then at the first handoff spot, you and he can practice your exchange. You can check out the mountain run course if you want."

"I want." It's always an advantage to see what you're getting into before you're in it.

"I'll bring my bike and the canoe. You and I can practice the canoe leg together, and I want to ride the mountain bike route, too."

He mentioned his bike, but not mine. "Don't I need to practice the road bike course?"

He shakes his head. "Most teams don't. The highway's not closed down except on race day. You can only practice if you want to bike alongside traffic."

That doesn't sound like fun, but I need to practice because that flash bike and I are not used to each other. "I want to ride the course tomorrow, even if I'm on the shoulder."

He shrugs. "Okay, bring your bike. We'll put it on the rack."

"Ten a.m. Here?" I glance at both X and JJ.

The three of us nod at each other.

As an endurance racer, I'm used to running across territory I haven't explored before. But endurance races are small, generally no more than fifty competitors. Running and biking and paddling courses simultaneously with hundreds of other competitors seems dangerous.

But not nearly as dangerous as what I plan to do in the morning before Jason picks me up.

Six

"How come I've never heard of endurance racing?" MacKenzie tosses back her blond hair, which is streaked with crimson and black, the school colors.

MacKenzie, Chloë, and Ashley are also staying with the Fitzgeralds for the weekend. They are on one of the recreational teams from Central Washington U in Ellensburg.

I shrug. "It hardly ever gets media coverage."

"Kinda like Ski to Sea. Except..." Chloë studies the ceiling for a second, then snaps her fingers and points to me. "Wasn't one of those endurance races in the news last year? On an island? Something about the President's son and some terrorists?"

"Yeah. I was his partner."

"That was *you*?" Chloë sounds incredulous, which seems slightly insulting.

"Oooh, Sebastian Callendro," Ashley croons. "Can you introduce me to him?"

"We're not in touch," I lie, shaking my head.

"Damn." She sighs. "He was a hunk."

I agree, and he still is. Note to self: tell Bash about this later. He won't enjoy knowing his fans are still looking for him, but he will appreciate the lust of college girls, even if it is reported secondhand in this case.

We are sitting on pillows around a coffee table in the family room, eating popcorn and drinking orange juice. My uber-fancy bike leans against the wall next to the television.

The Fitzgeralds, a retired couple, pointed us to two daylight basement bedrooms and a bathroom to share, and then left us to go upstairs and watch the evening news. Mr. and Mrs. F seem really nice. Except they keep calling me Zany, so these three girls do, too. Some days I think I should just stop caring.

The college trio tells me about the apartment they share with another girl named Trina.

"Furnished with Craigslist specials," MacKenzie volunteers. "Not a single piece matches anything else."

Chloë tosses back a handful of popcorn. "We splash red cushions around so nobody will notice."

I envy their camaraderie, and it's nice to be treated like one of their group for a little while. But when they start discussing upcoming final exams and comparing schedules on their phones, I feel like the dork girl who came without a date. I got my GED at sixteen because I needed to earn a living instead of going to school. If I ever get the chance to go to college, it'll have to be part-time in the evenings.

"I work at a zoo," I blurt. "And I live with a housemate out in the country, on sort of a farm."

They are startled by my interruption, but also intrigued, because they know I'm younger than they are.

"What's your favorite zoo animal?" MacKenzie pushes a crimson lock of hair out of her eyes.

I could talk about animals forever. "Right now, my favorite is the baby tapir—he has stripes and spots and the funniest little trunk nose that he doesn't know what to do with."

Ashley leans forward to scoop up the last of the popcorn. "Do you have cows and horses on the farm?"

"Mostly pygmy goats. People keep dropping them off at my gate."

The count is up to five goats right now. I wish it would stop rising; the browse is getting scarce and I don't know how I'm going to feed all these animals. "People get a kid, thinking a baby goat is a cute pet. Then when they realize how ornery goats are, climbing all over the place and getting into everything, they can't wait to get rid of them."

Chloë looks up from her cell phone. "That's sad."

"Three abandoned cats and two dogs have shown up, too."

"Even sadder," Ashley adds. "What do you do with them?"

"I keep some. I find others homes."

The cats are tolerated by Bailey, although the two species view each other with contempt. I can't even bring the poor dogs inside the gate. Maybe it's a species memory of packs of hyenas and wild dogs in Africa, but Bailey views canines with homicidal intent. When he and I first moved to WildRun, I heard coyotes howling at night. A couple of weeks later, I found one flattened into two dimensions in the orchard. Nothing short of a steam roller or an elephant could do that.

I no longer hear coyotes, and I cart the poor abandoned dogs off to a no-kill shelter a couple of miles away.

At eleven, I yawn and stretch. "I'm going to crash."

It's not like these three will even notice I'm gone. They're all glued to their cells, watching videos or texting. I take my juice glass upstairs and put it in the sink, then let myself out the front door. This neighborhood is quiet, although I can hear the white noise rush of the traffic on I-5 not too far away. The sky is partially clear now. A few stars peek out between the scuttling clouds.

I close my eyes for a minute and think about how grateful I am to be in Bellingham and on a Ski to Sea team. How glad I am that Jason survived. How nice it is to see Catie again, and find a new friend in Xavier. I breathe in the moist night air, listen to the squeaky croak of a tree frog in the tree beside me. Then I open my eyes to admire the stars.

Every night after dark, even if it's raining or snowing, I go outside and do this. Some consider it weird. I don't care. It's my way of appreciating being on this planet for another day.

I let myself back into the kitchen.

"Jeepin' Jehosafat!" Mrs. Fitzgerald yelps, clutching a dishrag to her chest. It leaves a small damp spot on her cotton sweater.

"Sorry," I apologize. "I needed some air before going to bed."

I thank her again for the place to stay. "I have to get up early tomorrow. I want to get in a bike ride before my teammates pick me up at ten."

She tells me she'll leave out breakfast for me.

"Thanks, but you don't need to. I'm used to fending for myself."

"It's no problem, Sweetie." She stares into my eyes. "You seem so familiar to me."

My breath snags on my tonsils. Did my parents know any

Fitzgeralds? Did Mrs. Fitzgerald use a different name when I was growing up here? Was I just so clueless as a youngster that I don't remember her?

"You're so much like Jamie Elson," she finally says. "She's a good friend of my granddaughter."

My shoulders relax. "No relation. Does she live around here?" It could be handy to have a double in Bellingham.

Mrs. Fitzgerald shakes her head. "Spokane."

We say good night and I descend to my assigned bed in the basement. Slipping into the top bunk, I pull my tablet computer out of my pack. It's last year's model. I can always count on discards from my pals at Dark Horse Networks.

I click on Wordage to see what it will throw at me next. My new word is *Doppelganger—an apparition or double of a living person.*

Freaky. Mrs. Fitzgerald and I were just discussing a possible double of mine. But I also think the word sounds like a German pastry—*would you like a piece of strudel or would you prefer the doppelganger?*

I could be funny if I only had an audience. But I don't, so I move on to my next task, pulling up a couple of old photos to refresh my memory. They say you remember best if you try to memorize just before you go to sleep.

These photos are some of the few reminders I have of my family, hidden on a USB drive left behind when the movers cleaned out our house. As well as a few photos, the drive held five scans of boring formulas and accounting spreadsheets, which I guess makes sense, given my parents' jobs.

The scans must be important. Why else would Mom bury them on a memory stick attached to our spare house key?

Maybe I'll run into someone in Bellingham who can help me decipher them.

I also loaded the photos—my mom in her lab coat with her colleagues at QTL, my dad at a cocktail party with some employees from the import-export company. I don't know if these photos hold any clues, but it's a place to begin.

I lie back on the unfamiliar pillow and try to memorize faces in the pictures. I wish I could recall the last conversations I had with my mom and dad. I remember whining to Mom about not getting some jeans I really wanted; I sure hope those weren't the last words I said to her. I'm pretty sure the last thing I said to Dad was, worst case scenario—"Whatever"—and best case, something along the lines of "See you later."

Why can't I remember? Add these sins to the fact that I snuck out of the house on that last night, and anyone can tell that I was the worst daughter any parent could ask for.

In the lab photo, my mother's expression is serious. She's in scientist mode, her face nearly as pale as her white lab coat, her chestnut hair pulled back into a low bun, her reading glasses perched on top of her head. I swipe across the touch screen to the next photo, and there's my dad at a company party, raising a wine glass, winking at the camera, the only black person in the group.

As Tanzania Grey, I tell people that my father was from Africa. In truth, he was from Chicago. He met my mom in Zimbabwe—that's where *she* was born.

Mom.

Dad.

God, I miss you.

Did I ever say, "I love you"?

Seven

I rise early, stuff my backpack with necessities, help myself to coffee, juice, and two bagels with cream cheese and strawberry jam in the Fitzgeralds' spacious kitchen. Then I mold my khakis to my legs with Velcro straps and head out on my bicycle. I want to be in place when employees start arriving for work at Quarrel Tayson Labs.

After chaining up the bike in the darkest corner I can find, I position myself in the underground parking garage with a pad of lined paper clamped to a clipboard on top of my tablet computer. I've done my best to dress like I think an intern would, with my hair neatly braided down my back and my teal silk blouse tucked into my pants. The write-your-own nametag on my left shoulder identifies me as Jenna Miller.

I wait until a few cars drive in, and then I approach a pair of women who are chatting as they walk together from their parking spot to the elevator. They look like they might be scientists. Their hair is severely pulled back, and they are dressed casually in slacks and tailored blouses, the kind of clothes you'd wear under a lab coat. Laminated QTL identification tags dangle from plastic tubing around their necks.

"Excuse me." I step in front of them. "Do you work in the lab?"

The redhead frowns. "Which one? There are a lot of labs."

I laugh nervously. "Well, I'm not sure. See, I'm a new intern."

I'm a little appalled at what a magnificent liar I have become over the last four years. Any story could come out of my mouth at any time.

"I'm supposed to be cataloging all these old photos for HR." I pull up the picture of my mom and her colleagues on my tablet and show them. "They told me to identify all these people and the settings, and I don't know what I'm doing."

"The light is terrible in here." The older woman glances up at the flickering light in the wire cage overhead. "Let's go inside."

We move toward the elevator. The redhead pulls her cardkey necklace over her head and then studies me with suspicion. "Where's your ID, Jenna?"

This morning, Wordage gave me *Unapt—not suitable or qualified, not appropriate.*

I feel pretty *unapt* right now, but I nonchalantly wave a hand. "Security said they'd have it ready at ten a.m. They said to ask any employee to let me in, or to call them if one wouldn't."

That seems to satisfy them. The redhead zips her cardkey through the reader, and then hangs it back around her neck, with the ID card flipped over, showing only the big QTL insignia on the back side. I'm tempted to twist it right side up for her so I can get a look at her name, but that seems a forward gesture for a brand new intern to make.

We get on the elevator and ride to the third floor. We stop

just outside the elevator doors, which makes me nervous, because it's kind of a public lounge, with a couple of couches and tables and bright abstract paintings on the walls. While much of Bellingham is filled with buildings that were in their prime a century ago, the modern QTL building is like a city unto itself, with state-of-the-art science labs and ultra-high-tech offices, many with views of Bellingham Bay and Lummi Island to the west and the snow-capped Cascades to the east.

The employees here have it easy, with three cafeterias to choose from, a half dozen lounges to relax in, endless free soft drinks and coffee at their fingertips. My mother told me there are even sleeping rooms and showers on the top floor. A complex climate control system keeps the air fresh and the temperature at seventy-two degrees, no matter what the weather is doing outside. I always hoped I'd work here eventually like my mom, that I'd be one of these important people doing a job that made a difference in the world. My daydreams never extended far enough to imagine what that job might actually be.

At this hour of the morning, we three women are the only employees in this lounge. We sit on a dark blue couch, with me in the middle, as the two women study my photo.

"I only recognize two people." The redhead hovers her index finger over my tablet and identifies them. I dutifully write down their names on my clipboard.

"Oh, I remember them all," says the older woman. Her ID card says *Dr. Marilyn Wigener*. Her eyes are almond-shaped, giving her a vaguely Asian look, which is emphasized by the mandarin collar of her blue blouse. "This must have been taken a long time ago, because these two"—she points to my mother and a tall woman standing beside her—"disappeared into thin air around four or five years ago."

"Disappeared?" I study Dr. Wigener's face for clues. "What do you mean?"

"Amy Robinson." She points to my mom, and hesitates as though deciding what to say next. "Amy was the star of this company. She created RT44."

"Really?" The other woman's head jerks up. Her voice holds a note of awe.

"Wow," I remark. As an intern in big pharma, Jenna Miller would definitely be wowed.

RT44 is Retaxafal 44, a vaccine used to prevent all the variations of Ebola from striking down populations all over the world. It has saved hundreds of thousands, if not millions, of people.

My mom deserved the Nobel Prize.

Instead, she got a death sentence. What the hell could have happened?

RT44 has to be constantly tweaked to keep up with the ever-changing virus, so sales rip along every year. My dad used to harp on what a great investment QTL stock was because of that.

"RT44 is the company's biggest product, isn't it?" I ask.

"Along with Plactate," says Dr. Wigener. "Another of Amy's formulations."

Plactate is a med that controls some nasty side effects of the vaccine, so they're always used together. I routinely get dosed with both when I travel to an endurance race in some disease-ridden country.

"Wow," I say again. "What happened to Amy Robinson?"

It feels so weird to say Mom's name like I don't know her.

The woman shakes her head and considers for another moment. Then she tells me, "It's hard to say for sure exactly what happened. She was here one day and gone the next. HR said she was transferred to Africa."

I must look confused, because Dr. Wigener informs me, "We have offices in Harare and Johannesburg."

Jenna would probably have done her homework, so I nod. "I read that somewhere."

Dr. Wigener hesitates for a second and purses her lips as if making up her mind whether to add more, but then she says, "It was all so abrupt, I figured they canned her."

The redhead bends forward to peer around me at her colleague, a perplexed expression on her face. "Why would they fire the star of the company?"

The older woman shrugs. "I didn't work with Amy. But I heard she had some sort of dispute with management."

Then her expression darkens as she abruptly decides that she has probably said too much to a lowly intern. Dr. Wigener shoots a stern look at her colleague. "We should get to work."

"So, okay, thanks." I rise along with them from the couch. "I've got everyone's name except for this one." I point to the woman by my mother's side.

"That's Maxine Newsome." Dr. Wigener strides quickly toward a door secured with another cardkey lock.

I trot alongside her. "Did Maxine get transferred to Africa, too?"

"No, I don't think so." She pauses briefly to zip her security pass through the reader on the door in front of us, which bears a huge red warning sign: RESTRICTED: LAB

PERSONNEL ONLY. "Maxine quit the day after Amy left. I heard she's still around here somewhere."

The door opens, and my informants hustle away, passing a man in a gray suit and a young woman in white pants and black jacket walking in my direction. I turn away to wait for the elevator in the little lobby.

Did I learn anything useful? Of course I know my mom left QTL abruptly; it's not like she had a choice. The dispute Dr. Wigener mentioned might be imaginary, a convenient excuse for Mom's sudden disappearance. But Maxine Newsome—that name might be an actual lead, as they say in the detective biz. At any rate, now I have another person to check out.

"Have a safe trip," a male voice says behind me.

I glance over my shoulder. Gray Suit has stopped at the security door, holding it open for the young woman to pass through. He squints at me.

I quickly turn back to the elevator and study the buttons on top. The elevator slowly descends from the twelfth floor.

The girl joins me. She's wearing a visitor's badge and she holds an important-looking briefcase in one hand. At least I think it's a briefcase—it's made out of metal, not leather. And now that I'm studying it, I see that a metal ring encircles the handle on the case. An identical ring is around this girl's wrist, barely visible below the cuff of her jacket.

She notices me looking at it. "Yes, it's a handcuff."

My gaze meets hers. She can't be more than a year or two older than me. Her light brown hair is braided neatly on the right side. A small pimple dots the middle of her forehead. It must be annoying.

She lifts her chin proudly. "I'm a courier. I'll be in Casablanca late tomorrow."

"Cool." My comment is drowned out by the chime of the arriving elevator. We step in, side by side. "I'm an intern," I tell her. "How'd you get to be a courier?"

She tosses her head nonchalantly. "There are lots of us, mostly from Western Washington."

She means the university in Bellingham.

"This is my second trip. The first one was to Istanbul, five weeks ago."

"Wow," I murmur. Apparently my intern self has a very limited vocabulary. Wordage should include more exclamations. "I think I applied for the wrong job."

The elevator descends to the parking garage. We both step out.

"QTL needs couriers all the time to take important shipments all over," she explains. "You don't get to stay long." She scrunches up her face to show her discontent about that. "But you get free trips all around the world. The hotels I've stayed in so far were rad. You can order whatever food you want, and the pay's great."

I almost blurt out that I've been to all sorts of exotic places, too. But then I remember that I'm Jenna Miller, lowly intern, and it seems unlikely that I've ranged farther than Canada.

The courier leans close and lowers her voice. "I exchanged the plane ticket so I could stop and visit a friend in Senegal on the way back from Casablanca. I didn't think I'd ever get to see her again. It's only for a few hours, but what they don't know, right?"

"Smart," I respond. Maybe I'll try that the next time Dark Horse Networks gives me a plane ticket to a race in another country. The snag is that Emilio is the only person I know overseas, and I usually don't know which country he's in. If I could find out, would the Army let me just drop in for a visit? The odds don't seem good.

I might have relatives in Zimbabwe, but I don't have a clue how to go about finding them without telling the world who *I* really am, which could lead the killers to me. Plus, I'm fairly sure that an extra stop would cost extra money, and I'm lucky if I can scratch up bus fare to the airport.

The courier girl leans away and says in a more public voice, "They give you these, too."

She raises her non-handcuffed hand to show me a large see-through zippered bag with two smaller ones inside, one bag bordered in orange and one in white. The small bottles and tubes in the bags look like shampoo and lotion samples packaged to go through airport security.

"Sweet," I remark. "I normally use a zip-lock baggie."

She laughs. "Those are all free goodies, too, from QTC's cosmetics branch. Fringe benefits. The travel bags add a little class, don't you think?" She tucks the bags under her elbow like a purse and strikes a pose.

"I really like the orange one," I tell her.

"I like the orange best, too, but I'm supposed to check that one in my luggage and give it to the woman meeting me in Casablanca. I get to keep the white, though."

We stop in front of a beat-up Honda Civic. She uses an electronic key to open the trunk and extracts a roller suitcase, then locks the car again.

"Who could I talk to about being a courier?" I ask.

"Mr. Pederson, in the Security Department."

I snap alert. "Peterson? Like Patterson, but with an e?" What are the odds?

She shakes her head. "P-E-D, not T."

Pederson, then. Still, it's close. "What's his first name?"

She gives me an odd look, like I just accused her of sleeping with the man. "No clue."

"No worries," I reassure her. "I'll figure it out; I want to be sure to apply to the right guy."

"Good luck." I walk alongside her as she pulls the suitcase toward one of the garage exits. A QTL minivan is waiting in the driveway.

"You get a ride to the airport, too," she tells me. And then, finally, she lowers her voice again and says, "I never told you any of this."

"Zipped lips," I murmur. "Have a great trip."

I figure I'm pressing my luck to stay longer, so I walk to my bike, peel off my nametag, and ride away. I wish the racing wheels weren't quite so colorful in the sunlight.

What if I applied to be a QTL courier? It sounds so cool. Maybe I could fly around the world on my days off from the zoo, delivering vaccines to save people.

Then I remember that I'm not exactly an upstanding job applicant for QTL. I'd probably have to pass a security check. Not going there. I can't even repeat this stunt. There are cameras everywhere in that building, and now I'm recorded on them.

Focus. Eyes on the prize. Maxine Newsome.

I head for the nearest Starbucks and park myself in a booth to use their wi-fi. The line at the counter is long, so the guy working there doesn't have time to give me the evil eye for taking up space without ordering anything. We Habitat Maintenance Technicians can't afford four-dollar coffee drinks, especially those of us who are supporting a menagerie at home. Really, there should be a special category for us on tax forms. Instead of Head of Household, maybe Herd Leader.

A woman towing a little boy by the hand walks past the window, and damn, if it isn't lithping Charlie and his mom from yesterday. I twist in my chair to turn away, but the little twerp spots me.

"Edna!" he chirps loudly enough for me to hear through the glass. And then he points to me.

His mom's gaze follows the kid's finger. I smile and wave. Good thing I took off Jenna's nametag. Even better thing that I haven't introduced myself to anyone in *this* place.

I brace myself for more used-to-live-here chitchat. Fortunately, Mom pulls Charlie past the coffee shop toward the grocery store. I turn my back to the window and hunker down over my tablet.

Wordage gives me *Farrago—a jumble or hodgepodge.* Really? Are there no normal words in this program? I've never heard anyone say *farrago.*

I tap Maxine's name into the local phone directory. Nada. *Dammit.*

Since I'm now a property owner myself, I know a little bit about recordkeeping and taxes—that stuff is divided up by county, and where I live, the office that keeps track is called the assessor's office. I find the Whatcom County Assessor's Office and then the online property records. I choose to search by owner and type in *Newsome,* hoping that since she had a good job, she bought a house somewhere in town. And yes, there it is—M.S. Newsome owns a house south of Fairhaven. I snip a copy of that address and send it to my email for safekeeping.

While I'm on the site, I check records for my family's old address, and I'm surprised to see that a sale *is* registered to Specialty Containers Inc. from Amy and Alex Robinson. It's actually dated a few days before their murders.

Why did my parents not mention selling the house? What happened to that $340,000? That pile of dough could buy a lot of hay for my beasts at home. Is it sitting in a bank account somewhere waiting for someone to claim it? How could I possibly find out without blowing my cover?

Then again, this record might not be accurate. Does anyone in the county office ever check to see if sales are real? Maybe they just file whatever papers land on their desks.

I know how it easy it is to plant details in public records. I learned that from my adopted mom Marisela Santos. If it's printed on official paper or posted online on a reputable site, people assume it's real.

Marisela never asked me who I used to be or why I needed a new identity. I didn't ask how she learned all these tricks to fly under the legal radar. We protect each other.

Tanzania Grey's online history is pretty bombproof, at least to the average citizen. Somehow it even passed the Secret Service test last year. Which intensifies my worry over P.A. Patterson—why does that person even *suspect* that Tanzania Grey knows Amy Robinson?

Checking out Maxine or Specialty Containers or P.A. Patterson will have to wait for tomorrow, because it's almost time to meet JJ and X, so I head for the Ladies to change into my running clothes.

Eight

I've always thought it's strange that the local ski slope is called the Mount Baker Ski Area. The ski runs are not actually on Mount Baker, although we can see that volcano from here: it's the spectacular snow cone gleaming in the sun to the southwest. To add to the confusion, Mount Baker is often called Kulshan, the native name for the mountain, so maybe, out of respect for history, this area should be called the Kulshan Ski Area.

Or maybe it should be the Shuksan Ski Area, because overshadowing the eastern flanks of the ski slopes is Shuksan, a craggy mountain that I personally think packs a lot more wow factor than Baker.

Shuksan is not a volcano. The mountain has all these sheer gray cliffs and glaciers that look like they might come crashing down any day now. People take a gazillion photos of it every year, especially at Picture Lake, because the water there makes a perfect mirror when the wind isn't blowing. When we drive past it today, the surface is rippled. A group of Japanese tourists with their cameras are crowded onto the dock at the edge of the water, waiting for the breeze to stop.

We park in a big lot that my family always used when we went snowshoeing. The starting gate and the parkour loop are marked with little orange flags that zigzag up the hill. The route leads to hay bales that must be climbed or leapt over, and a huge net that the contestants apparently have to crawl under. Small patches of snow and rivulets of running water cross the course. There's a lot of mud to navigate through before the racers reach the handoff area in the snowfield at the top. No wonder they had to replace the usual cross-country ski leg with this parkour challenge.

JJ helps X strap his snowboard onto his pack, which bulges with his boots inside.

"Don't forget this," JJ says to his brother, handing him an elastic band, which X snaps over his left wrist to simulate the timing chip bracelet we have to pass around on race day. After doing a couple of quick stretches and jumping jacks to warm up, X gives JJ a snappy salute and then turns to me. "Meet you at the bottom of the ski run, Z."

Then he sees the look on my face and changes that quickly. "I mean T."

So the Way2Go team is composed of alphabet soup. But the letter—or would it be a word?—sounds weird coming from Xavier's lips, because Emilio is the only one who has ever called me Tee. He says it stands for terrific and talented and any other compliment he can manufacture on the spot.

X dashes off into the muddy trail, running through the obstacle course uphill toward the crest, where he'll switch to the snowboard. We watch him leap the hay bales and then splat down under the net and do a fast crawl that reminds me of the way crocodiles move on land. The pack on his back makes it especially difficult to maneuver; he has to lie face down and slither through the mud to keep his gear from catching on the net. I'm glad this is not my leg of the race.

JJ and I drive to the bottom of the hill and park close to the ski lifts, where the handoff from the downhill skiers to the mountain runners will take place on race day. There's barely a trace of snow on the soggy ground, which is nice for me but not so great for X to slide down into.

"He'll be slow today because he has to switch from shoes to the board by himself," JJ tells me. "He won't have to carry all that gear on race day. We've got helpers."

This is news to me, so I wait for more explanation.

"Sasha, Linnea, and Kim. You'll meet them on Sunday."

"Didn't know you were such a player, JJ," I tease. "You got three women to come across the country with you?"

He shrugs. "Sasha's my cousin. She's the one who turned me on to Ski to Sea in the first place. She's a student at Western Washington U. Kim and Linnea are her housemates. They'll take care of our gear and do some of the driving."

"Good to know. I wondered how I was supposed to handle my bike between the running and canoeing legs."

We lean against the car and stare at the ski slope while we chat about what we've been doing since the Verde Island Race. For JJ, the last year has been mostly rehab, but I find out he's studying math at Kenyon.

"What's your major?" he asks.

"Life." I remind him that I work in a zoo, and tell him a funny tale about Hiram, our tamandua that escaped from the nocturnal exhibit and somehow ended up sleeping among the stuffed toys in the gift shop.

JJ raises an eyebrow. "Tamandua?"

"A little anteater from South America." Most of the time I feel like an ignoramus, but when it comes to zoology, I can hold my own.

I guess JJ's not too interested in animals, because he changes the subject. "What do you hear from the First Son?"

A few years ago, Bash—Sebastian Callendro—was outed as President T.L. Garrison's 'love child,' much to everyone's surprise. Especially Sebastian's. Although 'horror' would be a more accurate description of how *he* took the news about his bio-father and the pack of aggressive paparazzi that hounded him after the story broke.

"I hear nothing," I tell Jason.

"I don't read much about him now. There are rumors that he's doing charity work in Bolivia."

"Interesting." I work to keep my expression neutral. I planted those Bolivian rumors myself.

I may be the only person on the planet who knows that Bash is hiding in a small town in New Mexico. Before he left, he sent a terse text message to the Prez from a burner phone: *Going off grid 4 one year. Pls do NOT search. Contact u on return.*

My opinion of Garrison shifted up a notch when he actually honored Sebastian's request. At least the man gets how uncomfortable it is to live in a fishbowl.

"Now that Garrison's in his last term," I say, "the media's too busy chasing the candidates to focus on him or his relatives."

That's what Bash is counting on. As soon as Garrison is out of the White House and the national spotlight, Sebastian Callendro plans to resume his original life again. I envy him that.

If by some miracle Way2Go wins the Extreme Team competition, I could use my plane ticket to go see Bash in New Mexico. Or I could use it to go to Michoacán, Old Mexico, with Emilio. We have long promised each other to visit the winter refuge for millions of monarch butterflies there, but we never simultaneously have money and spare time.

With a free ticket, we could probably make that trip on his next Christmas leave. It's been so long since I've seen Shadow in person. I try to recall what his kiss feels like.

"Top of the hill," JJ murmurs.

Ack! I was so wrapped up thinking about Bash and Emilio that I forgot to be on the lookout for Xavier, but sure enough, there he is, shooshing down from the crest toward us on the slushy snow.

I hastily tear off my jacket, do a few quick toe-touches, make sure my laces are double-tied, and then jog over to the exchange area just in time to nearly collide with X. He slides in, then falls over on his side.

He's streaked with mud from his ankles to his hairline. I reach a hand down to help him, but instead he pulls off the elastic band, snaps the slimy thing onto my outstretched wrist, points to the road, and yells, "Go!"

I take off running down the side of the road to get to the big red flag that marks the beginning of the mountain run. The road is littered with loose gravel and wet leaves. Yuck. I'm used to all sorts of obstacles when I run cross-country, but I'm also used to choosing my own route, and being confined to this narrow strip feels claustrophobic.

I focus on the asphalt beneath my running shoes and try to make the best of it. I am so glad there are only three-quarters of a mile on asphalt this time—in previous years, the downhill running leg has been eight miles of nothing but road.

A car comes up behind me. It slows and parallels my course. X rolls down the passenger window. "Meet you at the bike exchange area."

I nod and wave to show I heard, and then my teammates zip off down the mountain with our two bikes strapped to the rack on the back of the car. As they disappear around a curve, I feel a bit...well, abandoned. This is odd, because I'm used to running by myself. I guess it's because I am on a road with cars passing me, so I feel like a lonely jogger right now instead of an intrepid endurance racer conquering rugged, dangerous terrain.

The terrain under my feet right now is plenty dangerous, though. I skid in a patch of loose gravel and do an impromptu tap dance to avoid crashing down on the asphalt. The road is rippled in spots, too, and there are potholes and lumpy patches everywhere. I focus on placing my feet carefully while fretting about how I will have to practice my ride on the shoulder of the highway, too.

After I round another bend, I see two runners practicing in front of me. I'm pleased when I pass them just before we reach the red flag. Then I'm off and all alone as I gallop down the mountainside through the forest. When I'm running, I feel free. I don't have to pretend to be anyone else. I remind myself that I'm not free to choose any route in this contest, though. I have to keep a sharp eye out for the orange tags tied to trees along the way to stay in the assigned area as I gallop down the mountainside. Drones will be keeping track and I don't want to get disqualified by straying out of bounds.

At a bend in the trail, a ptarmigan and I startle each other. She—I think it's a hen—flaps off in a noisy flurry of wings and I have to catch myself from falling as I sidestep onto a slippery rotten branch. A few minutes later I see the back side of a deer as it flashes off through the woods, but I don't see any more humans.

I am in my element, jumping over fallen logs and dashing around giant ferns. This is a much shorter run than I'm used to, but if I have a hope of getting out front in this competition, it will be during this mountain run.

When I reach the valley below, I see JJ and X standing near the road. JJ's hands are on my bicycle handlebars. I'm pleased to see there's a water bottle in the holder beneath the main tube, and when I reach them, X hands me a cup of water, which I gulp down as I shake out my feet and hands, strap on my helmet, and then climb onto the bike.

"See you at the canoe start," says JJ. He and X jog back toward the car.

After slamming my feet into the ground on that downhill run, pedaling feels awkward at first. But my leg muscles are well warmed up, and as I pass a couple of other cyclists on the road, I realize this might be an advantage. Maybe the extreme threes will beat the regular eights on race day after all.

I'm riding on the highway through the Nooksack River valley in the foothills. The road zigs and zags and has a lot more ups and downs than I ever noticed while driving along it in a car. The overhanging trees transform the asphalt into a patchwork of sun and shadow, making it hard to see the bumps and holes in advance. Bikers and cars on the road ahead flash light and dark like they're dancing under strobe lights.

I'm used to riding long distances to work, but my route is a lot flatter and straighter and sunnier than this one. I have more time to think while I'm commuting, because I don't normally ride as fast as I could. But this bike naturally wants to race and I'm pumping along, trying to get used to this faster speed on a twisty highway. I hope race day will be less nerve-wracking. At least I won't have to ride on the shoulder then, but I may be riding my bike in a pack of competitors, which I've never done before. I zoom past the pullout area on the right where a narrow trail heads off into a grove of giant trees. I don't know why nobody has ever marked that trail, but most people in the area know it's there, so it's not precisely a secret. I wish I could stop and look at those massive old-timers again, but I'm past in a flash. A little way down the road there's the turnoff to Nooksack Falls. I'd like to turn off there, too, and see that awesome waterfall again. But these landmarks would mean nothing to Tanzania, and her partners are waiting.

A black pickup passes, its side mirror so close that I feel a gust of air on my left arm as it speeds by. I have a dizzying vision of my body hurtling off into the forest on my right and not being found for days. I search for a ninja in the side mirror, but I can't see the driver. It's a long hour and a half to the rendezvous area, enough time to fret about who was driving that truck and who might be driving the next one, so my brain is as tired as my legs when I reach the canoe rendezvous area. I almost ride right past JJ's car on the riverbank.

A shout—"Whoa, Tana! Over here!"—makes me slam on the brakes and veer into the riverside park. I follow Xavier as he jogs to where JJ stands beside a green fiberglass canoe. He's wearing shorts, and the stump of his leg is in a plastic bucket thing. I can't see the foot part because he's wearing a shoe over it, but I guess this is his biking foot in place for the mountain bike section that follows this one.

X picks up a bright orange PFD. JJ is already wearing his own life jacket. I jump off my bike, lay it on its side in the dirt, and trot over to them.

"You okay?" JJ asks.

"Good to go." In truth, I'd like to sprawl on the ground and give my leg muscles a rest, but I won't be using them in the canoe, anyway, so I put up with the burn. I'd also really like a nice juicy cheeseburger right now, with fries and a chocolate shake, but the sooner I get this over with, the sooner I can eat.

"Arms out!" X commands, unzipping the PFD.

It takes my brain a second to interpret what he wants, but then I stand spraddle-legged and fling my arms out. Xavier wraps the life vest around my sweaty torso.

"You cannot remove or even unzip this during the race," he reminds me as he fastens the Velcro straps over my shoulders and snugs up everything like he's pulling corset strings tight. Then he leans in and croons, "Was that good for you?"

This is the way alphabet soup is going to talk? "Yeah, baby," I say. "I like it like that."

JJ groans and rolls his eyes, all superior since he's older, I guess. He leans down and grips the side of the canoe. "To the river?"

I bend and grasp the other side. "Let's do it."

"You're in front."

X takes the back end. The three of us walk the canoe to the bank and shove the bow into the water. JJ's limping. I wonder what it feels like to carry a load with an artificial foot. Does the extra weight hurt his stump?

The Nooksack River is running high. No surprise, with the snowmelt coming off the mountains. My anxiety level ratchets up as I watch the noisy water rush by in standing waves raised by rocks beneath the water surface.

A river almost killed me and Bash on Verde Island. I haven't forgotten what it was like to be trapped underwater, seeing nothing but a blurry brown infinity, wondering if I'd ever breathe again.

Nine

JJ uses a hand to haul his leg over the edge before he slides into the canoe. His artificial foot makes a thunk on the bottom as he moves into place. Can he balance in a canoe with an artificial foot?

I don't feel like I can question that, so I ask, "Can you swim?"

"PFD," he mutters, annoyed.

My brain is still on Verde Island, remembering how Bash's personal floatation device did not function when he needed it, how he disappeared beneath the roiling water, how I held my own breath as I waited for him to come up. I nearly passed out, and *I* was on land.

As JJ and I shove off the bank into this dangerous river, I remind myself that both Bash and I survived that experience. I pick up the wooden paddle at my feet.

JJ's voice comes from behind me. "Gel pack on your left."

Huh? I glance down at the metal seat, and sure enough, at my left hip is a see-through plastic squeeze bag filled with honey-brown goop. It's energy gel, the high-calorie-vitamin-mineral-protein-glycerin mixture racers swallow in long cross-country runs. It's disgusting at other times, but during a race, it works miracles on tired muscles and empty stomachs.

"Go ahead," JJ says, "I can steer alone for a minute or two."

"Yay." After sliding my paddle between my knees, I pick up the gel pack with both hands, yank open the valve, and squeeze a third of the bag into my mouth. I've never had a brown mix before. I try to analyze the odd flavor as I work it around my dry tongue and gulp it down. I finally decide it's supposed to be root beer.

"Figured you should have something. X and I had ham sandwiches and chips," JJ tells me.

I groan as best I can with my mouth full. We are bouncing through the waves, and my aching thigh muscles are already growing stiff as I try to balance in the exact middle of the seat. At the same time as I squeeze the last mouthful out of the bag, I see a bend in the river ahead, with the water swirling up against the rock-lined shore. I toss the empty bag into the bottom of the canoe and quickly snatch up my paddle as we slip-slide toward the far bank, where cottonwood branches dangle into the water, waiting to grab us. I lean to the left and jam my paddle blade into the current.

"Right side!" JJ yells.

I quickly switch sides.

"Paddle hard!"

I'm relieved that he seems to know what to do, because I certainly don't. I may be strong, but I have paddled a canoe exactly three times in my life, and never on a river moving as swiftly as this one. I dig in with all I've got. We make it around the bend without getting tangled in the drooping trees, and end up more or less in the middle of the stream.

The trees on the banks flash by. We startle a couple of girls sunning themselves on a boulder at the river's edge. One advantage of such high water is that we are really zooming along. But on race day, all the other competitors will be traveling just as fast, and now I realize we will have to avoid hitting each other as well as all these obstacles in the water.

JJ shouts, "Strainer ahead!"

Which means nothing to me. I see only a long strip of brown that reaches halfway across the river.

Next, he yelps, "The log!"

Aha. The brown strip *is* a log—or actually, it's the trunk of a fallen tree, submerged only an inch or so under water that rises to flow over it. Branches erupt from its trunk near the bank, shimmying as the current bounces them.

"Paddle hard left! Now!"

I switch sides. The canoe tilts slightly, which makes me gasp, but I dig in my paddle again and again. We slide left but the canoe is moving forward much faster, headed directly for the strainer. As we near, I see there's a lot of debris—twigs and trash—piled up in front of the log. It's a damn *farrago* of river garbage with water pouring through it. I guess that's why it's called a strainer.

"Harder!"

My shoulders and elbows burn with the effort. I think we are just barely going to pass over the end of the strainer, but then the bow thunks and a shudder passes down the length of the canoe.

"Shit!" we yelp in unison. Great minds think alike.

We are going to flip. I am going to feel exactly how cold this river is. But then the canoe begins to swing sideways and peel away from the log.

"Backpaddle!" JJ yells.

We both reverse paddle, and the bow clears the strainer. Then the current catches the canoe and we begin to bounce down the river, sideways to the flow and headed directly for a giant boulder parting the water in the middle of the stream.

If a tree in the river is a strainer, then what the hell is a rock? A grater? A washboard? Right now, it looks like a tombstone.

I'm pretty sure that in another second I will be flung out of this canoe. And then I will probably drown. After I crack open my head on a rock. Why did I volunteer for this?

"Paddle left!"

Left is toward the boulder. It seems like we should be paddling away from that death trap, but I'm only the inexperienced co-pilot in this doomed craft, so I paddle on the left.

"Give it everything you've got!"

The canoe actually straightens out and we zip past the boulder, only inches from its jagged flank, and we ride into a relatively quiet portion of the stream, where the river flows straight, with no obvious obstacles waiting for us.

"Wahoo!" yells JJ. "Eee-haw! Isn't this great, Zany?"

I'm shivering, half from being splashed with glacier meltwater and half from adrenalin. I twist my head to scowl over my shoulder at my overly enthusiastic partner. "Call me Tana."

He grins and winks at me, and I can't help but forgive him. While this is my third leg of the race, it's his first. He'll be a lot less manic a few hours from now.

I turn back around in time to see a bald eagle swoop down

and snag a fish. He—or she—carries it, sunshine flashing off its wet flanks, back to a nest of twigs high in a broken-off Douglas fir. Some eaglets are going to get a fresh lunch. Jason's right, it is pretty great out here.

Shouting erupts behind us as another pair of canoeists practice skirting that boulder, but we're way ahead of them.

Then, all of a sudden, there's the sound of a waterfall ahead, which starts my adrenaline surging again. It turns out to be only a small drop, though, less than a foot. I thunk over first and the bow splashes me with a shower of icy water. Then the river shoves the rest of the canoe over into the next pool.

We have a few more obstacles to navigate around, a submerged rock and branches that droop from trees leaning out over the water. As we shoot between a couple of these dangling branches, I notice the tree's roots are barely hanging onto the rocky shore. It's worrisome to paddle beneath tons of precariously balanced wood. But I'm getting the hang of the way the canoe moves now, so I can mostly anticipate what I should do next.

I'm reasonably calm and really tired when we finally see X waving from the river bank ahead. We beach the canoe on the sandbar between the barrels the race organizers have placed here to mark the end of the canoe route.

And then, unfortunately, the rules say that the canoeists must *carry* the friggin' canoe up the bank to the exchange point. The rules also say the mountain biker can help, but since my paddling partner is *also* our mountain biker, that's of zero benefit to the Way2Go team.

After running and biking and then sitting for miles on this river, I'm so stiff I can barely crawl out. JJ doesn't look like he's feeling rusty Tin Man-like the way I am, but he has trouble balancing and getting his fake leg over the side of the canoe. I have to reach across the canoe and brace his shoulder to save him from doing a faceplant in the sand.

"I'll get out on the other side on race day," he mutters, embarrassed.

Note to self: Remember to switch sides when exiting the canoe so we'll both end up where we need to be for the carry.

We manage to stagger—half carrying, half dragging the fiberglass beast up the bank to JJ's parked mountain bike—at which point I collapse onto the ground to observe Xavier unzip JJ's PFD and yank it off, help JJ position his mountain bike foot in the pedal stirrup, and then hand him a gel pack. JJ squeezes some goop into his mouth and swallows, then pulls his water bottle from its holder and squirts in some water as he rides away.

X and I hear the shout, "To infinity and beyond!" as he vanishes down the trail through the trees.

"Freak," comments X, his hands on his hips as he watches his brother vanish into the forest.

"Let's see what he's like at the end of the kayak course," I suggest.

"Yeah."

"Has Jason always been like this?"

X snorts. "He's down; he's up. Last year was pretty intense."

"I can imagine." What would I feel like if suddenly I had only one foot instead of two? "No, that's a lie; I really can't imagine."

Instead of collecting designer feet like Jason, I think I

might ask Bailey to stomp on my head the same way he crushes melons.

I try to unzip my PFD, but the zipper pull is in an awkward place and my left hand is cramping instead of working like it's supposed to.

"Need help undressing?" X pulls off my PFD. Thank heavens, a mountain biker waiting for his canoeist to arrive volunteers to help Xavier load the canoe on top of the car. I'm happy to sit with my butt in the dirt, my back against a tree, and a water bottle in my hand. I just completed three of the longest legs of the race, and I'm not too proud to say that I am spent.

A few other teams are practicing today, too. A man with the QTL logo on his jacket sits in a folding lawn chair near the parking area, his gaze bouncing back and forth between the river and the young woman sitting next to him. She's decked out in the latest biking get-up, all synthetic sleek, with a QTL patch sewn onto her sleeve. One of those alien-style helmets rests at her feet, and what looks like a brand new mountain bike leans against a car a few feet away. I've never seen the woman before, but when the man turns to glance at the river, his face is familiar.

I quickly look away and take a long pull from my bottle of water. I pretend to pick some dirt off my pants leg while I study him out of the corner of my eye.

There's a shout from the river. "Cue-tee-ell coming in!"

The man stands up, along with the biker girl, and now that I see his erect posture, I recognize him. Shit, it's Gray Suit from this morning! The guy with that courier girl. He looks very different now in his jeans and windbreaker. I hope I look *completely* different to him.

X reappears at my side, having packed and strapped down all the canoe gear. I feel only slightly guilty as he pulls me to my feet. I moan a little for effect.

"I'm tired, too," he informs me as we slide into the car.

The QTL guy is clapping his hands, cheering on the canoeists as they stagger up the bank with their canoe. The biker gal is astride her bike, strapping on her helmet.

"Do you know those people?" I ask X.

"What people?"

"On the QTL team?" I tilt my head in their direction.

He studies them for a second. "I don't even know what a QTL is."

I shrug. "Just wondered. QTL seems to be big in Bellingham."

"Where I don't live," he reminds me. He puts the car in gear as the QTL biker streaks off beside us, disappearing down the path.

"Food?" I ask, hopeful.

"I left a ham sandwich on the passenger seat."

I feel beneath my thigh, and sure enough, my cold fingers identify a plastic bag. I pull out a sandwich that looks like a steamroller passed over it.

"Sorry." X shoots a grin at me. He pulls the car out onto Mount Baker Highway and heads back toward Bellingham.

I rip open the baggie. Never has a lukewarm two-dimensional sandwich tasted so good.

Then I must have zonked out, because the next thing I notice is that I'm alone in a car in the parking lot beside the Bellingham marina. The side of my forehead has left a smear on the passenger window. I rouse myself, extract my stiff limbs, and shamble into the park in time to see JJ come screaming in on his bike, covered in mud.

X waits by the kayak, ready to help carry it down to the dock. A couple of other practicing competitors and a cluster of families with wide-eyed kids stand by, watching the exchange. JJ screeches to a stop and leaps off. Or actually, he attempts to leap off, but he ends up nearly toppling over and then hopping on one leg as the small crowd gasps. A woman claps a hand over her mouth.

A little girl wails, "Mommy, the man ripped his leg off!"

"Awesome," adds a twerp at her side, probably her brother. His eyes are huge.

"Shit, shit, *shit*!" JJ bends and yanks his bicycle foot from the pedal cage, then lets the bike fall with a clatter as he collapses onto the damp grass, yelling "The blade! Gimme the blade!"

Beneath the dollops of mud that cling to his cheeks and chin, his face is beet red.

X tosses his brother an even weirder-looking contraption, a plastic bucket attached to a piece of metal in the shape of a J, and JJ yanks this artificial foot onto the stump of his leg. Grabbing his brother's hand, Jason vaults to his feet, wincing as he smacks the heel of his artificial foot hard on the ground.

Seizing the bow handle of the kayak, he straightens and growls, "Let's go, slacker." He and X carry the kayak down the ramp to the dock.

I shift my weight from foot to foot as I wonder if I should be doing something other than just watching. My teammates seem to have the situation in hand. X helps his brother with his PFD and then steadies the boat as JJ squirms into the cockpit. Then JJ abruptly shoves his kayak away from the dock and nearly tips over.

"Shit!" He recovers with a nice brace and then paddles off into the bay. The water is choppy. X watches, one hand cupped over his eyes to shield them from the sun.

"That poor boy," a woman standing beside me says. "He's so brave."

"He's super," the twerp says. "Like a robot man."

That sounds like something my little brother would have said. I cross my arms and shift my gaze to the far horizon.

Aaron and I used to come to this windy park to fly kites. One afternoon the gusts were so strong that the kite pulled Aaron off his feet and he almost ended up in the bay. At the time, I thought that was hilarious.

"Are you okay, honey?" The woman touches my forearm with her cool fingers.

"I'm fine." I wipe away the tear rolling down my cheek. "The wind makes my eyes water."

The Way2Go team made really good time on our practice relay, and we weren't even giving it our all. So after X and I collect JJ at the finish line in Marine Park, we three teamsters wipe off the worst grime and then celebrate with brats and brews at an outdoor beer garden downtown. The place is breezy even though it's sandwiched between buildings, but that's good because we are all ripe with sweat and dirt. Jason is twenty-one, so he buys the beer. It's unlikely the guy manning the counter will check IDs for Xavier and me. Maybe things are a little more fluid here because Bellingham is only a twenty-five-minute drive south of the border. Half the population here is

Canadian, and the drinking age up north is nineteen instead of twenty-one.

The twenty-one business is truly insulting when you think about it, anyway—at eighteen, you can vote for whatever politician you think is the least corrupt, you can die fighting in a stupid war that only corporations care about, but you can't buy a beer?

I bet they don't check IDs in Army base camps. Emilio has been in the Army since he turned eighteen, and he's been drinking for years. As I sip my beer and chomp through two bratwursts with piles of sauerkraut and extra hot mustard, I try to imagine what he's doing right now. I hope he's in his bed, not out on patrol. He seemed kind of down the last time we videochatted. I hope he's having pleasant dreams. His days are horrible enough.

After we discuss the course we just finished, JJ and X and I don't find much to talk about, since we don't really know each other. So as soon as we're done eating, we agree on a start time for Sunday, wish each other a good rest day tomorrow, and then my teammates drop me and my bike off at the Fitzgeralds' house a little before nine p.m.

The college girls are out. They're probably at a party somewhere. How can they have more energy than I do? Then I remember that they were all still asleep when I got up this morning. And they are on a regular eight-person team, so if they practiced at all, each of them did only one leg of the race.

I take my time in the bathroom, enjoying a long shower with lots of hot water. Wordage teaches me *Rhapsodize—to express oneself with enthusiasm,* and Geographastic informs me that Shiprock is a sacred Navajo peak in New Mexico, which makes me think of Bash. I wonder if he's ever seen that mountain.

I go out in my PJs to say goodnight to the world, letting myself into the backyard this time so I won't freak out Mrs. F again.

There are no clouds tonight. It's a new moon, only a curved sliver, with the ends pointing up. I read somewhere that a new moon is considered a lucky time to start something new. Ski to Sea is a new experience for me, and this is my first return to Bellingham, too, so I hope the shining silver smile above is a good omen. Just in case it will increase the odds, I make a wish on the brightest star before I turn in for the night.

Ten

I sleep so hard that I don't hear MacKenzie come in and slide into the lower bunk beneath me, which is unnerving for a hyper-vigilant girl like me. I rise and dress as quietly as I can and tiptoe to the kitchen, only to find that Mr. and Mrs. Fitzgerald are already there. I wolf down a big glass of OJ and two bagels with peanut butter. Mrs. F wants to know what I will do today. I tell her that I will rest up for the big race tomorrow and I rhapsodize over a fictional day I will spend around town with fictional friends. Then I cut out early with my pack stuffed full of clothes and a clipboard and my tablet computer.

"Maybe I'll see you at the parade," I suggest to Mrs. F as I back out the door.

No way is that going to happen. The Ski to Sea parade is the usual smallish town gig, and I'm too likely to run into someone from my old life there. No, I plan to spend today sleuthing.

When I turn on my phone, Wordage serves me *Eldritch—unearthly, weird, ghostly*. Eldritch? Really? I'm beginning to think somebody *eldritch* selects the vocabulary for Wordage. It can't be a normal human.

Maxine Newsome's house is perched on a cliff overlooking Chuckanut Bay, in the swanky area south of town. The house is modern style, all square blocks and glass. Maxine must have a rich husband, or else QTL was paying her a whole lot more than my mom. There's no way my family could have afforded a place like this.

Even with its expensive rainbow wheels, my racing bike looks out of place chained to the railing of the porch, which isn't exactly a porch but sort of a fancy entryway that overhangs a decorative creek below.

A very obvious security camera juts out over the ornate front door, and there's no way to avoid its scrutiny. I press the doorbell button. I don't hear anything from inside. I'm about to knock when the little glass peephole in the door goes dark. Should I wave? I opt for simply looking earnest and unthreatening. After a couple of seconds, the door opens.

In the doorway is the tall woman who was standing next to my mom in the photo, although now she looks older and more worn.

I smile, introduce myself, and tuck my notebook under my arm in case she wants to shake hands.

She doesn't. She seems uptight, although my interpretation might be partly due to her clothes: a gray turtleneck that reaches her chin, and a calf-length gray skirt. She looks like a governess character out of an old movie.

Her dark hair is twisted up in back and shot with streaks of silver, so I guess she's older than my mom. I don't remember ever seeing her before, and I sure hope she doesn't remember me.

She frowns, making a vertical crease appear between her brows. "Who did you say you were again?"

"Claudette Campbell," I tell her. "From the Journalism school at Western."

I know that next she's going to ask how I found her, so I quickly add, "We're supposed to write an article on women in the sciences; I picked you out of *Who's Who*."

The suspicion drains from her face and is replaced by...well, it doesn't look exactly like happiness, so maybe it's pride or at least satisfaction.

I continue my charm offensive. "I'm sorry not to call in advance, but I couldn't find your number." This much is true; her number is unlisted. "If you can spare a few minutes this morning, I'd like to ask you a few questions."

I am relieved when she steps aside and gestures me through the slate-tiled foyer into the living room beyond. "Come in."

She points at a sleek off-white leather couch that looks uber-expensive. As a matter of fact, everything in the room looks pricey, all leather and glass and chrome. Huge paintings cover one side wall, an array of photos in fancy frames on another. Small sculptures are scattered here and there on the side tables. A giant red Oriental rug on the floor gleams in the light filtering in from the wall of glass that faces the bay. I've never seen a rug so glossy; it must be made of silk instead of wool.

The most expensive thing in the room is that incredible floor to ceiling view of Chuckanut Bay. It's breath-taking.

"What a beautiful house," I comment.

She murmurs a thank you.

I perch on the edge of the couch, pull my clipboard and paper out of my bag, and sit with my pen poised above the lined page. "You were one of the leading scientists at Quarrel Tayson Labs, right?"

The compliment makes her face light up. "You could say that. Although there were several of us."

"I know QTL makes vaccines and other drugs. What was your specialty?"

"I isolated different strains of virus mutations."

I'm not quite sure what that means, so I scribble it down on my notepad as I say, "That sounds dangerous."

"It is." She nods. "But to make effective vaccines, you have to be able to target specific strains of a virus."

Maxine might be the perfect person to show my mom's scans to—she could probably decipher all those chemical alphabet codes or whatever they are. But I can't start off with that request, so I ask about how she did her job.

She smoothes her skirt over her thighs as she gives me a long description about cultivating viruses.

"You mean they keep all those viruses in the labs?" I ask.

"Of course."

Yikes. I never imagined that Mom worked among live viruses. My horror must be evident on my face, because she quickly explains, "They're stored at very low temperatures in special sealed containers, and when we work with them, we are locked into special rooms. The scientists wear special protective gear. We go through decontamination procedures every time we exit the labs. It's all very safe."

Maxine rises from the couch. "I was just getting ready to make myself some tea. Would you like a cup, Claudette?"

"That would be nice." I usually drink coffee, but I suspect Claudette would like tea.

She leaves the room, her heels clacking on the expanse of hard floor—it's black and shiny, maybe polished cement—as she heads for the kitchen. I peel myself up from the leather couch to enjoy the expansive view.

A big sailboat with all its sails tucked up tight drifts through the glassy water of Chuckanut Bay. The large crowd gathered on the deck seems to be watching one man up toward the bow. Science class? Tourist cruise? Then a woman steps forward out of the crowd, holding a flower-covered pillow in her hands. After a brief hesitation, she surprises me by tossing it into the bay.

Then I know that wasn't a pillow. I've seen this ritual once before, when the ferry service through the San Juan Islands stopped for a few minutes to allow a family to conduct a funeral ceremony.

That pillow was actually a packet of ashes.

I don't have ashes of my parents. I don't even know if they wanted to be cremated, or if they did, where they would want their ashes spread. Bellingham? Africa? In the wilderness? In the city?

When you're a kid, you never imagine that you won't have time to ask these things. I was so selfish that none of the questions even occurred to me.

I pull my gaze away from the bay to the photos on the side wall. Some of them are artsy black-and-whites of twisted trees and endless mountains, some are clearly family shots. There's a photo of a younger Maxine with a man—presumably her husband—and two teenage girls. There's another of a young boy pulling on the oars of a rowboat. He looks to be about the same age Aaron was when I last saw him.

And that thought makes me even sadder. I turn away from the photos back to the view.

Maxine returns, sets two steaming cups and saucers on the glass coffee table, and then joins me at the window. She lays a gentle hand on my shoulder. "Are you alright, dear?"

I take a deep breath to pull myself together, and then I swallow hard to make my voice work again. I tilt my head toward the window. "That's a funeral, isn't it?"

She studies the boat in the bay for a minute. It has started up its engine now and is moving away from the floating flower pillow, which swirls in the wake. "I suppose it is."

She turns to me and examines my face, which makes me nervous. I wrap my arms around myself and study the toes of my shoes for a few seconds. Finally, I say, "I'm sorry. I lost my brother a few months ago."

Another lie, although 'lost' is a good description for Aaron. It gets harder each year to remember his face, but the pain doesn't feel like it's going away any time soon.

"He was about the same age as that boy there." I point to the photo on the wall.

"Oh Claudette, you poor thing. I'd be absolutely crushed if I lost my grandson." Maxine moves her hands to my shoulders, and for a minute I'm afraid she's going to hug me, but then she simply asks, "How did your brother die?"

"Car accident."

The lies never stop. Since that night, my whole life has been a work of fiction. I can't exactly tell her about the ninjas that dragged Aaron screaming from his room. There are days when I'm not sure if that was real or I just imagined it.

I turn again to the window. The sailboat has rounded the peninsula and disappeared from view. Chuckanut Bay is empty. The pillow is nearly out of sight, too, the dark waters swallowing the fabric rectangle.

I suppose those pillows are designed to sink. Otherwise, the ashes of your loved one could end up on the beach among plastic bottle caps and six-pack holders.

"I'm sorry for your loss," Maxine murmurs, patting my shoulder.

Those TV words sound so fake, so rehearsed and formal, that they sober me right up. I sniff and say, "I'm sorry for losing it in your living room."

She nods toward the cups of tea on the coffee table. "Shall we continue?"

We sit again. The steam from my cup feels good on my cheeks as I sip my tea. The brew is good, flowery and slightly sweet, even without sugar. Maybe Claudette knows what she's doing with this tea drinking.

I pick up my notebook. It's time to get what I came here for. "Who did you work with every day?"

Maxine seems startled by the question. "What?"

I shrug. "I mean, you didn't work alone, did you? There were other scientists and maybe lab techs and such on your team? I remember reading something about..." I pretend to be scanning my notes. "...Amy Robinson?"

After keeping our names secret for so long, it always feels like violating an oath to say Mom's name out loud.

Maxine's eyes go dark. "You don't want to write about her."

"Why not? A lot of people tell me Amy Robinson is a hero."

She shakes her head like she's trying to dislodge the name from her brain. "Amy and I didn't work in the same lab. I worked on the viruses; she worked on the vaccines."

"But you knew her, right?" I press.

Maxine clenches her jaw and shoots me a look that could drill a hole through my head like a laser beam.

I squirm under her intense glare. Does she suspect something? Is she looking for similarities to my mother in my face? Thanks to my dad, my skin and hair are several shades darker than my mother's, and my hair is curly, whereas my mom's was flatiron-straight. The only feature we have in common is our eyes, a hazel color that tends toward green in certain lights.

"Amy Robinson. That woman!" Maxine almost spits the words. If she were a dog, I'd be backing up now, afraid of the bite that's coming. "That woman is not a hero. That woman ruined everything."

I am paralyzed by the venom in her voice.

"We had security. We had good-paying jobs for life. We were well respected." She twists around on the couch, making the leather squeak, and stares out the window again. "But Amy was determined to muck up everything."

Her anger is so harsh that I struggle to keep my cool. Never in my life did I imagine that my parents did anything wrong. After an awkward moment filled with static electricity, I finally find my tongue again. "What did she do?"

Maxine works her jaw for a second, takes a sip of tea before she looks back at me. "Actually, she didn't succeed in *doing* anything, but she wanted to take down QTL."

"Why would she want to take down the company?"

A look of alarm settles on Maxine's face. Her shoulders rise and fall, and then she quickly says, "Who knows?"

"How could she ruin QTL?"

Maxine sighs, exasperated. "By talking trash about the company's vaccines. By ruining the company's reputation." Her expression flattens as she says, "It doesn't matter now. She didn't get away with it."

"What happened?" I'm having a hard time staying present in this room, because now instead of the red Oriental rug here, I see Mom and Dad's bodies on our living room floor. Mannequins swimming in blood.

"She got herself canned. Her meddling husband, too."

"Her husband worked for QTL, too?" I know this is not true, but Claudette would ask.

"He handled shipments and accounts for a subcontractor. That company dumped him at the same time. Good riddance, I say."

I keep my gaze on my notebook so Maxine won't see the anger in my eyes. "Where did they go?"

She stares out the window for a long moment, then shrugs again. "Nobody knows. The whole family just skedaddled in the middle of the night like the vermin they were. Here one minute; gone the next."

You can say that last part again. I still can't believe how quickly the Robinson family was obliterated. But—*vermin?* Why would anyone lump my family in with rats and cockroaches?

I pretend to jot down a note. I obviously cannot show my

scans to Maxine; she's not a friend.

Maxine is not finished. "Amy wrecked my life."

I have to stop my gaze from bouncing around the room from the amazing artwork to the expensive furniture and jaw-dropping view. Apparently Maxine's version of having her life ruined isn't very close to mine. I lost my family, my home, and my future.

She's on a rant now. "Do you have any idea what this town would be like without QTL?" she asks. "Or for that matter, this country? Or the whole world?"

I nod and scribble more on my pad. My brain is still stuck on the idea of my mom trying to take down a company and wreck someone's life. And my dad was in there somehow, too?

"QTL saved hundreds of thousands of people! RT44 and Plactate are still saving thousands of people every day!"

I pretend to scan through the pages on my clipboard. "I saw the name P.A. Patterson somewhere," I tell her. "Did you work with someone named Patterson?"

She looks annoyed at my interruption of her soliloquy on the nobility of QTL, but pauses to ponder my question. "I believe there was a Michael Peterson in Sales for a while."

Why doesn't she mention Mr. Pederson in Security? Maybe he arrived after she left.

"The name I heard was definitely Patterson," I tell her. "Maybe some connection with Africa?" The latest email message came from Kigali, but the packages I got last year were postmarked in Johannesburg.

"QTL's parent company does own some sort of subsidiary in South Africa, I believe. And I think the company also has some connection with Zimbabwe, because that was a hot spot for Ebola mutations decades ago." She takes a sip from her teacup. "But I wouldn't know the name of anyone who works over there. Maybe someone at QTL could help you out with that. Try the HR department."

I nod. "Thanks. I'll do that."

I want to ask more about what happened with my mom and the company, but due to my unaptness, we've veered away from the subject and I can't think how to get back. "Anything else you'd like to tell me about your work at QTL, or about your colleagues there?"

"My colleagues," she repeats. "Most were great. Most knew how important, how *crucial* our work was."

But Amy Robinson ruined your life? I want to repeat. *How? Why?* None of this makes sense to me. Talking trash about vaccines? I don't remember my mom or my dad ever saying anything like that.

I do remember something weird I heard my mom say on the phone only a few days before she was killed, though: "That's not only unethical, it's immoral."

What could be unethical or immoral about vaccines? I thought Mom was talking to a coworker. Was she even talking about *vaccines*? She could have been talking about some sort of affair or unequal pay or...

"Quarrel Tayson is the *heart* of this city. Bellingham was *dying* before they came. No work, no future for kids like you graduating from the university. You want to get a decent job someday, don't you, Claudette?" Maxine waits for my answer, her teacup half way to her mouth.

I shut down my mental meandering and focus. "I sure hope so," I say. "I'd love to stay here after I graduate."

After a few more statements about how QTL is the only life raft keeping the region afloat and how everyone in the whole wide world should be so damn grateful for everything the company does, Maxine winds down, her wrath gradually evaporating like smoke.

She stares at her teacup for a couple of seconds. "I probably shouldn't have said any of that, but I can tell you're a smart girl who knows what's important. There's no need to include any discussion of Amy Robinson in your article, Claudette."

So many questions are running through my brain, but I don't know how I can ask them without blowing my cover. After all, Claudette came here to do an interview about Maxine Newsome. I wrap up our talk about her work, ask why she took early retirement. She flashes a tense smile. "The company made it worth my while."

"Is your husband retired, too?"

Her eyes cloud over, her jaw tightens, and she mutters, "He killed himself, three years ago."

Shocked, I lean forward, uncertain about what to do. "Oh, I'm so sorry. I shouldn't have asked."

When she doesn't respond, I figure I better get out of here before I get myself in trouble. I rise from the couch. "It was great to meet you, Miz Newsome. I'll send you a copy of my paper," I tell her as she walks me to the door. "Thank you so much for your time! And the tea, too. It was delicious."

Am I overdoing the chirpiness? I'm relieved when she closes the door.

The neighboring house is a twin to Maxine's, another interlocking set of concrete boxes with plenty of glass. As I bend over to unchain my bike from the railing, a black-haired man comes out the neighbor's front door. I assume he's headed for the sleek BMW parked in the driveway, but he stops just outside of the door, leans on the chrome railing there, and gazes in my direction.

A chill zings down my spine. It's Mr. Gray Suit from QTL, the same volunteer I saw at the canoe site yesterday. He lives next door to Maxine Newsome? Why do we keep running into each other? Does he recognize me as intern Jenna and racer Tana?

I have the crazy thought that he has seen me through Maxine's security camera, and it's all I can do to stop myself from looking at the lens above the doorway again. My fingers are shaking. I have a hard time twisting the cylinders on the bike lock to match up with my code. Finally, I have the cable undone, and as I wind it around the tube under the handlebars, I sneak a look at him again.

He's still staring. Actually, glaring would be a more appropriate word. His expression is intense. We're too far from each other for me to say hello without shouting, so I smile and give him a friendly little wave.

He doesn't even twitch one of his heavy black eyebrows, which form an irritated vee above his beaky nose. My stomach does a somersault. I turn my bike to go and swing onto the seat. He leans forward another few inches and grips the railing with what looks like fury, making his arm muscles stand out under his black tee shirt. Now that I see him without his suit coat or a windbreaker, I can tell he's lean and fit. He looks like he could be a hit man. I try to imagine him with a ski mask pulled over that glowering face. His neck is clean, though—no V shapes, no tattoos.

I feel his eyes on my back as I ride away. At the top of the driveway, I risk another glance over my shoulder. He aims a cell phone at me, taking my photo.

Eleven

When I reach the parking area for Arroyo Park, I stop to catch my breath. Nobody is following me.

I lock my bike to a signpost warning about car prowls and walk into the woods. Crossing over the creek, I step off the trail and climb up to one of my old favorite spots, an almost flat rock shaded by the limbs of a giant Doug fir.

It's only eleven a.m. I don't know what to do next. The only thing I know for sure is that I'm hungry again. I have two aging cheese sticks in my pack. They shine with grease because I've been carrying them around in an unrefrigerated backpack for a while, but they're probably still edible. As I peel back the plastic, I replay Maxine's words in my head.

How the hell could my mother have ruined *her* life? How could my mother have brought down QTL? I guess criticizing the products could ruin a company's reputation, but I don't know why Mom would do that; she created the original vaccine, for godssake.

I am so confused. I was expecting a hint that threats had been made, that a stalker had followed my mother or my dad, that there was some sort of black ops hit team out there. I sure as hell never thought I'd hear that either one of my parents was guilty of anything.

I pull out my tablet and bring up the old photos. Mom looks happy. Maxine looks happy. All the other employees do, too. Dad looks happy, and so do *his* colleagues from World Cargo West. What the hell could have gone wrong?

I pull up one of the mystery scans. I've stared at these things thousands of times, and they never reveal any secrets to me. Just like the other, this one is a mix of letters and numbers and strange symbols, all Greek or Martian to me. No matter how hard I stare at it, it's meaningless. I'll bet Maxine knows exactly what this is, but I don't trust her. She doesn't seem exactly objective about my parents.

Maybe if I email this scan to P.A. Patterson, he could decipher it? But that seems way too risky. While P.A. Patterson seems to connect the Robinsons with me, I don't have a clue who he is. I might lead a murderer straight to my own door.

Maybe I should try to connect with someone at World Cargo West. What would I ask? *Who* would I ask? I can't traipse into their offices and announce that I'm here to find out what happened to Alex Robinson, the freelance accountant who worked for them four years ago. Besides, it's Saturday and Memorial Day weekend, and their offices are closed.

I bring up the accounting scans. At least that's what I think these lists are. The pages have WorldCargoWest.com in the header, and the columns have labels: Pkg, Travel, Imp/Exp Fees, Shpmt, Value, Return, Notes. There are dates and names and notations like 'Del 514887 – 398 uts' and 'RRT.' What use can these possibly be to me? I could never understand how my dad did this boring work. Oh, I know that accounting is important, because order is important. And measuring. If we can't measure things and don't keep records, then how would we know if we're making progress or slipping backwards? How would cheaters ever get caught? So, yes, I understand that my dad's work was important. It's just that spreadsheets make my eyes cross, and these are no exception. Plus, the dollar amounts under Travel, Value, and Return seem astronomical. Life is so much simpler, at least on paper, when you have zero funds to manage.

My brain goes round and round in circles, one idea chasing another and getting nowhere. All that I've accomplished so far is to make myself feel stupid. And apparently, make Mr. Gray Suit suspicious.

Why was he taking my photo? That creeps me out. I hope he's not going to ask anyone about me. I've been Jenna the intern at the company offices and Tanzania Grey on the race course, and before that I called myself Edna and Sunita. What will he think if Maxine tells him about Claudette Campbell stopping by? How can I possibly come up with a plausible excuse for all these identities?

When my cell buzzes, I answer it, grateful for the distraction.

My housemate and zoo co-worker Sabrina starts right off with, "You can't come back too soon."

"The race is tomorrow. I won't be back until day after. What's up?"

"Sending you a photo."

After a second, the screen fills with an expanse of gray wrinkled skin and two mahogany-colored eyes, framed by the striped curtains that hang around our living room window.

I laugh.

"It's not funny!" she protests. "Bailey is pacing round and round the house, looking for you. He's trampled all the flowers into mush and wiped snot all over the glass. I'm afraid he's going to break a window."

Okay, that would be serious. And expensive. "Distract him."

"How?"

"Give him a pumpkin?"

Bailey loves to roll them around with his trunk. When he tires of that, he stomps on them, and finally, he eats the pieces. To Bailey, a pumpkin can be a source of entertainment for several hours. Other round melons and squashes work, too, but we generally have to pay for them, while we filled up the barn with free pumpkins last fall.

"He ate the last one six weeks ago, and in case you haven't noticed, it's not exactly pumpkin season now."

"The tire swing?" It's a favorite toy of his.

"He ripped it down this morning and tossed it into the pond."

I sigh. "Let me talk to him. Take your cell outside and put it on videochat."

"Worth a try. Hang on."

I hear her walk across our creaky wooden floor. The screen door on the front of our house bangs shut.

"Bailey!" she shouts.

After a few seconds I hear the low rumbling sounds that Bailey makes, asking what Sabrina has for him. She switches the phone to video. I see my elephant rocking slowly from foot to foot, staring expectantly at my housemate.

"Go," Sabrina says to me.

"Bailey," I say in a loud voice. "You be a good elephant, you hear? I'll be back soon. Play with Salt and Pepper." His friends, two pygmy goats. "Be good for Sabrina."

His trunk comes up and I get a close-up view of his nostrils in the tip and then all I can see is a blur of slime. I hear a snuffling noise and Sabrina shouting, "Bailey! No! No! Bailey!"

The screen reveals a brief blur of gray and then there's darkness and a flash of white as Sabrina continues to yell, her words now muffled and distant. "Give me that! Bailey!"

I'm laughing so hard that I can barely join in, but I try. "Bailey! Bad elephant! Bad!"

The clip-clop of hooves calls my attention to the trail a few yards away, where a woman riding by on a bay horse shoots me an amused look. I'm a crazy girl sitting under a tree in a northwest forest, shouting about elephants. Obviously I need to lower my voice.

Then there's a loud clunk from my phone and for a second, I see nothing. Oh jeez, please don't let that flash of white have been elephant *teeth*. Please don't let Bailey have swallowed the phone. I can't afford a vet bill and neither Sabrina nor I want to sort through mountains of elephant poop to find the cell phone.

Then finally the screen shows movement, a swipe across denim. "*That* worked well," my housemate drawls. "It's a damn good thing this cell is practically indestructible."

"Sorry," I tell her. "I thought maybe he'd listen and believe I was coming home soon."

"Right. Because elephants are so good with phones and calendars."

I laugh again.

"Any more brilliant ideas?"

"Take the goats into the back pasture. If Bailey follows, shut the gate to keep him away from the house."

"And hope for the best."

"And hope for the best," I agree. We both know Bailey can walk right through a locked gate if he wants to. "I'll be home on the morning train on Monday."

"You better pray there'll still be a house here then."

"Thanks for holding down the fort. And thanks for the laugh."

"Next time I'll juggle goats for your entertainment. Speaking of which, dammit, Pepper!" She abruptly hangs up.

I go back to staring at the scans on my tablet. The letters and symbols in the chemistry formulas still mean nothing to me. I switch to the accounting scan. Totally beyond my comprehension. But they must be significant in some way, if my mom buried them on a thumb drive along with our spare house key. Clearly, I need help, an expert in chemistry or math or maybe physics. The most logical choice would be one of those women I met yesterday morning. Maybe Dr. Wigener?

Way too risky. She might talk to Maxine. And what sort of story could I possibly make up about where I got these scans? Finding a discarded USB drive on the street seems a little implausible. An errant email? No, that could be traced. If these scans *are* important, anyone from QTL is likely to take them from me, and—oh yeah, *major* reason not to go there—check into *my* background and identity.

There is only one person in the world I can truly trust, because there is only one person who knows my history. He's almost twenty-two now, and he's studying some sort of bio-engineering having to do with recycling waste materials. That has got to include a bunch of chemistry and math. I check the time on my phone. It's almost noon, which means that it's close to one in New Mexico. I highlight José Alvarez on my People list (I would never list his real name) and press Talk.

I listen to the phone ring five times. It's weird how we all hear old-fashioned rings on one end when the person on the other might be hearing Beethoven's Fifth or a rooster crowing. I love my loon call ring tone; it reminds me of a tranquil sunset on the water.

A gruff voice interrupts my musing. "Yeah?"

In the background, I hear hammering. Bash is hiding out in some undisclosed poverty-stricken place in New Mexico, helping the community build a recycling center and water treatment plant.

"Hail, Royal Son Bash. Are you working?"

"Why wouldn't I be, Tarzan?"

Hearing his voice puts a grin on my face. He's the only person I'd let call me Tarzan. "Uh, because it's Saturday?"

"Coincidentally, that's the day most people have off to volunteer on projects like this."

Duh. I would trust my life to Sebastian Callendro, but he does have this irritating way of making me feel like an idiot pretty regularly. It's that older and wiser thing, not to mention the much-more-worldly turn his life took after he was outed as The President's Son.

Into my silence, he asks, "Qué pasa, amiga? You need bail money or something?"

I snort. "Or something. I need a chemistry expert."

"You planning to sell designer drugs for money to feed that massive beast wandering around your yard?"

"You know me too well. You got any of those recipes?"

"Let me check." There's a brief pause punctuated by the whine of a power saw. "The closest I can come up with is a recipe for date bars."

"That sounds better, anyway."

"And not nearly as likely to blow up your house."

"Another plus," I respond. "No, seriously, I need someone who understands chemistry—actually, it's probably biochemistry—to look at some scans of formulas. Could you do that?"

"Don't know until I see them," he says. "Send 'em on. Seeing as how it's you, I presume this is all hush-hush?"

"Seeing as how it's me," I confirm. "Hey, guess what—I'm getting ready to race in the Ski to Sea and you'll never guess who my partners are."

He waits, and my phone bleeps a call waiting signal into my ear. Probably Sabrina again. Another second passes. "Give up?"

"You said I'd never guess."

"Jason Jones! And his brother, Xavier."

"The same Jason Jones whose foot was obliterated last year?"

"He has a whole suitcase full of feet now. Or maybe it's a footlocker."

Bash groans at my pun. "Who'da thought? I'm envious. Not of the feet, but man, I sure miss racing."

"You'll get back to it next year. You're too good to stop."

On Bash's end of the call, I hear a female voice. "Stan? Stan? Oh Stan the Man, I neeed you!"

Her voice is melodious, her tone flirtatious. I envision a blond babe in a skin-tight tee shirt and tool belt that molds to her shapely hips.

Another bleep chirps in my ear.

"Coming!" Bash yells back.

"*Stan?*" I ask. "Don't they know who you are?" Most Americans have seen photos of Sebastian Callendro; they've been plastered all over TV and cyberspace in the last two years. Millions of people know his name. Hundreds, if not thousands, of paparazzi are on the lookout for The President's Son.

"Some of them know," Bash says, "But I don't want people shouting out my name for everyone to hear, do I?"

"Good point."

"I better get back to it."

Another bleep. I lower the phone from my ear and see that the call waiting is *Emilio Santos*. "Gotta go, too. Will send those scans in a minute. Ciao!"

I flash over to the other call. "Shadow!"

"What's up, Tee?" he asks. "Took you so long, I was getting ready to leave a message."

"I had to dig out my phone. I'm hiking in the woods in Bellingham. I'm running in a race tomorrow, remember? I sent you email."

There's muffled silence for a beat. "You were talking to *him*, weren't you?"

Why is it that the only person in the world who suspects when I'm lying is my jealous boyfriend, Sergeant Emilio Santos?

"Sebastian and I are just friends," I explain for the nine-hundredth time. "I needed to ask him a question about chemistry." I figure it's safe to say that, because Emilio knows virtually nothing about that subject.

"Why would you need to know anything about chemistry?" His voice is full of anger.

"Can we switch to video?" I press the icon so he can see my face, and after a second, I can see his. The top half of his forehead is pale from wearing his helmet, while the rest of his skin is tanned dark from the sun. His face is haggard, with creases across his brow, chapped lips, and about two days worth of stubble on his cheeks and chin. He could be forty instead of a few months shy of twenty-one.

"Nice to see you, Shadow." I flash him a smile. "Sabrina and I are worried about the herbicides they use at the zoo," I explain in a chirpy tone, reasonably certain this topic will quickly bore him into a stupor. "I wanted someone to read the formula on the container and tell me if anything was dangerous. Nobody at the zoo is gonna do that."

Sure enough, his eyes glaze over and he grunts, "Uh-huh."

"Enough about me. What's new in the peacekeeping industry?"

"Same old." He sighs heavily. "They kill each other. Sometimes they try to kill us. We ride around and try not to kill too many of them." He rubs a finger across his left eyelid.

There's a window behind him, and I can see it's dark outside. "Is it late there?"

"Almost ten p.m.," he says wearily, which tells me he's in the Middle East somewhere. "Are you really in Bellingham?"

"Yeah—we talked about it last time, remember? I'm on an extreme team in this Ski to Sea race tomorrow with two guys. I'm running, biking, and canoeing."

His jaw tightens. "Guys?"

Oh please. "Jason Jones, the guy who lost half his leg in the Verde Island race? And his younger brother, Xavier. Or JJ and X, as they're calling themselves now."

"You're running with a guy with half a leg?"

"*He's* not running. And even if he was, we wouldn't be running together. It's a relay. X hands the baton to me and I hand it to JJ. Except it's a timing chip, not a baton."

Shadow rolls his eyes. "The things you do for fun, Tee. How's the elephant?"

Aiming for a lighter note, I tell him, "I need to find Bailey some chores to do around the place before he gets into trouble. He seems interested in gardening."

Bailey is famous for ripping up plants just to taste them. I laugh at my own joke, but Emilio doesn't even crack a smile. Suddenly, his somber face scares me. "You okay?"

He sighs and rubs his fingers over his close-cropped hair. "Just tired. And you're so far away. We're in two different worlds."

"What did you do today?" I ask.

"Flattened two houses and then toured the area in the tank for a while. Show of force."

I don't know what to say to that. It does not sound like peacekeeping to me. It doesn't even sound constructive.

"The kids here throw rocks," he says. "The women spit and give us evil eye signs."

Small wonder. Flattening houses is probably not the best way to make friends. But I don't say that. I don't know the whole story. I'm not sure I want to.

"Things are heating up here; we're moving out tomorrow to a new base."

"I hope your new digs are nice."

He grimaces. "God, I miss you, Tee. I miss my real life."

I try to think of an appropriate way to respond. The military *is* his real life right now; he has two more years to go. "I miss you, too, Shadow. When's your next leave?"

He groans and scratches the bottom of his chin. "Who knows?"

"We'll do something fun then."

He leans close to the camera so his whole face fills the screen. "You know I love you, don't you, Tana?"

I gulp. "Yes, I know you do."

He's waiting for me to say it back. I owe Emilio Santos so much. I'd be crushed if he died, but I'm not sure I love him the way he wants. He knows only the hardworking Tanzania Grey part of me. I don't know what would happen if he knew about snooty cowardly Amelia Robinson's past.

What I do know is that he needs someone from home to hang onto. He needs someone to plan a future with, so I murmur, "Stay safe, my hero."

"I'm trying." He leans back, and through the window behind him, I see a flash of light. A searchlight? An explosion? He glances that way and then looks back at the camera. "Some days I'm not sure if it's worth it."

What does he mean by that? He's really frightening me now. "Think about Michoacán," I urge him. "We have to go see all those monarchs."

He scrubs both his hands over his face for a couple of seconds. I don't have a clue what's going on in his head. He's either really tired or really sad, or maybe he's trying to rub the vision of trees full of butterflies into his brain. Finally he puts his hands down and stares at the camera for a long second before he says, "Good luck tomorrow. Good night, sweet Tee."

He kisses two fingers and presses them against the lens. And then my phone goes dark and silent and I'm sitting all alone in a beautiful forest on a sunny day, feeling anxious and guilty as hell.

After I send the chemistry scans to Sebastian, I still have the afternoon to myself. The parade downtown is over, so I bike through the area, heading north to Bellingham's small airport. The city sidewalks are practically empty now, with only a few Ski to Sea volunteers doing litter cleanup along the parade route. There were obviously horses involved; I have to swerve to avoid piles of grassy manure. The historic buildings of downtown quickly give way to residential neighborhoods crowded with working class homes; some beautifully maintained Victorians, some worn-looking rentals. Then all the properties thin out to the warehouses and small manufacturing facilities that surround the airport.

When my dad worked for them, World Cargo West had an office near the airport, but I can't find it now. I ride around in a circle for two circuits, peering at all the buildings. Unfortunately, one of these structures is the local highway patrol office, and an officer is standing out front. He's still there on my second go-around and he's staring at me. He waves me over, which starts my heart pounding. I debate for a second about taking off, but I make myself stop beside him in the parking lot, still straddling my bike.

"Can I help you?" he asks. His nametag says Collins. He studies my face like he's memorizing it.

"Uh..." is the first thing that comes out of my mouth. His

scrutiny makes me squirm. I've often wondered what the Bellingham cops would do if I confided in them. Based on my experiences right after my parents were killed, I'm pretty sure it wouldn't be good.

Finally, he smiles hesitantly and says, "You're Zany Grey, aren't you?"

I almost fall over on top of my bike. It's not often that I run into someone who knows me, especially by that stupid nickname. "Tanzania Grey, yes. Most people call me Tana."

"I remember you last year from the Verde Island race."

"Yeah?" A few people might remember me because of the terrorist incident there, but nobody has ever told me they saw the race.

"Tober Collins is my nephew."

That explains it. He followed the race because he was close to one of the other competitors.

"Here for Ski to Sea?"

"I'm on the Way2Go Extreme Team. Running, road bike, canoeing."

He whistles a low note to show me he thinks that's impressive. "Good luck."

"Thanks; I think I'll need it." I tell him that I'm looking for World Cargo West.

He tilts his head toward the building across the street. "World Cargo West used to be over there, but they went out of business about two years ago. Couldn't hack it after the big scandal, I guess."

"Big scandal?" I know nothing of this. You don't get a lot of news when you're in the fields picking crops like I did for the first two years I was on the run.

"They were in the import-export business."

"I know." My dad spent a lot of time figuring out the most cost-effective ways to move goods around the world. He was forever boring dinner guests with talk about the fluctuations of pesos or yen or euros.

"Turned out one of their major clients was importing not only coffee beans from Colombia, but also cocaine."

I don't have to pretend that I am shocked. "No!"

"It's true."

Another highway patrol officer emerges from the building and stops to cast a look in our direction. "Ready, Collins?"

"Ready." Collins gives me a final nod, says "Take care," and gets into a patrol car with the other officer.

I ride my bike across the street and study the old World Cargo West building for a couple of minutes. The sign out front reads SeaStone Enterprises. Did World Cargo West know their client was dealing in drugs? Did my father stumble on that information? Did it cost both my parents their lives? My jaw clenches with frustration. At QTL, I could find employees like Dr. Wigener and Maxine and the courier, but now there's not even a company to start with to find out more about my dad's work.

I pull my cell out of my pocket and check my messages before getting back on my bike. Only one from Sabrina, wondering where I hid the sugar. I used the last of it to make some hummingbird nectar. *We're out*, I text back, *sorry*.

For once, Wordage gives me a word I've actually heard before: *Innocuous—harmless, innocent, safe.*

I try to believe that word applies to everything I've been up to today.

Twelve

The preparation for the race starts well before dawn, and for the first time, the three college girls get up at the same time as I do. I dress in the long-sleeved Way2Go shirt and pack the short-sleeved tee in my bag, along with some other clothes. We eat a huge breakfast (Mrs. F is a big believer in complex carb loading, and bananas), and wish each other luck before JJ and X arrive to pick me up. They explain that they unloaded the canoe and kayak and JJ's mountain bike yesterday, so there's only my racing bike to carry on the rack. Way2Go drives up the Mount Baker Highway to the starting point. As the miles roll past, I find it incredible that this distance will be covered in a race that will be over before sundown. People power to the max.

My nerves are jangling, and the electrical current bouncing around the inside of our car tells me that my teammates feel the same way. We don't find much to say to each other, so I pass the time by checking into my education apps. The *eldritch* server at Wordage delivers *Anabranch— part of a river that diverts from and then rejoins the main stream.* Huh. Who knew such a thing even had a name?

Geographastic tells me that there's a debate about whether the longest river in the world is the Amazon or the Nile. I probably saw an *anabranch* of the Amazon on my last Jungle Run, or maybe that was a river on its own? Who decides these things?

The parking lot near the race start is a mass of RVs and cars. A few tents are perched on the soggy grass between patches of snow. We meet Sasha, the WWU sophomore cousin JJ and X mentioned. She has freckles like JJ and X, but her hair is red, not sandy blond. She's wearing a wool turtleneck under her Way2Go tee, and a long fuzzy scarf is wrapped around her neck. Even with gloves and a stocking cap, she stills stamps her feet and swings her arms to stay warm in the dawn chill.

"I've been here for almost an hour," she says.

"Linnea? Kim?" Jason asks.

"Kim couldn't make it after all. Linnea's up at the first relay point with Xavier's skis." Sasha points toward the top of the mountain. "We'll grab X when he's done, and then as soon as they'll let us through, we'll drop him off at the canoe leg and drive to the kayak start to meet you there."

JJ turns to me. "Let's go. I gotta drop you off before they close the highway."

Just getting the equipment and volunteers in place sounds like a secondary relay to me. I'm having a hard time keeping track of who will be where. "Wait—who will meet me at the road bike start?"

The cousins toss a glance around their family circle. "I'll drop off your bike on the way down the mountain," JJ tells me.

"There won't be a volunteer there?"

JJ shakes his head. "No cars on the road while the bikes

are racing, and we don't want to get stuck. You can get on your bike by yourself, can't you?"

"Yeah, but…" It will cost valuable seconds for me to unlock my bike. Seconds can make the difference between winning and losing the race. *Stop with the competitiveness*, my conscience nags, *this is supposed to be fun.*

JJ reads my mind. "I'll make sure your bike is right at the checkpoint. Nobody will steal it."

I sure hope he's right; I wouldn't want to explain otherwise to the guys at Dark Horse Networks. "Okay."

A loudspeaker announces fifteen minutes till the start. X begins his stretches and jogs in place to warm his muscles. He pulls on fingerless biking gloves to help with leaps over rocks in the parkour course.

JJ holds out a fist. "Kill it, bro."

"Consider it dead." X bumps his knuckles against his brother's.

I'm not sure what "it" is—maybe the competition? I envy their sibling closeness.

The chatter of the contestants is nearly drowned out by a steady background buzz. All around us, drones rise from the ground like miniature helicopters. I can't decide if it's cool or creepy. Maybe a little of both.

"We'll have to keep in mind all these cameras," X comments. "No rearranging the junk; no scratching of crotches."

His brother laughs.

I hope I've peed all I need to for the next several hours. I'd hate for a drone vid to feature me crouching in the bushes with my tights around my ankles.

Another announcement. "Five minute warning. Contestants, please approach the starting line."

"Way2Go." JJ puts his hand out. X puts his on top, and then the brothers look at me. It takes me a millisecond to realize what they want, but then I put my hand on top of X's, and we grin at each other and bellow a loud "Way2Go!" before we part ways. The camaraderie feels good.

X is quickly lost in the melee, and JJ and I start down the road. We hear the blare of the starter horn a few seconds later—it sounds like one of the Washington State ferries leaving the dock.

Parking is nonexistent and there are hundreds of people at the bottom of the ski area, so JJ drops me off and then I have to walk quite a distance before I reach the exchange area. The other mountain runners are stretching and dancing around and grabbing quick sips of energy drinks. I scan the crowd for the QTL runner. It takes a while, because I don't know whether to look for a man or a woman. When I finally spot the distinctive company logo on a black shirt, I'm surprised to see the redhead lab scientist wearing it. Damn. I can't ask her for more details about the company or Amy Robinson's reputation. I don't even want her to see me, so I slide behind a group of college kids to become less conspicuous.

Then I spy Catie Cole in her yellow Femme Fatales Extreme Team shirt and black running tights and walk over to say hello.

"Good luck, Catie."

She straightens from her stretch and holds out a hand for me to shake. "You too, Tana. Let's show 'em what the extreme ladies can do."

"We will."

The volunteers are all gathered around a big screen, which seems an odd thing to have on the mountain. They abruptly break into a cheer. Then a couple of them turn and point to the mountain top, where half a dozen skiers are spilling down the slope.

I shield my eyes from the bright morning sun with my hand and scan the snowfield. It's a rainbow cascade of downhillers and snowboarders going every which way—black, red, blue, purple, lemon yellow.

I spot X's green Way2Go tee shirt. He slides down the hill on his snowboard, narrowly missing a skier, and then cutting in front of another snowboarder. It looks like he might come in fourth or fifth, which is miraculous, considering that hundreds started at the same time.

I jog in place, swallow a gulp of water from a paper cup that a volunteer hands me, and then position myself as close to the timer checkpoint as I can get without being in anyone's way. Catie lines up right beside me.

Wristband past the sensor, I remind myself. I watch as three skiers hand off their wristbands to their runners, who pass through the starting gate. As each holds out the wristband toward a bulls-eye, the sensor beeps, recording the team's starting time for that leg.

X slams into place, spraying me with slushy snow. He's slimed with mud and icy grit. As he falls sideways on his snowboard, he rips off the wristband and tosses it to me. Ugh. The elastic is as wet and filthy as he is, but I clutch it tightly as I point the timing chip at the sensor. As soon as I hear the beep, I race away, because Catie's skier is sliding to a stop.

After I put fifty yards between myself and the starting point, I manage to pull the band over my hand and onto my right wrist.

I dash to the flag where the course leaves the road. The mountain run leg follows a hacked out path that zigzags down the flanks of the mountain, but since this year's rules say I can choose my own course as long as I stay in the designated area, I leave the trail whenever it seems more efficient, leaping over downed logs and descending in a straighter, steeper downhill route.

I hear Catie's footsteps and rhythmic breathing behind me, and as I round a bend in the trail, I catch a flash of her yellow tee and blond ponytail. She's not even a second behind me, and she seems to be gaining. This feels like old times. We exchange places several times as we descend the mountain, always within view of each other. With all the cars and crowds and buzzing drones, there's no wildlife in sight today. I'm thankful that Miz Redhead from QTL isn't within view, either.

The ten miles of the mountain run route pass quickly, and soon I emerge back onto the Mount Baker Highway and spot the road bike checkpoint ahead. Catie leapfrogs me again as a volunteer hands her a bike and helmet and I have to locate mine leaning against a nearby tree. I pass my wristband through the checkpoint a few seconds behind her.

Her bike is even spiffier than mine, and she's fast on it. She probably has a bike coach and a dedicated track at home.

On a downhill slope, I manage to bend and grab the water bottle from its holder and squirt some of the precious liquid into my mouth. Today the bikers have the entire right lane to themselves. I don't know why we don't get the left, too, but since I'm near the front of the pack, I'm not squeezed anyway.

Still, on this twisting road, this leg feels plenty dangerous at this speed. Careening down a highway on this racing bike feels too fast and more than a little dangerous. I'm so glad there are no cars on the road with us today.

Unlike running, bike riding requires complete focus for me, especially at this speed. The shoulders along the highway are narrow and lined with thick trees on both sides. I could end up splattered against one of those Douglas firs just from hitting a patch of gravel or even one of the many pinecones that litter the road.

My legs burn, but I keep pumping as fast as I can. When the highway straightens, my helmet mirror reveals a big group of riders closing in behind me like a pack of wolves. I focus on the road ahead and pedal harder than I ever have before. The wind rushing past dries some of the sweat I worked up during my downhill run. My head itches under my bike helmet; I can't wait to yank it off.

Catie finishes the road bike leg at least fifty yards in front of me. I watch as she leaps off her bike (gracefully, of course), letting it fall as she races to pass off the timing chip to her teammate down at the canoe launch area. Skidding into the gravel parking lot, I also hop off my bike, but since it's a loaner and I don't have a garage full of extra sports equipment like Catie does, I hold onto the handlebar with one hand until a kind woman in an orange volunteer vest grabs it from me. Then I dash through the timer gate and down to the river bank where JJ waits with the canoe, one foot already inside, yelling "C'mon, Tee! Move it!"

Xavier holds out my PFD. I jam my arms through the holes. He's still pulling on a tab to tighten it as I jump into the boat. As we push off, I remember to unsnap my bike helmet and toss it at him, and then we are off.

My right buttock cheek plops down on an energy gel pack and as we back away from the bank, I take a second to squeeze some gel (cherry) into my mouth, followed by a squirt of water from the bottle at my feet.

Then I drop everything and paddle hard. We pass by the trees overhanging the river and zigzag between a couple of rocks and branches that I don't remember from two days ago. The river is moving just as swiftly as it was then. The weather yesterday was warm and the snow has been melting in the mountains, so maybe the current is even faster.

"Strainer ahead!" JJ yells from the back of the boat.

At least now I know to look for a log jam. It might be my imagination, but I think the damn thing is even bigger than it was during our practice run. It is a colossal obstacle that reaches halfway across the stream, and the Nooksack is swiftly sweeping us toward it.

We nearly upset the canoe as we frantically paddle on the same side to pass the log jam. But just as I think we'll make it, our back end starts swinging in the direction of the strainer like a nail pulled toward a magnet.

"Damn it, Zany, paddle like you mean it!" JJ shouts.

What the hell does he think I've *been* doing? I want to yell back that I ran ten miles and then I biked forty-two miles before I even got into this canoe, but what good would that do? So I switch sides and dig in, but the current has us in its clutches, and we slam broadside into the logjam of debris. I swear that this farrago has tripled in size since I last saw it. It's a gigantic dam of branches.

"No, no, no!" JJ bellows as we hit. And then we both lean right to dig our paddles into the water.

It's a fatal mistake. The canoe tips sideways and the current pushes the icy water inside.

Jason goes into the river first, and although I try to hang onto the upward side of the boat, I get only a second more of air before I'm sucked under the surface, too.

Thirteen

The force of the river is unbelievable. Jason and I are both wearing life vests, but the horrific current still sucks us beneath the surface and jams us up against the strainer.

I am nearly impaled on a mass of sticks and roots that gouge my stomach and breasts and face. The water shoves up against my back, plastering me against the log jam, while at the same time flowing downward, tugging my feet and legs toward a black void below. I open my eyes in the swirling current to see dark green and darker shadows. The glacial meltwater scours my eyeballs with icy grit.

I kick as hard as I can, but my legs are being sucked down under the debris jam, and if I move upwards at all, it's no more than an inch or two. My lungs are already burning. Where is Jason? At first I can't see anything but the green blur, but as I frantically grope my way along the wood pile, I finally identify a pale shape among the sticks. A hand. Jason's holding onto the strainer, too.

I grab hold of my partner's wrist and pull. After I yank hard, he lets go of the branch he's been clinging to. I try desperately to claw my way up the debris dam with my free hand, but the force of the water shoves my head down as effectively as a giant hand holding me under.

I'm getting desperate for air. My lungs feel like overinflated balloons that could pop at any second. I'm afraid to look at Jason. He went under a second before I did. Is he drowning? Has he already drowned?

Then I feel a tug on my hand. Jason is still alive. Above my head, I can see a lighter shade of green that has to be the surface, and I try again to kick up. A broken branch stabs me in the neck and rakes across my shoulder. I'm as stuck in this fierce current as if I'm swimming through hardening cement.

Our extreme team may just extremely die here.

Then a crazy thought blasts through my oxygen-deprived brain. If I can't swim up to air, I should try going down. At least it would be less embarrassing to drown in deep water instead of three feet from the surface. So I struggle to turn, pulling myself along the strainer with my free hand, pushing my head downward into the violent flow. Jason tugs back, trying to stop me, but then he either understands my intention or gives up on living, because he stops pulling. I kick with all my might, and finally try to brace my feet against the strainer to gain some leverage, which causes me to lose my shoes to the tangled mess.

Dark shadows dance in front of my eyes, and something long and slick—a fish?—darts from left to right in front of my face. My lungs are bursting. I can't hold my breath much longer. My back scrapes against branches or rocks or something else that is sharp enough to dig trenches through flesh.

Then, abruptly, we are swallowed down and flung sideways into the current.

We tumble with the swirling water. I lose Jason's hand. I can no longer tell which way is up. Everything's black and green with flashes of white. I keep kicking and cursing the PFD manufacturers about how useless their so-called life vests are.

There's a roaring in my ears that's bigger than the river, bubbles are escaping from my lips, and what little I can see is going black. Just when I think I can't stand it anymore, that I have to open my mouth and suck in a fatal breath of cold water, my head breaks the surface. Jason pops up beside me, choking and gasping.

We can't do anything except struggle to breathe for at least a full minute. I don't think there will ever again be enough air to satisfy my lungs. How long were we under? Seemed like at least half an hour. It's truly amazing how long you can hold your breath when your only alternative is dying.

I hear a weird buzzing. Which doesn't seem so surprising, given that I just almost drowned. It probably indicates some sort of brain damage.

When the air hits my brain again, I notice we are not floating down the river, but treading water in an eddy behind the strainer, holding onto branches at the back of the log jam. Water is moving through the strainer at the surface, but it's a sluggish flow, nothing like the torrent moving around and under it.

Jason seems to be floundering. Both his hands are curled around branches. I guess it's harder to tread water with an artificial foot. I look downstream, but I can't see our canoe. Which means...

"Hang on," I tell him. I claw my way up the back side of the strainer. As my head clears the top, sure enough, I spy our canoe still broadside to the biggest log. My bare feet and ankles are scraped and punctured by sharp sticks and thorns. It seems completely unfair that thorny blackberry vines are tangled with the rest of the wood debris—aren't tree trunks and broken branches enough, for godssake?

"Zany!" Jason yells as I climb over the top. I hope it's only my imagination that he sounds desperate.

I forgive him for his second relapse. I can barely remember my own name right now.

"Getting the canoe!" I bellow back over my shoulder.

The boat is half full of water and one paddle is still inside. I manage to dump out most of the water as I crouch unsteadily on the bouncing log jam and haul the canoe upside down out of the river. Amazingly, I find the other paddle among the branches of the strainer. I toss both into the canoe.

"Way to wipe out, Way2Go!" Two men wearing Iron Men tees and orange race bibs flash past in their canoe, not even close to this damn log jam. I stick out my tongue at their backs.

"Tana!" Jason shouts from the other side. At least he remembered to use the right name. He must be recovering.

I stand up on the biggest log, teetering a little because the footing is nowhere close to steady, and then I lean back and use all the strength and leverage I can muster to haul the canoe, bow first, up over the top of the strainer. A flash of light stabs my eyes. At first I think it's sunlight reflecting off our canoe's metal trim, but the angle isn't right, and then I realize the flash is related to the buzzing I hear, which is not river water in my ear canals. A drone is hovering only a couple of yards away. The sun glances off its metal skin as it zips around, filming our disaster in living color.

Wonderful. I'm so glad JJ and I both still have clothes on. At least we won't look like *naked* idiots.

"Grab the canoe!" I yell to my partner as the bow of our boat slides down into the water.

Thankfully, Jason manages to grab the edge of the canoe as it slides past him. My plan is to jump in as the canoe moves past, like a cowboy leaping onto a moving horse. But instead I end up barely catching onto the stern as the boat and I simultaneously fall off the log jam into the water.

I have to do a fast hand-over-hand maneuver to the side opposite Jason so we won't flip the damn canoe over again. The current pushes us out into the main channel. Soon we'll be completely out of control once more. When my hands are even with my partner's on the other side, I yell, "Hold on as tight as you can."

When I see Jason's knuckles whiten as they grip the side of the canoe, I kick hard and pull myself up. The canoe tilts scarily toward the water. But Jason probably weighs a few pounds more than I do. He manages to anchor the boat, and I belly-flop inside.

Now that I'm upright, I see we're headed directly for the big gravestone rock, so I snatch the paddle from the bottom and stroke hard to get our canoe back into the center of the flow. Then it's time to pull my partner into the canoe.

Right. I try to plant my butt on the opposite side for counterbalance, but Jason can't kick hard enough to get up, and every time I lean over to pull him, the canoe tilts toward him and we threaten to flip again. He's shivering. His teeth are chattering. He won't be able to hold on much longer. We're both still wearing our PFDs, so he's not likely to drown, but our race is over.

I am about to stroke toward shore when I spy a rescue kayak headed our way. To my surprise, the man with the paddle is Mr. QTL, Gray Suit, Maxine's neighbor. I guess I misjudged him. He's a good guy after all, coming to help.

But as he nears, his face doesn't show concern or reassurance. Am I reading him right? His eyes are cold. His lips are set in a determined line. He exudes pure malice.

The other competitors are gone; there's nobody else in sight. I'm making myself dizzy glancing back and forth, trying to keep an eye on Jason, the river hazards, and Mr. QTL. As he brings his kayak alongside our canoe, he raises his paddle toward me. He's going to knock me out of this boat, and there's not a lot I can do about it.

What will happen then? Will he hold me underwater with his paddle till I drown? Will he kill Jason, too? Why is he doing this?

As the kayak nears, I glance up to be sure that our drone will capture this attack.

Fourteen

Mr. QTL notices me looking up. When he spots the drone, his expression abruptly morphs from Psychotic Killer into Selfless Rescuer. He quickly lays his paddle along the top of his kayak and grabs onto the side of our canoe, rafting up.

"Pull him in!" he shouts.

I am reluctant to turn my back to Mr. QTL, but Jason's a goner if I don't. I kneel in the bottom of the canoe, reach over the edge and curl my fingers under the shoulder straps of Jason's PFD. With my assistance and Mr. QTL counterbalancing our combined weight, my partner is finally able to heft himself over the side.

Now I see what all the floundering was about. Jason's artificial foot is gone. Probably stuck in the strainer alongside my shoes.

Jason won't look at me; I know he's ashamed and embarrassed. I can identify; I feel weak and incompetent at my inability to pull my partner out of the water. As soon as Jason has flopped into the bottom of the canoe, Mr. QTL lets go and peels his kayak off into an eddy.

I add confused to my list of feelings: did I imagine those swiftly changing facial expressions? But there's no time to check out what he's up to behind us, because our canoe is about to go over the drop.

Jason pushes himself upright, grabs his paddle, and we both stroke hard to stay in the middle of the current. We've switched positions. Now he's in front and I'm behind, copying his paddle strokes. He's shivering. I'm surprised he can move at all after all that time in the icy water. But then, he's an extreme like me.

"You okay?" I yell.

He doesn't answer but instead holds up his paddle, positioning his hands to give me a brief double thumbs-up before we both have to paddle again. The rest of the canoe leg seems downright anticlimactic until we beach the boat on the sandy shore at the finish point. That's when I realize that between us we have only three and a half legs to carry the canoe up the slope.

For a few seconds I wonder if we can both go down onto our knees and drag the boat up that way, but Jason manages to hop-drag-hop-drag his side. I lurch-and-drag as hard as I can, and together we jerk our canoe up the slope.

Behind the thundering of my pulse and the locomotive chug of my labored breaths, I hear cheers from the onlookers. I can't decide if this is the ultimate celebration or the supreme humiliation. I glance at Jason. The expression on my partner's face is a mix of pain, embarrassment, and determination. The sharp gravel jabs into my bare feet and I can feel at least one blackberry thorn in my left heel, so I'm pretty certain the expression on my own face is mostly pain.

When we finally reach the exchange point, X hands his brother a different artificial foot, shoes, and a pack of energy gel, yanks off Jason's PFD and helps him into a fleece-lined windbreaker. After sucking the last of the gel from the pack, Jason mounts his bike and pedals off.

"Way2Go!" X and I bellow at his back.

"To infinity and beyond!" His voice sounds more hoarse than two days ago.

The crowd of canoeists, bikers, and volunteers roars in approval. I marvel at how our competitors can be so enthusiastic. Personally, I can barely stand up. X throws an arm around me and helps me stagger to the bench of a nearby picnic table. My legs and feet are criss-crossed with bloody scratches, and when I raise my arms to help X take off my PFD, I realize my hair is a mass of sticks and leaves.

"You won't believe what happened," I whine.

"We saw it all, Tana." He points to a large screen that is showing two canoes frantically maneuvering to avoid the strainer and each other.

I stare at it, open-mouthed.

Xavier hands me a sandwich. "They have screens set up at every exchange point so the teams can see when their racers are coming in. Didn't you notice them?"

The big screen at the ski-to-runner handoff seems so long ago. "I was a little busy running and then getting on a bike and then I was in a canoe."

X grins. "Fair enough. Now you're done; you can catch up on all the action."

I take a big bite out of the sandwich. "Hell, I'm happy just to be alive. I can't believe JJ can still pedal."

We look at each other for a second, then high-five and yell in unison, "Way2Go Extreme Team!"

A volunteer brings me a most welcome cup of hot chocolate. After checking out my legs and feet, he says, "I'll get First Aid," and wanders off to find whoever or whatever that might be.

After a couple of gulps of hot chocolate, I'm more interested in dry clothes than anything else. I limp to the bathroom, use my fingers to rake the biggest chunks of debris from my hair, and change into my clean short-sleeved Way2Go tee shirt, shorts, and flip-flops, which is all I have now that my running shoes are at the bottom of the river. When I get back, our canoe has been loaded on top of the car, and my bike is on the back rack.

I inhale a second sandwich and five cookies while the First Aid lady cleans my scratches and punctures and pulls the thorn out of my heel.

"How many teams have come through?" I ask her.

"Twelve, including yours. You were eighth."

Not exactly champion material. But to be in eighth place after nearly dying feels pretty good right now.

She sprays down my legs and feet with some sort of sticky instant bandage stuff. After a few seconds, it dries to a plastic skin that makes my legs look as if they're encased in shiny pantyhose. Thankfully, that stuff doesn't sting nearly as much as the GluSkin that med teams have used to seal gashes in my other races. X pulls me to my feet and we take off in the car, headed to the finish line of the race. He tells me Sasha and Linnea are waiting at the marina to assist JJ as much as they are allowed when he transitions from mountain bike to kayak.

I hope he doesn't pull off his foot this time.

The finish line is at Marine Park in Fairhaven. Of course there's no parking within a half mile, but we finally find a spot several blocks away in a residential neighborhood. We shrug on ball caps and windbreakers and pin our race patches over the outer layer. Then we walk (actually, Xavier strolls and I limp) through the off-leash dog area and across the railroad tracks to join up with the crowd on the beach. When people spy our race patches, they respectfully step out of our way, which makes me feel important.

A vendor selling beer under a big canopy has a line of customers. His assistant is checking IDs before each sale, so X and I cruise on by. We walk along the fringe of the crowd to the seawall so we can peer out over the water, passing a balding man with a big cooler.

Baldy holds out two brown bottles of beer. When we hesitate, he says, "You earned it, Way2Go."

We use his church key to pop off the tops. He holds out a third. "For your teammate."

"Appreciate it, man." X sticks the extra bottle in his jacket pocket and then does a fist bump guy thing with the man.

A drone whirs overhead, circling over the crowd, filming. There's a big screen here on the beach, too, and as a cheer goes up, the three of us turn to watch it. A kayaker rounds the last buoy in the bay, waves breaking across the bow of his boat. He streaks for the finish line, his paddle glinting in and out of the water. Two other kayakers are close on his stern, paddling like maniacs. With everyone leaning forward and hands and paddles flashing back and forth and caps pulled down low on their heads, it's hard to tell who is who until the drone captures the scene from the back. Then their team colors and emblems are revealed.

I don't recognize the leader, but a cluster of onlookers clad in red, white, and blue shirts cheer, "Go Aussies!" so it must be an Australian kayaker. I'm disappointed that the leader is from one of the regular teams, not an extreme. But the second kayak—actually an uber-sleek surf-ski—belongs to Catie Cole's Femme Fatales extreme team, and I spy Catie down the beach with another blonde, dressed identically in their yellow and black team colors and doing cheers they must have practiced beforehand, because their moves are synchronized. They even have black and yellow pom-poms. After they finish a shake and twirl and final graceful gazelle leap, I look up again and focus on the third kayaker.

Which is, unbelievably, Jason.

"Way2Go!" X and I jump up and down and scream at the screen.

"How did he move up to third place?" I ask his brother. Jason is ahead of the next paddler by only a foot, but he's giving it his all.

X shrugs, but our beer supplier fills us in. "Collision in the mountain bike segment. A whole bunch of bikers piled up. Your guy actually jumped his bike over the tangle. Then he slid past the guy in third position, who had a lot of trouble skidding out on the downhill curves." He shakes his head in appreciation of Jason's skill. "You gotta see the replay."

"Can't wait," I tell him, raising my beer in acknowledgment to the man.

"And you, young lady," he says. "I can't believe you could drag that canoe over that log jam."

"I can't believe it either." Personally, I find not drowning in the strainer a lot more impressive, but apparently there were no underwater drones to capture that feat.

As the first kayak hits the sand, the crowd surges toward the beach like a tsunami. Xavier and I have to watch the screen to see what is actually happening down there. The first to land is the Australian, but he's barely out of his kayak before the black-haired gal on the surf-ski leaps onto the beach. They race up the slope to the finish bell, where, with a mighty leap, he grabs the rope a millisecond before she does. With a clang, the Aussie becomes the first to finish this year's Ski to Sea race. A hundred camera shutters click simultaneously. The bell is still ringing when the second racer gives it a fast yank, and the Femmes Fatales Extreme Team finishes a fraction of a second behind the winner.

The scene on the screen is still focused on the gorgeous gals hugging each other when X and I see two more kayaks hit the beach.

"Way2Go!" we scream. The camera switches to show Jason and an Iron Men Extreme Team kayaker pulling themselves out of their kayaks. Down the beach, the other two Iron Men teammates are yelling just as loud as we are.

People gasp when they see Jason's metal springy foot hit the sand, along with the running shoe on his other foot. Iron Man is lankier, so it takes him a second longer to unfold himself out of the cockpit, and that's all Jason needs. He reaches the bell first, and Way2Go finishes third.

I couldn't be more proud, but I remember to pull down my cap to hide my face from photographers as X and I swim through the crowd to scoop up our exhausted but exuberant teammate. Catie and her teammates do their cheer routine again, this time chanting "Way2Go, Way2Go!" as they shake their pom-poms.

The Aussies join in, finishing off with a "Good on ya, mates!"

X cups his hands around his mouth and shouts, "All hail Australia!" and we all bow in the winning team's direction. Then I yell, "Hail the Femme Fatales Extreme Women!" and we turn and bow to them. And then, finally, JJ turns to the Iron Men and slaps them on the back. They reciprocate, pounding him and Xavier, but they give me strange Boy Scout salutes, two fingers snapped from their brows.

Sexism or gallantry? Whatever.

And then we leave the beach to make room for the hundreds of other teams to come in. Besides, there's a huge party starting near the stage at the other end of the park, and we know we'll be welcome there.

First, we are swept into an awards ceremony. The Aussies get the overall award, the Herald Trophy, which will travel to the Land Down Under this year. It's not the extreme team, either, but a traditional team. I feel a twinge of jealousy when all eight of them are also handed vouchers for the free airline tickets.

Then the announcer calls the Femmes Fatales, Way2Go, and the Iron Men extreme team to the stage. We all get plaques as the top three winning teams in the Extreme Class. I stash my plaque near the edge of the stage to pick up later, because the party is starting to heat up.

The band is loud and the players are the age my grandparents would be, if I had any, which makes me pause for a minute, wondering if I might still have relatives in Zimbabwe or Chicago. But there's no way to know, so, whatever. The music these graybeards are playing is great for dancing.

The local Mexican restaurant has set up a big buffet in the closed-off street, and when the guys manning it see our race patches, they wave us over, yelling, "Free for *you!*"

We are thrilled to take advantage of their generosity and load up on enchiladas and tacos and refried beans.

A huge screen on the stage behind the band shows highlights of the race. I have to say that I look damn good in most of my scenes, although no woman except maybe Catie could look movie-star pretty after going through the strainer.

JJ exchanges his running blade for his party foot and dances with his newfound fans. Xavier looks like he's having a great time with some college girls, too. At least I think they're college students; they're wearing tees that advertise the Huskies from the University of Washington.

I am so happy I don't know what to do with myself. I not only raced in the Ski to Sea, but my team came in third! I hear a group talking about the footage taken by the drones. *Stellar,* one says. *Superb,* says another, *why didn't we ever do this before?* Two others talk about entering the final film in the Banff Mountain Film Festival. Everyone at this party agrees that there should be more extreme teams and more drones next year.

"Right on!" I chime in, high-fiving a stranger with a moustache and a soul patch and a camera around his neck.

I drink a few more beers (two? Okay, maybe three) and shake my booty with three exuberant Australians, who keep yelling "Cooo-eee!" for some reason that makes sense only to them. I can feel my firefly tats light up with joy, and I take off my windbreaker and tee shirt to set them free while I dance in my sports bra and running tights. The gouges and bruises from the strainer that decorate my back and arms make the partiers around me wince, but I'm proud to be battle-scarred. I'm really getting into partying and eyeing another beer when Mrs. Fitzgerald materializes beside me.

She holds out my jacket, my shirt, and my plaque, and suggests a ride back to her house.

Damn. I should never have told her I was eighteen.

I guess that means I'm busted. "Give me ten minutes to say my good-byes?"

She nods.

I have to push my way into the throng of admirers around Jason to give him a good-bye hug. I even kiss him, right on the lips, a big smack. "I have to go. Thanks so much for making me part of this, JJ."

His smile is lopsided. I can see he's slightly drunk, but his eyes say he's also super happy.

"Way2Go, T," he says, and holds out a fist. I bump it as he adds, "Next year, first place!"

"To exfinity and beyond," I reply.

"*In*finity!" He laughs.

I snort in embarrassment and then laugh harder. "Whatever. Next year, Jason."

Xavier is harder to locate, but eventually I find him dancing with a girl in a belly dance costume in the middle of the crowd. I grab his wrist and twirl him around. He grins, raises his arms above his head, and then does a silly Egyptian move that makes me chuckle.

I dance up close and then stop him by putting a hand on

each of his shoulders. "Have to say good-night, X."

"Really? I don't want this party to ever end."

I know what he means. It feels so good to let loose and celebrate with friends. Our team did well, but everyone here seems happy just to be part of Ski to Sea.

I position my lips a couple of inches from his ear so I don't have to bellow. "Xavier, thank you. Way2Go wouldn't have made it without the incredible start you gave us."

When I pull back, I see his eyes are glistening. He runs his fingers through his spiky hair. Then he wraps his arms around me in a sweaty bear hug, lifting my feet from the ground. In my ear, he murmurs, "Thanks for noticing, Tana."

The swift kiss X and I give each other feels like a natural way to say good-bye to a teammate.

A thought of Shadow's jealousy flits across my brain. *The hell with that.* Emilio Santos is halfway around the world. I'm not going to let him piss on my parade tonight.

Mrs. F shepherds me to a Volvo, which somehow already has my bike strapped onto a rack in the back. She even snaps on my seatbelt. Although it's kind of embarrassing, it's also nice to have someone looking out for me.

Fifteen

I have no memory of getting into my pajamas and into bed. I get up barely in time to catch the train back home. Mrs. F hands me coffee and a bagel sandwich and offers to drive me and my bike to the station so I don't have to pedal my way there.

The college girls are still snoring when we leave; Mr. F tells me they crawled in about two a.m.

As we walk out the front door of the Fitzgerald house, a young woman trotting up the sidewalk intercepts us. She aims an index finger at me. "Tanzania Grey?"

"Maybe," I say. *Depends on who is asking.*

"I'm so glad I caught you." She hands me a hot pink paper bag with the word *Congratulations!* and a big bow on the front. "Specialty Containers is donating these gifts to the top three winning teams in each class. Our rep couldn't find you last night."

When I look inside, I find one of those cute transparent travel bags. Mine is aqua, which I like even better than the orange and white ones I saw the courier carrying. Mine has a gold and crystal zipper pull, a nice classy touch. Inside are tiny bottles of sunscreen, lip moisturizer, shampoo, conditioner, and lotion, all bearing the QTC label from Quarrel Tayson Cosmetics. Everything looks innocuous enough. I ditch the screaming pink paper sack in the garbage can at the Amtrak Station and stuff the travel bag into my backpack.

After I deposit my bike with the baggage handlers, I occupy a restroom stall to change into my salwar kameez and paste on my bindi—a black lotus design this time. It's impossible to cover the scratches on my face with makeup, so I keep my scarf pulled across my nose like a modest Asian woman. It's reassuring to travel as Sunita Brown again. When I wear this getup, strangers tend to leave me alone.

I'm tired. Sore. Hungry. I have a headache from partying, but I miss the revelry. So we didn't win Ski to Sea. So there's no plane ticket or prize money. I'm pleased with myself and my performance. I felt like such a winner last night. I felt like I belonged.

Wordage, at last, delivers a word I already know: *Divine— relating to a deity, superb.* Last night I felt *divine* in the second sense, or maybe even a little bit in the first. But I'm surprised to find that the word can be used as a verb, too—*to discover by intuition or insight.*

I wish that I could *divine* more details about my parents' murders. Did I actually get anywhere with my bumbling investigation, or did I just raise suspicions about myself? Now I have even more questions about my parents. How could Mom have wrecked Maxine's life? Why was my mother in dispute with QTL? Did Dad know World Cargo West was transporting cocaine?

I have to come back to Bellingham. My logical brain asks, *and do what?*

I don't have an answer.

I close my eyes and wish for aspirin. This morning I couldn't find my ball cap. I wonder how many photos and videos I appeared in without it last night.

I think about Maxine's scowling neighbor, Mr. QTL, and how he took a photo of me. Was he really going to attack me on the river, or was that just my paranoia kicking in? I wish I knew more about him. Then I realize that I do know something that might be valuable: his address. Pulling up the Whatcom County Assessor website, I look up his property. At first I make the mistake of thinking the address would be off of Maxine's by only two numbers, so it takes me a while, but I finally stumble across a map that shows me the property to the south is Maxine's address plus six.

That house belongs to a Phineas Pederson. The name sets my mind spinning. P. Pederson. Kayaker killer/rescuer Pederson. Pederson could be P.A. Patterson. If he is, he's been cyber-stalking me for years.

Thank God I've never answered his emails. Thank God he doesn't know where I live. I focus on my surroundings and try to relax. Amtrak. Going home, back to where I am always Tanzania Grey.

I always have a hard time coming back to my ordinary life after a race. Grocery shopping and household chores and going to work seem so...well, pointless, when there's no competition and no clock and no prize to win. I knew going in that there was no big Ski to Sea prize, but I still want one, or at least a continuing celebration. Or maybe a vacation.

Instead, I'm going home with bruises and scratches and the crawly feeling that I may have blown my cover in Bellingham.

Geographastic tells me that the Pacific Ring of Fire includes the volcanoes of Washington State. I already knew that. The race started off near one of them yesterday—Mount Baker—and when we get past the Chuckanuts, I might be able to see Mount Rainier to the south from the train.

I text Emilio. *We came in 3rd!*

Although I wait a couple of minutes, the screen stays blank. There's nothing like blasting out a message and getting no answer to make me feel all alone in the world. Emilio's probably out demolishing villages.

I've just zipped up my backpack when my phone chirps. But it's not Emilio answering me, it's an email message forwarded from Dark Horse Networks:

Saw you on news. Amelia? – P.A. Patterson

My stomach does a flutter-kick.

What's with the Amelia reference? Clark at Dark Horse wants to know.

No clue, I text back. *Can U tell where tht msg came frm?*

There's a long pause, and then *Somewhere n Africa* appears.

Spam 4 sure, I respond. *Or mistakn ID.*

Why is Patterson contacting me again so soon? That's more than his usual creepy style. It's scary-creepy. Screepy. Or did the message really come from Pederson, who is pretending to be Patterson?

No way in hell am I ever going to respond to P.A. Patterson or Phineas Pederson or whoever is sending these messages. That could be like inviting a snake into my bed. I wish I could think of a way to discover who P.A. is without revealing who *I* am.

I'm zipping my phone away again when it makes its loon call. Yeesh, I don't normally get this much phone traffic in a week. It's freaking me out. I don't recognize the number on the screen. U.S. Army? I hesitantly squeak, "Hello?"

"Hello, is this Miss Tanzania Grey?"

The formality of the unfamiliar voice makes me instantly suspicious. I don't spread my number around, so I rarely get spam calls. "Who is this?"

"This is United States Army Lieutenant Tim Owen, ma'am. Am I speaking to Miss Tanzania Grey?"

"Yes." What the heck could the Army want with me?

"Ma'am, we usually do this sort of notification in person, but we were unable to find a physical address for you."

Even more suspicious. I don't like it when anyone tries to find out where I live. "That's right," I say.

I hear Owen take a breath. "Miss Grey, it is my sad duty to inform you that your fiancé, Sergeant Emilio Santos, has been declared missing in action."

First, my mind trips over the word *fiancé*. I know that this relationship has existed in Shadow's imagination for more than a year now. My adopted mother Marisela and her kids assume Emilio and I will get married eventually. But Emilio has never officially asked me, and I've never made that promise.

The loudspeaker in the train car announces my stop is next. I have to mash the phone against my ear to hear what this guy is saying.

"Please rest assured that the United States Army will do

our best to locate your fiancé. You will be notified as soon as we do."

My brain skips back to 'missing in action.' I talked to Emilio only two days ago.

"What?" I blurt like I suddenly became hard of hearing. "Wait! When did this happen?"

There's a rustle of paper on the other end of the line. "Sergeant Santos was last seen at 2300 hours on Saturday."

Oh God, that was only an hour or so after I talked to him. "Where?"

"In a rural area just outside Damascus, ma'am."

"What happened?" The train is slowing to a stop. People around me are collecting their belongings.

"That's all the information we have at this time, Miss Grey."

I don't believe that for a second. I start to say so, but Lieutenant Owen cuts me off. "You will be notified as soon as we have additional information. Thank you for your time."

The conversation reverberates loudly in my head, the sound of Owen's words clanging the way cymbals do after the percussionist claps them together. Feeling as if I've just been slapped, I grab my backpack and step off onto the station platform. I am so disoriented that I exit the train station and walk a hundred yards down the sidewalk before I remember to go back, change my clothes, and claim my bike.

The twenty-one miles I have to bike between the Amtrak station and my home give me time to reflect. When I talked to Shadow two days ago, he looked exhausted, and he sounded so depressed. He told me he loved me and I didn't say it back. Oh God, what did he do after that?

I try to convince myself that he'll be fine, that he just wandered away. But the Army doesn't exactly allow soldiers to take a break whenever they feel like it. A sludge of dread and guilt settle to the bottom of my stomach.

Fortunately, my elephant is waiting just inside the second fence on my driveway to greet me. Either he's been standing watch there every day, or he heard the security gate roll back after I punched in my code. The sight of him makes me feel a little lighter.

He trumpets and flaps his giant ears, signs that in a wild elephant could mean 'I'm going to kill you,' but in Bailey mean 'I'm going to kiss you.' He smacks me gently on my arms and shoulders with his trunk and snuffles me all over, messing up my hair and nearly knocking me off my bike. When he judges me to be sufficiently covered in welcome-home snot, he allows me to walk my bike to the porch. I spend a few minutes patting his shoulder and scratching him behind his ear.

"I'm happy to see you, too, Bailey."

He makes a rumbling sound and leans against me. I stagger backwards. Elephant affection is not always easy to take.

Sabrina emerges through the gate from the back pasture, carrying an empty bucket. She is trailed by Salt and Pepper and our growing flock of nameless goats. My housemate is the opposite of me, short and sturdy with pale skin and bleached white-blond hair that she highlights with colored streaks—today, they're lilac.

She greets me with a question. "How was it?"

"Third place."

"Good for you!" Then she cocks a pierced eyebrow at me. "Third *is* good, isn't it? Was Bellingham cool?"

I nod a couple of times in answer to both questions.

"Then why don't you look happy?"

I tell her about Shadow.

Her face clouds over. She met Emilio the last time he was home on leave. "Lord have mercy," she says. And then she sets down the bucket, strides forward, and puts her arms around me.

Sabrina doesn't know a lot about my history, but she knows what it's like to be on her own so early in life. Her druggie mother is in prison and she has never met her father. She doesn't try to tell me that everything will be okay, but just murmurs, "Hang in there, Tana."

When Pepper butts over the metal bucket, the loud clank startles us both. Sabrina rolls her eyes as she steps back. "I'm so glad you're home. Bailey's been crazy."

I decide I might as well act like everything's normal, too. "And that's new?"

"There's leftover pizza in the fridge," Sabrina offers. "It's all yours."

"Yay." That pizza was there when I left for Bellingham. But I'll probably eat it anyway; food is food and it's already paid for.

I pull off my backpack. "I'm hitting the shower."

My cell phone informs me that Marisela, my foster mom and Shadow's aunt, called while I was biking home. I can't face talking to her yet, so I wash and put on my jeans and gulp down the pepperoni-flavored cardboard that used to be pizza. Then, screwing up my courage, I call her back.

She answers with tears in her voice. "Tana."

I swallow. "So you know."

"They wouldn't tell me anything," she wails.

"All I found out was that he vanished outside of Damascus."

"Syria?" Her voice rises an octave. "*Dios mio*, so many journalists have been kidnapped and killed there!"

"Emilio's not a journalist."

Not a helpful thing to say, my mind informs me too late. Not a *hopeful* thing to say, either. Journalists can plead that they're impartial observers; soldiers can hardly argue that. Their uniforms are obvious declarations of which side they're on.

"He's only missing," I tell her. "Maybe he simply walked away."

"Why would he do that? Did he say anything to you?"

You know I love you, don't you?

I bite my lower lip hard. I should have told Shadow I loved him, even though I'm not sure what that means. I should have told him I couldn't wait to marry him, even though I'm not fit to marry anyone.

Some days I'm not sure if it's worth it.

"We have to have hope, Marisela." My voice sounds strangely hoarse.

"And pray."

"Whatever works." After everything that has happened to my life, I find it difficult to believe there's a caring God watching over us mortals. "Call if you hear anything."

"I will, *m'hija*."

"Me, too. Stay strong." I end the call and then blow my nose and wipe my eyes.

I wish I *were* the praying kind, because at least that would be something to do.

Sixteen

y nerves are jangling too much to sit, so I go for a walk through my acreage to make sure the fence is secure. Maintaining a barrier strong enough to deter an elephant from escaping is a never-ending job.

I lead a slow, quiet parade around the perimeter, trailed by one elephant and five pygmy goats. There's an inside electric fence, ten feet high. A belt of fir trees occupies the twenty-five-foot strip between the inner fence and six-foot-high exterior fence. The trees frequently block my view of the outside fence, but everything seems to be fine, and our computerized security system hasn't registered any breaches, or Sabrina would have said something.

The sixty acres of WildRun are a mix of pasture, woods, and old farm fields. The fence was what attracted me to the place; previously the property was home to a small herd of bison, who are also escape experts.

It's hard to believe that I competed in Ski to Sea yesterday. Today the world seems like a completely different place. There's nothing I can do about Shadow except wait for more news, so I resign myself to doing just that. I'm feeling slightly less jittery when I return to the house. Bailey must be, too, because he stays in the barn, happily destroying the bale of hay I give him, shoving the goats away with his trunk.

At sundown, I'm in my room checking my email, hoping for a message from Emilio, or for some word from Bash on those scans I sent him two days ago. Patience is not one of my virtues.

Sabrina squeals from the living room. "Tana! Come here! Hurry!"

I rush in, my gaze bouncing around the room to spot the problem. Sabrina is on her feet in front of the television. The news is on, but it's the weather report; nothing to get excited about.

"There!" My housemate points to the window behind the TV.

I see nothing unusual through the glass.

"It was just here, I swear it!" She dashes to the window and peers up toward the darkening sky.

When I join her, I hear a faint buzzing sound coming from somewhere above the roof.

Sabrina turns, shrieks, and points. "There it is!"

A small helicopter-like box hovers just outside the window across the room. A flash of light blinds us, and then the machine whirs away.

I gallop out onto the front porch and down the steps. It's times like these that I wish I owned a rifle that fires real bullets, not just tranquilizer darts. The invader is already far overhead, but it spirals out over my property, flashing a burst of bright light downward every few seconds. Then it rises into the sky and vanishes.

Gritting my teeth, I walk back inside.

"It's a drone," I tell Sabrina. What the hell is one doing over my house?

"Thank you, Captain Obvious," she responds. "Think someone's out there?" She's standing at a different window now, peering out into the growing darkness. "Aren't the drivers or pilots or whatever you call them supposed to stay near those things?"

"They're supposed to stay where they can see them, but there's a long way between 'supposed to' and actually obeying the rules." I try to act nonchalant, like this happens to everyone all the time. "Maybe it was one of the neighbors checking to see if we have more than one elephant."

"Hmmph," she snorts. "It's probably Dreck trying to catch us having pagan sex with farm animals."

She means Tom Derek, a greasy lech down the road who is always telling us how uber-concerned he is about 'two such young and attractive women living all alone.' I wouldn't be surprised to find out Derek is a registered sex offender, but he doesn't scare me. Bailey would flatten him in a heartbeat if Dreck slithered onto my property.

Sabrina flops down on the couch again and turns up the volume on the TV. I'm walking back to my room, trying to tell myself that a drone dropping by is no big deal, especially in comparison to a boyfriend going missing in Syria, when she shouts again. "Hey, your race is on television!"

I return to the living room and lean against the back of our decrepit couch, watching the screen from above Sabrina's purple-streaked head.

"Despite losing a leg last year during a perilous cross-island running contest, twenty-one-year-old Jason Jones proved during the recent Ski to Sea Race that he hasn't lost his competitive drive," the reporter intones as the vid shows Jason and me pushing our canoe into the river. *"It wasn't*

easy, though. Jones and his partner took a life-threatening tumble in the Nooksack River."

The camera dips down almost to water level to highlight the slam of our canoe against the strainer. I hold my breath as we tip and Jason is sucked beneath the surface. I vanish a second later. *Tumble* does not seem adequate to describe our experience in the river.

"Although Jones lost his artificial foot during that incident, he was undeterred." Next is a couple of seconds of Jason and me hop-dragging our canoe up the bank, then he's riding off into the woods on his bike.

"When a major collision occurred right in front of him, Jones deftly avoided becoming collateral damage and surged ahead." There's a pileup of five mountain bikers on a downhill slope, and it looks for a second like Jason's going to join them, but he somehow defies gravity and manages to lift his bike into the air, sailing over their heads.

Through the magic of creative editing, the film flash-forwards to Jason paddling his kayak onto the beach. He runs up the slope on his racing blade foot to ring the bell. On the screen, X and I whoop and slap JJ on the back as the newscaster wraps up the story with *"Jason Jones, former endurance race champion, is now an extreme canoeist, mountain biker, kayaker, and never-say-die competitor. Having only one foot is no handicap to this young man. And that's why Jason Jones is our Person of the Week."*

The film ends with a close-up of Jason's exultant face, quickly replaced by a singing hamster in a car commercial.

Sabrina twists around to look up at me. "That *was* you in that canoe, wasn't it?"

"Yeah. And that was Xavier, Jason's brother, our other teammate, at the end."

She frowns. "They never even mentioned your name."

I'm actually glad about that, because I worry that little Charlie's mom or Dr. Wigener or Maxine Newsome might see this footage and wonder if that racer is the same girl they talked to. "S'okay," I tell Sabrina. "They're right, Jason *is* amazing."

Even though we spent only a few days together, I miss Jason and Xavier. I have a sudden, silly urge to raise a fist and shout "Way2Go!"

But that would be weird, so I bite my lip and watch the fat rodents zoom off in their new green hamstermobile on television. Sometimes I just don't get advertising.

As I undress for bed, I can't stop fretting. Who sent a drone to check on us? Sabrina's right, it could be Dreck. He's a creep. But this feels different somehow. Was someone trying to spot Bailey? I know some of the neighbors wonder what's behind all my fences.

My thoughts leap to Mr. QTL, Phineas Pederson. Or P.A. Patterson. Who might be the same person. A high-tech company like Quarrel Tayson would know how to keep tabs on a suspicious girl like Tanzania Grey. Was that drone sent to check on me?

The flashes of light worry me. I think those mean the drone was taking photos. For what purpose? Dark Horse Networks set me up with a great security system around my place, but electric fences and computer-controlled gates can't protect any of us from an attack from the sky.

I pull down the shades on my bedroom windows just in

case that drone comes back. Ten minutes later, I get up to raise the shades. If a drone is snooping around out there, I want to know about it.

The next day I have to report to my job as usual. During the long days of spring and summer, I actually don't mind starting work at six a.m. In the dark winter months, riding my bike to and from the zoo can be a harrowing experience.

The zoo is usually peaceful in the early morning. The animals act more naturally at this time of day than when hordes of kids hang over the fences and scream at them.

This morning, one of the reticulated giraffes leans down to look me in the eye as I shovel dung from his pasture into a wheelbarrow. I love giraffes. The skyscrapers of the ungulate world are gentle and quiet, and they have the prettiest big brown eyes with long lashes. I imagine them as the deer of Africa, gliding silently through the forests of that continent, shoulder to shoulder with all kinds of exotic antelopes and zebras and elephants.

Mom used to tell us exciting stories about growing up with wildlife in Zimbabwe. I hope I get to see all those animals in the wild someday.

Unfortunately, Africa has few endurance races. There's one in Egypt every now and then, and one across the desert of Morocco, but I don't know of any in places that might have giraffes. That's probably because most places that have giraffes also have creatures not so friendly to runners, such as lions and leopards.

Two of the assistant keepers, Karrie and Dave, want to know where I've been for the last few days. They know I'm a runner, but they've never heard of Ski to Sea, so I'm not going to get any kudos there.

"A cross-country race," I tell them.

"Guess that explains the scratches." Dave eyes the red stripes that decorate my arms and face, mementos from the strainer.

Karrie makes a face. "You do things like that on purpose, Tana?"

That's how it is in the lesser sports. Each competition seems like a life-and-death contest to those of us who participate, while nobody on the outside of our circle is even aware it's happening. I may be a champion endurance racer, but to my colleagues at the zoo, my skills with a pitchfork and shovel are the only talents that count.

I dump my load of giraffe and zebra doo and work my way down my habitat maintenance chore list as I continue my worryfest about everything that happened yesterday. I haven't received any news about Shadow, so I try to focus on the drone. Dreck is techie enough to own a drone and icky enough to spy on us, and since he lives nearby, he could fly it in from his property. I hope he was the pilot, and I hope he was just playing around. I can't think of any way to check up on that, short of asking the creep. It's pretty hard to follow a drone. It's not like they leave tracks behind.

During my morning break, I check my phone. No miracle messages from Shadow. Geographastic tells me that the capital of Lithuania is Vilnius. I wonder when I'll ever need that piece of trivia.

Ennui is the word of the day on Wordage. *Dissatisfaction from lack of excitement.* Totally appropriate for me. I am *ennui* personified today, although I think maybe there needs to be a word that combines ennui and anxiety. Ennuixity? Unhappiness due to lack of excitement *and* bad news.

My happy buzz from Ski to Sea is completely gone. I wish it could have lasted longer. I miss my teammates. So when my phone sends out its cricket chirp, I'm glad to see a message from J. Jones on the screen. He and Xavier are back home in Ohio, but he has more than just college to get back to. He texts me that he's received an endorsement offer from a mountain bike company and another from a prosthetics manufacturer.

Yes 2 Conquest Bikes, but I dont want 2 B a famous gimp, he writes.

R U nuts? I text back. *U R a gimp hero! Nspire othr gimps 2 fame!*

After a minute, he texts back, *U R right. X says so 2.*

The film compilations I've seen so far have included brief clips of me floundering in the river or me helping Jason haul the canoe up or down the riverbank, but X didn't get one speck of recognition for his part in the race. During the parkour and downhill ski legs, he was one among hundreds on camera. He seems relegated to be Jason's personal assistant.

Crapola! I am every bit as shallow as the media hounds that covered the race. *X is a hero 2*, I text back too late.

I stare at the screen for a minute. No response. JJ has already moved on.

Sighing, I shove my phone back into my pocket. Clearly, I need to find something to look forward to. I resolve to check out the list of upcoming endurance races tonight, and to improve the training course that circles my property. I'll build some climbing obstacles—based on my canoe experience, my arms and shoulders could use some more beefing up, in spite of all the shoveling I do here. Maybe I'll throw in more hurdles, too. Swimming would be nice, but it's not as if I can afford to build a lap pool. I wonder if Dark Horse Networks would spring for a gym membership I could use on my days off.

The bonobos glare at me from behind bars, complaining bitterly about being caged as I hose down their enclosure. After I turn off the water and put away the hose, I take the time to tickle the youngest baby through the bars with a long piece of straw, relishing his laughter. We play tug of war for a few seconds until the dried grass breaks and he scampers away, proud that he has won the game. I've just closed the gate behind myself and let the bonobos out of their sleeping quarters when the cricket chirps again from my back pocket. I park the wheelbarrow next to a spectacular variegated canna plant and dig out my cell.

No news, says the text from Marisela.

Damn. I had actually managed to lose my worries in work and monkey business for a couple of hours. Now I feel guilty about that, too.

No news, I echo back to her.

Nathan Ransek strolls past, giving me a worried look. I wave him away. He vanishes around the corner.

I wheel my latest load of poop to the compost area and empty it onto today's pile. There's a line-up of little stalls full of excrement and dirty straw and food rinds and such. After the oldest piles are completely composted, the results are packaged and sold as Zoo Doo, which local gardeners buy as fast as it's produced. There's always a waiting list of eager customers who believe that exotic manure trumps livestock manure. Gotta love capitalism. Even poop has value when cleverly packaged and marketed.

When I wheel my barrow past the butterfly exhibit, my eyes are drawn to the colorful display outside the building depicting the life cycle of a monarch butterfly.

Oh, Shadow. Remember the monarchs. I can't go to Mexico without you.

My never-ending loads of manure seem like a metaphor for my life. Mom. Dad. Aaron. Now Emilio, too. How much crap is one girl supposed to endure? My throat cramps up, my vision gets all blurry, and I have to bite my lip hard to keep tears away. I inhale a long, slow breath to try and head it off, but a moan comes out of my mouth. I park my cart and clap a hand over my lips to prevent more embarrassing sounds from escaping. Tears course down my cheeks without my permission. I have to hunt through my pockets for a tissue.

A few minutes pass before I can pull myself together and end my private pity party. A chubby woman pushing a sleeping toddler in a stroller takes a wide detour around me, like my troubles might be contagious.

Finally, I manage to suck it up and grab the handles of my cart again and round the corner of the Nocturnal building to get back to business. Ransek blocks the pathway, feet spread and arms crossed, his expression all fatherly and concerned.

"You okay, Tana?"

"A soldier friend of mine went missing in Syria," I confess.

"Then you got good reason to be upset," he commiserates, nodding. "I think the beheadings there are up to nine now."

Ransek is known for having no filter on his mouth.

"Thanks so much for telling me that," I say.

He twists his lips sideways and then brushes an invisible piece of lint from his shirt, embarrassed. We turn away from each other and get back to our jobs.

Seventeen

I don't seem to be able to get away from shit. Literally. Even my home life is full of crap. The next day, after supper, Salt and Pepper and Bailey accompany me and my wheelbarrow full of dirty straw and poop from my barn to the big maple tree. Some people have dogs that follow them around. The creatures that shadow me have hooves and trunks.

I started a big compost heap at the tree's eastern shade perimeter, because the morning sun and then the afternoon shade from the maple's leaves keep the debris pile at the right temperature to compost quickly. I try to lose myself in physical labor, hoisting forkfuls with my pitchfork to turn the compost heap, but my mind is thousands of miles away, in Syria. Has Emilio been captured by the enemy? I know something about held by terrorists, and I don't want to believe that Emilio is going through that horrific experience right now. Is he lost in the desert? Lying comatose and unidentified in some field hospital?

I jab the pitchfork into the manure pile again and again, trying to work off the tension. Then Bailey decides that activity looks like fun and tries to pull the pitchfork out of my hands.

"No!" I scold, jerking it away from his trunk. He's fascinated by the pitchfork, or maybe he's just bored, but it's definitely not a good idea to arm a bad-tempered elephant with four sharp metal tines.

The pygmy goats play around the base of the tree, chasing each other from one side to the other, until they end up face to face, and then they butt their heads together over and over again. It's a game only goats can appreciate.

Is Shadow alive? Is his body decaying in a ditch somewhere? Is he buried under the rubble of a bombed building? Am I somehow to blame? Did my lack of loving words inspire him to do something desperate?

I feel so helpless. I wonder if there's any way I can get more information out of the Army. Then I wonder if there's any way to go *around* the Army to get more information. Maybe there's an #MIA hashtag on Twitter?

The animals and I hear the buzz from the sky at the same time. The sound is unmistakable; a drone is flying somewhere above us. I scan the closest fences, hoping to catch a glimpse of the pilot. Nothing out of place there.

The buzzing gets louder. Overseas, the military uses drones to shoot people. Shadow has told me about watching "targets" get obliterated on monitor screens, like characters in a video game.

I'm caught out in the open. If I run for the house or the barn, I have to cross at least a hundred yards of open space.

I can't decide whether to run or hide or give the drone the finger. I'm not even sure if I should look up, because then my face might be recognized. The goats bounce around stiff-legged, unnerved by the strange noise. Bailey raises his head and extends his ears to appear enormous and threatening. The buzzing sounds as if it's directly above my head. I'm about to drop the pitchfork and run into the house when the machine abruptly descends from the sky.

Fleeing the monster, the goats gallop off to the shelter of the woods. I'm inclined to follow them.

The drone drops into the space between me and Bailey and hovers there, slightly more than five feet above the ground. My heart rate triples. The contraption is black and looks like a cross between a helicopter and a mechanical spider with a box for a body.

Whoever is piloting this drone decided they wanted a close-up. Or maybe they want to be sure they can't miss with a bullet or a laser beam. But is the drone pilot aiming for me, or for Bailey? There are killers out there that might want me dead, but there are also thrill-seeking hunters who shoot exotic animals for fun. Bailey was destined to be a high-priced target before I bought him. Killing an elephant with a drone would be the ultimate turn-on for those types.

I stare at the drone, frantically trying to determine where the lens or the weapon is aimed. My elephant snorts and flaps his ears once, blowing my hair back over my shoulders and making the drone bounce in the air. Then Bailey charges two steps forward and swats the drone with his trunk.

The machine slams into the maple tree with a loud pop. The buzzing stops. The drone crashes to the ground with a clunk.

"Yes!" I pump my fist in the air. "That was a home run, Bailey." I take a tentative step toward the wreck.

My elephant's anger management issues are the reason

that he lives with me instead of in a zoo. Bailey's lack of impulse control can be pretty scary, but right now I'm thrilled he's here to defend us. I'm also glad he never slaps me or Sabrina that hard. A brief vision of that two-dimensional coyote I found in the orchard flashes across my memory.

Gingerly, Bailey explores the black body of the drone with the tip of his trunk, and then, for good measure, he stomps on it with his right forefoot. The machine shatters into a dozen pieces. He carefully examines the remains, shuffling them around with his trunk. He even picks up one of the spider legs and puts it into his mouth, then rolls it around for a second before he spits it out.

Satisfied that he is finished with his examination, I sort through the pieces. I think it was armed with a camera, not a weapon. The wreckage contains bent circuit boards and a couple of glass lens-type things and pieces of twisted metal, mixed with shards of plastic. Drones are supposed to have registration numbers painted on them, but this one doesn't. I can't find a company logo or anything to tell me where it came from, only a piece of plastic with what looks like a serial number of some sort, and another with a long string of letters and numbers.

I put the circuit boards and two pieces of plastic with markings on them in my pocket. Then I go to the barn to get a bag to collect the rest. Goats will chew on almost anything and I don't want them tasting this new toy.

When I'm done picking up the evidence, Bailey rumbles low in his belly, as if to say "Is that it?"

I wonder the same thing. *Portent* was my word this morning—*an omen that something wonderful or disastrous is about to occur.* Somehow I can't believe that the mechanical *portent* Bailey just destroyed is predicting something good is about to happen.

Back at the house, I type the serial number into my computer's search box. And get nothing back except some more numbers that aren't even particularly similar.

I type the string of letters and numbers-X4NUQ55T1. The search engine coughs up the info that this is most likely part of a model number—it's missing a dash and the last three numerals-001, which Bailey probably stomped into dust. X4NUQ55T1-001 is a drone model from a company called UAV4U. Clever name for a company that creates personal unmanned aerial vehicles.

The front door bangs and Sabrina comes in, home from work, her khaki pants splattered with greenish stains. As she stands in my bedroom doorway, she spies the piece of plastic on my desk and the numbers on my screen. "What's up?"

"Bailey killed a drone."

"It came again? Yay, Bailey! Elephant, 1; Dreck, 0. Serves that freak right." She grins, raps her knuckles on my doorway for punctuation, and then heads off for the shower.

I copy down the main phone number for UAV4U, but I'm not sure what to do with it. Drones are expensive, so I'm guessing they come with warranties, and registering a warranty usually involves a product ID number. Maybe if I call the manufacturer with the right story and give them the numbers on the other piece of plastic, they could tell me who owns—owned—this drone?

But what is the right story? And would they tell the owner where the drone crashed? I'm glad Bailey destroyed the thing, but now I'm worried that I could be billed for the cost of the drone. It's illegal to use drones to spy on private property, but that doesn't mean that the owner wouldn't try to get the money back. Cops get sued for shooting criminals all the time, even when they catch them in the act.

If the drone was sending photos in real time, the owner has photos of me and Bailey, and will be able to guess that it bit the dust on my property.

I consider calling the police. But a police report would be available to the public, which includes the press. Not to mention that visitors to my place tend to obsess about the fact that there's an elephant wandering around out here. If Bailey gets labeled as dangerous to people or property, the county could revoke my license to keep him.

No, I need someone to call from a phone that can't be traced to me. Preferably someone who doesn't have an obvious link to me. I rack my brain for a good candidate who might be willing. Bash? No, he's in hiding, too.

Emilio? *Oh, God.* I feel like a total dinkwad for forgetting, even for a second, that I may never see Emilio again. Forgive me, Shadow.

My stomach hurts. I rub my belly. Can eighteen-year-olds get ulcers?

I finally settle on calling Xavier Jones. We had a connection at Ski to Sea, I think. He seems up for almost anything.

I spin him a yarn about the drone peeking in my bedroom window and me swatting it with a baseball bat but still wanting to find out who the pervert behind it is. X is enthusiastic about the undercover job, and even goes a step further to keep to my cloak and dagger theme.

"I'll ask Sheena—she's a friend of mine at school—to call UAV4U tomorrow," he offers. "So the call will come from Ohio, and nobody will know that I'm even involved, and they'll certainly never trace it to you. Can Sheena use your pervert story?"

"Sure. But please don't call him *my* pervert."

He chuckles. "I'll get back to you mañana, then."

"Thanks, X. Say hi to Jason for me."

I wake up in the wee hours of the morning, thinking I hear the buzzing of a drone outside. But it's only a honey bee that wandered into the house and is now batting its tiny brainless head against the window screen. I get up and push out the screen, liberating the bee. After I watch the precious insect disappear into the dark, I stand there for a minute looking at the night.

Clouds obscure the moon and stars, and it's raining lightly. I can't see much beyond the bushes below my window. A snuffling sound causes my pulse to stutter for a few beats before my eyes identify the solid dark mass of Bailey standing just behind the garden fence.

Unless an intruder gets past my vigilant elephant, Sabrina and I are okay for tonight. I hope that Shadow, too, has a guardian spirit looking out for him, wherever he is.

Eighteen

It's Wednesday, one of the three days that Sabrina and I work the same shift at the zoo. We carpool in her old pickup.

X calls me on my cell when I'm hiding food and toys in the chimp habitat. The staff calls creating a search like this an enrichment activity, or in other words, something for captive animals to do other than sit and scratch or harass each other. I can't talk on my cell while inside a cage. It's a basic safety rule. So X and I end up playing phone tag for more than an hour. On my third attempt, I finally connect with him.

He's proud of himself for getting an answer for me. "That drone is registered to SeaStone Security."

"Thanks, Xavier, that's a big help." I do my best to sound grateful. Although it sounds vaguely familiar, the name means nothing to me.

When I research SeaStone Security on my break, though, I see that it's a branch of SeaStone Enterprises, the company that took over World Cargo West's building out by the airport in Bellingham. No wonder the name seemed familiar. Listed among SeaStone's testimonials is one from Quarrel Tayson

Labs. And an older one from World Cargo West.

And then I see that Phineas Pederson is listed as Director of Operations for SeaStone Security. I still can't get over how he took my photo at Maxine's house. I don't think that was just neighborly interest.

So Pederson is not Mr. QTL, but Mr. SeaStone Security. Since his company worked with both World Cargo West and QTL, he could have known both my parents. His photo on the SeaStone corporate site shows him in a suit, smiling slightly, all professional and polite, the way he looked when I first saw him at QTL. But I've seen the other faces he sometimes wears. Although he can't be the ninja I saw with the tattooed neck, there were two murderers. He could be the other man in the ski mask.

How did he find out where I live? I have a terrible feeling I've opened Pandora's box. Maybe if I just continue on with my normal life, if my days prove to be as uninteresting as they usually are, maybe SeaStone will simply go away. That's all I can think of to do—nothing. I feel spectacularly useless.

As I go about my usual duties in the afternoon, my imagination veers back and forth between fretting about what sort of hornet's nest I poked during my Bellingham visit, and worrying about Shadow.

It's been nearly four days since he disappeared. It no longer seems possible that he got lost or is just hanging out someplace more interesting than the Army base. I'm really, really worried that Sergeant Emilio Santos is going to be listed as the next Army suicide, and I'm really worried that I contributed to his depression. Will I never learn to be more sensitive?

I've still got several hours to go at work. Today, that

means checking and cleaning the water filters in the penguin, otter, and sea lion habitats. As I insert my key into the lock to open the door to the habitat maintenance area, my phone chirps to signal an incoming message.

I thumb the phone on, and I'm startled to see a photo message from Emilio. Seeing his name on the screen makes my heart do a tap dance of happiness. But then I focus on the image. It's so shocking that I almost drop the phone. I have to stare at the photo for a minute to realize what I'm looking at.

A soldier in Army fatigues, on his knees, arms twisted behind his back. Two hands grip his shoulders, and another holds a machete across his neck. The soldier's head is lowered, but his eyes look up toward the camera, although the right one is nearly swollen shut. Streaks of blood run down his face from gashes on his head. The features are so dark and misshapen with whiskers and bruises that I can't be positive it's Shadow.

But it has to be him. This is coming from his phone. Below the photo is a message: *100.000.00 USDollar or KILL!!!*

Following that is a string of numbers.

Omigod, omigod, omiGOD.

Did Marisela get this message too? I think about calling her, but I don't want to shock her with this if she doesn't already know.

What the hell was the name of that Army guy who called me? I scroll back through the caller list until I find Owen, US Army.

When I call the number, I get a voicemail saying he's away from his desk.

"No, no, no!" I scream into the phone. "Pick up! Pick up! Call me! I just got a message from Emilio Santos! The enemy has him!"

Out of sight behind the building, a sea lion barks in response. I forward the photo and message to Owen's phone number, but I don't know if he gets texts or emails that way.

Then I can think of nothing to do but stare at the awful image on the screen. There's no deadline. There's no date. Is the string of numbers a bank account? Would they really release Shadow for 100.000.00? Is that supposed to mean one hundred thousand dollars? There's no way that Marisela and I could get that much money, even if we asked everyone we knew to pitch in. My heart hurts.

President Garrison's words during my own kidnapping incident echo through my brain. *The policy of the United States stands: we do not do business with terrorists.*

My loon sings out an incoming call. It's Lieutenant Owen. His voice is too calm as he says, "This is good news, Ms. Grey. Now we know what happened to Sergeant Santos."

He sounds as if he thinks Shadow is already dead. "Can you get the money?"

"The Army will take it from here, Ms. Grey. I need your phone."

I experience a quick hot wave of my usual paranoia, and then I grasp that any message to the kidnappers needs to come from my cell phone. Still...

"We will clone the SIM and then give it back. I assure you that no personal information will be copied."

Yeah, right.

"We can go through the phone company to do the same thing, but that might take days."

Shadow's life may depend on my phone. I tell Owen where I am.

"I'll have someone there within thirty minutes," he tells me. "You are to do absolutely nothing—do not respond, do not share this news with anyone else. I'll get the phone back to you ASAP and let you know when I have further news. Thank you for your cooperation."

There's a click, and he's gone. I'm standing alone in the alleyway behind the aquatic habitats, shaking with the adrenaline flooding through my veins. Somewhere a peacock is crying in a nasal tone, sounding as if it's screaming, "Help, help, help!"

"Shadow," I say to the horrible photo. "I love you. I do." The words sound pathetic now. I shut off the phone so I won't have to look at my tortured boyfriend.

Then I quickly turn the phone back on and erase Bash's number and all the messages I got from him. I trust the Army to go after one of their own, but I don't trust any government institution to keep the location of The President's Son a secret.

I finish emptying my contacts and messages of all my sensitive information, which leaves me barely enough time to reclaim my key from the lock before the loon sings again.

I'm almost afraid to look at my phone. But it's only the zoo director's office.

"There's an officer from the U.S. Army waiting here, asking for you," the director's assistant tells me. "What's going on, Grey?"

"On my way." I jog to the zoo offices.

The officer turns out to be a young woman in a dress uniform, probably from the nearest recruiting station. Her light brown hair is twisted up under a smart uniform cap.

"Where's Lieutenant Owen?" I ask.

She's startled for a second by my question. "The other Washington," she tells me.

She zips my phone into a plastic bag before placing it in her briefcase. My stomach knots at the thought that the Army might take my fingerprints—Amelia Robinson's fingerprints—from the phone case. Why didn't I wipe it down?

"Follow Lieutenant Owen's order...er...instructions. Please." She pats me on the shoulder. "Try not to worry. We'll be in touch."

Then she picks up her briefcase and strides toward the exit gate.

The zoo director stands in the doorway, looking over his assistant's shoulder. Two sets of eyes on me.

"Are you in some sort of trouble, Grey?" He makes it sound like I've been caught distributing kiddie porn with my phone.

I shake my head. "Not at all. My boyfriend, he's in the Army, and he sent a..."

I'm not supposed to talk about this.

"...a sensitive Army communication," I finish. It sounds lame, even to my ears. "By accident," I add. "So I let them know." Which sounds even lamer.

I check my watch and then head back to the penguin pool. I keep seeing Emilio's eyes, one swollen shut, the other staring at the camera. What was he thinking? *Help?* Or *Don't cooperate; I'm already a dead man?*

I focus on diligently scrubbing the penguins' water filter, cleaning off the odiferous brown-green scum. It's a great relief to have something useful to do while I wait to find out if Shadow is dead.

Nineteen

By the time the workday is done, my head is throbbing. On the way back home, I feel strange in the truck sitting next to Sabrina and not telling her about the ransom note. What would it hurt? It's not like she's going to spread the news to anyone who is going to destroy our national security. While my ulcer and my headache debate whether to tell her, we chat about the antics of our zoo creatures and colleagues, and we arrive back at WildRun before I make up my mind whether or not I should violate Owen's instructions.

When we drive through the gates, nothing looks out of place, but our home seems unnaturally quiet.

I realize with a jolt that's because no creature has come to greet us. Occasionally Bailey is off rearranging the landscape in a far corner of the property, but usually there's a goat or two underfoot, begging for a treat the instant we get out of the truck. Or at least a cat lounging on the porch swing and disdainfully ignoring us.

I squint at the pasture to see as far as I can. I detect no movement.

Sabrina grabs the sack of groceries we bought on the way

home and starts for the front door.

"I'll be back in a few minutes," I tell her. "I want to see what new destruction Bailey is into."

I make my way along the western fence line, checking the wire mesh and the electrified top strands for breaks. "Bailey? Where are you?"

There's no trumpeting. No belly rumbles. No thundering footsteps. Has my elephant gone AWOL?

I have a really bad feeling about this.

Speeding up to a trot, I jog around the border of our sixty acres, turning now and then toward the interior to shout. "Bailey!"

Finally, I spot an unfamiliar hill among the trees. Smaller objects flit around nearby like insects scrapping over a corpse.

With my heart in my throat, I run to the site. Bailey lies on his side, his trunk flung out toward the fence. Salt and Pepper, his constant comrades, butt their heads against his flanks, trying to rouse him. Nearby, the new goats bounce around, clearly feeling worried but not understanding why.

"Bailey!" I fall to my knees and flatten the palm of my right hand against the skin between his eye and his ear. My left hand rests at the top of his trunk.

"Bailey!"

He doesn't even bat an eyelash. His eyes, usually weepy at the corners, are dry. His skin is cool to the touch. I jump to my feet, my pulse in overdrive.

"Bailey!" I run my hands along his side, searching for a wound. An elephant is a large territory to explore, but eventually I find a large dart deeply embedded near his tail. A trickle of blood, now mostly dry, runs down his hip.

Ohgodohgodohgod, some bastard shot my elephant!

I take hold of the dart with both hands and yank it out in case it's still sending out its poison. A gobbet of flesh comes with the hooked barb needle, and a swell of dark blood rises into the crater left in Bailey's tough skin. My elephant shows no sign of life.

"Bailey!" I smack his shoulder. What was in that dart?

Is he asleep?

Is he dying?

Is he dead?

I slap him again. No response. I straighten and stand beside him, shifting from foot to foot, one hand knotting the hem of my tee shirt, terrified and uncertain about what to do next. I scan the area, but see nothing out of place. All I hear is my own heartbeat thundering through my head.

This cannot be happening.

I reach for my cell, but my fingers slap down on an empty pocket. The Army has my phone. And even if I held it now, what would I tell 9-1-1? *My elephant is dying?* What a shit storm that would unleash.

I risked everything to save Bailey's life. So did Bash. Saving Bailey is the only good thing I've done in my life.

I bought WildRun for him. I paid the zoo to save him from being sold to an exotic animal game farm. But some crazed shooter still killed him.

Then my elephant takes a long, shuddering breath.

"Bailey!" I scramble over his foreleg and drop to my knees again beside his head. Slapping him hard on his wrinkled cheek, I shout, "Bailey! Wake up!"

I tug on his ear and smack him on his trunk with my open

hand. These are two of the most sensitive body parts on an elephant. "You've got to get up, Bailey!"

I've heard the veterinarians at the zoo talk about how dangerous it is to tranquilize creatures as big as Bailey. If the dosage isn't just right for their weight, they can die. If an elephant ends up lying on top of his leg or trunk, his massive weight can do irreparable damage to that appendage. Bailey's left rear leg is tucked under his body. I can't let him end up a three-legged elephant.

"Bailey! Bailey!" I scream at him until I'm hoarse. Then I grab hold of the edge of his ear with my right hand, wrap my left hand around his trunk, and lean back, trying to budge him. Which is ludicrous. Bailey's massive head weighs far more than my whole body.

Salt tries to assist by butting his skull against Bailey's. Pepper bashes his head into Bailey's backbone.

Apparently I exert enough pressure to irritate him, or maybe it's due to the goats' efforts, but Bailey raises his head a few inches in my direction. His trunk flails in the dirt like a wounded python. He snorts, raising a cloud of dust.

Ever helpful, Pepper butts my thigh. I'm glad my adopted goats are de-horned.

"Up, Bailey," I urge, pulling again. "Up!"

And finally, with a thunderous groan, he rolls to his belly. His back legs are now bent beneath him in a kneeling position. His front legs are stretched out beneath his head. He flops his trunk between his legs and rests his whiskery chin forward on his knees, exhaling a massive gust of air. Sort of a Downward Dog yoga position. Crouching Elephant.

"Good enough for now." A wave of relief washes through

me, making my knees quake. I can finally breathe again. I rub him behind his ear. His rumbles sound sad.

"Rest up for a minute." I push myself to my feet and pace around him in a circle, spiraling outward as I examine the ground. A tan-colored goat accompanies me, and then the spotted one decides to tag along, too. The small clearing has been thoroughly trampled by animals and people. There's no way to read all the prints on top of prints.

On my fifth orbit, I spot a rifle in the weeds. It's mangled beyond repair, the stock shattered and bent thirty degrees sideways to the barrel.

Distinct boot treads are pressed into the soft dirt a few yards beyond that. At first, the deep imprints are spread far apart—a running man. Probably fleeing a charging elephant. The prints lead me toward the fence, drawing closer together and becoming more shallow as the man slowed to a walk. I guess that at this point, Bailey was staggering as the tranquilizer took effect. Finally the boot prints stop. And then they turn and head off toward my house.

The house. Sabrina!

I glance back at Bailey. My elephant has raised his head. He looks wobbly, but he seems to be recovering.

"Stay, Bailey." Tonight, he might actually obey that command for a change.

I race back to the house, fearful that I'm going to find my housemate lying in a pool of blood. Instead, she's standing in the living room, her hands on her hips, anger darkening her face.

"They were neat about it," she snarls. "But someone's been here, Tana. My laptop was plugged in, and I didn't leave it that way. Damn good thing I use a passcode. Look at this!" She points to a faint outline of dust on the floor—a partial of the boot print I found in the pasture. When I back up and look at our oak plank floor from an oblique angle, I see multiple prints in the slanted light from the setting sun.

Bailey was not the target. Or at least not the only one.

In my bedroom, I check my laptop and my tablet. I think I discern finger tracks on the screens. I use passcodes, too, and I'm not especially worried about what an intruder might find, but now I need to have Dark Horse Networks check my computers for hidden programs that might have been planted there.

Good thing I'm paranoid. I already deleted my photos and notes from my Bellingham trip. I store my sensitive materials on two thumb drives, and I keep those in very weird places that not even Sabrina knows about—one buried next to the third fencepost from the house between the yard and pasture, another duct-taped to the back of our washing machine under the cold water hose.

My housemate waits in my bedroom doorway, tapping her foot like a fifties housewife. "Who the hell?" she asks. "That pervert Derek, you think?"

"Maybe. Although it looks like he brought a friend."

"Should we call the police?"

"Let's think about it for a little bit first." Then a frightening thought slams into my brain. "Are you positive they're gone?"

"I checked. Nobody's hiding in the closets." Sabrina sighs. "Where was our guard elephant?"

Should I tell her about Bailey and the tranquilizer gun? I

decide not to, for now—it's too scary and it's all my fault, and I can't think of how to explain it without telling her who I really am. "I found him at the other end of the property; he probably didn't even hear anything. I'll go get him now."

On my way back to Bailey, I find another double set of boot prints. And then I stumble across two deep parallel grooves next to the old orchard. The surrounding vegetation looks as if it was hit by a sudden windstorm.

My mouth goes as dry as the Sahara. Now I know how they got in and out. A helicopter landed here.

I have a sneaking suspicion who *they* are, and I think I know what they're looking for. The ninjas from my past know where their drone crashed and now this is retaliation. They have been here, searching for evidence of what I know about the Robinson murders.

Which is still practically nothing. But clearly they *believe* I might know something important.

Someone or something followed me home from Bellingham. Pederson? Patterson? I have led danger back to my innocent animals and housemate. Guilt descends on me like a dense fog. But I don't have a clue what to do about it.

I'm taking a shortcut through the woods when there's a sharp crack and then a crash, and a massive hulk abruptly rears up in front of me. I nearly wet my pants before I realize it is Bailey, crashing through the trees in the dark with even less than his usual grace. Together we walk back to the barn and I give him a giant ration of kale that the local supermarket saves for me when it's no longer pretty enough to be human food.

As he chews, Bailey rocks, shifting his weight from side to side on his front feet, distressed about what happened earlier.

I'm still freaked out, too, so I stay and scratch him and we talk about it until we're both calmer. The goats seem to have already forgotten the whole episode.

I'm torn between spending the night out here with my elephant and sleeping in my bed. Neither seems a safe choice right now. But my housemate will wonder what's up if I don't come back, and I need to protect her too, so I head for the house, where I work to convince Sabrina that it must have been Derek or neighborhood kids on a lark.

"But how could they get in?"

"Maybe a carpet over the electric fence?" I suggest.

"And Bailey didn't notice?"

My memory shoots the horrific image of Bailey, unconscious, onto my mental screen just in case I need a reminder. I shrug. "We have a lot of acreage. Bailey can't be everywhere. The intruders didn't take anything, did they?"

"I haven't noticed anything missing."

First Emilio, then the spy drones, now a home invasion. I feel sick. It's a race to see which explodes first, my head or my stomach.

I check Sabrina's face to see what she's thinking. Should I confess to her what might be going on?

I need Sabrina. Her rent, miniscule though it is, helps to pay for groceries and animal feed and small comforts like electricity and water. She helps me take care of the animals. But she doesn't have a clue who I really am. Is it fair to put her in danger because of my past?

She surprises me by saying, "I know who might be behind this, Tana."

I am flabbergasted. "What?"

She chews on her lower lip for a second before she answers. "I should have told you before, but I really thought we were safe. You know my mom's in prison, right?"

I nod.

"Her druggie boyfriend's doing time, too. And I helped put him there. I testified against him."

"But he's still in prison, right?"

"Yeah." She scuffs the side of her shoe against the floor. "He has a lot of friends on the outside, though. They might be looking for me. Revenge, you know. Maybe we should tell the police."

This is a twist I wasn't expecting. Sabrina has been feeling guilty about not telling me *her* secrets. I know Sabrina Vasile was a street kid. Now she's a tough twenty-year-old who hides her natural beauty behind tattoos and piercings and bleach and fluorescent hair dye. I try to think the situation through. "But if they found you, Sabrina, wouldn't they do something?" *Like kill you?*

"Probably." She frowns and thrusts her hands out to her sides. "I don't get it."

I can't let her feel guilty. She's my best girlfriend. But it would probably put her in more danger if she shares my knowledge about what happened to my family, so I say, "I don't think this has anything to do with you. That piece of plastic I found the other day? It was part of a drone that was registered to a company in Bellingham. I think the drones might be looking for me. Probably a paparazzi thing after the race. Could be they're looking for clues to find Sebastian Callendro."

A wave of relief passes over her face. "Maybe we should still tell the police."

If I tell the police, that would unleash a volley of questions about who might want to hurt me and why. It takes a lot of power from on high to erase a whole family like they obliterated mine. The authorities in Bellingham completely bought the story about my family suddenly relocating to Africa. The cops might have been part of the plan.

Even if my local police here believed me, they'd probably talk to the Bellingham law enforcement agencies, and then, I have no idea what might happen.

My brain hurts. My heart does, too. I'm so tired of being scared. I'd like to run off and hide somewhere, but I can't leave Bailey. I can't leave Sabrina, either. Or my job.

My fear slowly burns into rage. How dare anyone invade my house! How dare they shoot my elephant! I have to think of a way to make this stop.

But I can't do anything without solid evidence that someone—someone *specific*—is truly after me. And there's a chance that they—whoever *they* are—will simply decide to leave me alone. Pederson could have killed me by now if he wanted. So it seems unlikely that *they* have uncovered any evidence that I am Amelia Robinson.

I remind Sabrina that the police would want to come to WildRun and they'd have a million questions about Bailey and the two of us.

"You don't have a name you can give them, do you? Someone who'd be after you?" I ask.

She shakes her head.

"Neither do I." The police would never believe that Phineas Pederson might be stalking me.

So we decide to leave it at that. We will both be on guard.

Then, later that night, as I'm getting ready for bed, I can't find my hairbrush.

That can't be good.

Twenty

All night I obsess about the hairbrush. I get up three times to check the window to make sure nothing scary is going on outside. As soon as dawn breaks over the horizon, I call Marisela so I can hear a comforting voice. She's caretaking an orchard right now and supervising a small army of farm workers as well as her kids, so I know she's up before sunrise. I can't tell her anything about what happened last night. But we still have plenty of worry to share.

"Nothing," she answers sorrowfully instead of saying hello. "The Army still says they know nothing about Emilio."

She's talking in a low voice, practically whispering, which tells me that ten-year-old twins Kai and Kiki don't know that their cousin is missing in action overseas.

My conscience does a whirling dervish dance before I decide that it's kinder to lie to her about the kidnapping than to tell the truth. "I haven't heard anything, either. But, you know, Marisela, no news could be good news." *At least they haven't found Emilio's body.*

"I am praying," she says, her voice breaking. "He should never have gone."

"He's a good soldier," I tell her. "I'll keep in touch."

She murmurs, "Te quiero, m'hija."

It always brings tears to my eyes to hear Marisela Santos say she loves me. She's the closest thing I have to family. She's had so much sorrow in her life; she doesn't deserve this latest bad news. Who does?

"I love you, too, Marisela. Kiss the twins for me."

I take a deep breath and wash my face before I join Sabrina in the living room.

When I commute by bike, I don't have time to do anything except grab a cup of coffee and a banana before leaving the house, but on the days we share a ride, Sabrina and I usually take our cereal bowls to the couch and watch the morning news while we eat breakfast. This morning, when I flick on the television, a voice starts off with *"...the latest blow to the terrorist network in Syria with the rescue of Army Sergeant Emilio Santos and journalist Nathaniel Timmons."*

The video shows a dozen commando types inside a building. We watch two hooded, handcuffed prisoners being dragged through the flying dust toward a doorway. There are dark humanoid shapes lying near the walls, presumably dead terrorists.

And one dead prisoner, too, according to the report. Guy Tibodeaux, an aid worker from France, did not survive, although it's not clear whether he was dead before the commandos arrived or if he's collateral damage from the raid.

Next, President Garrison appears on screen to take credit and tell us he's proud of this victory over terrorism and of the rescue of our gallant military heroes.

I can hardly believe that the military managed to rescue

Shadow less than twenty-four hours after I got the ransom message. Owen wasn't kidding when he said the photo told them what happened to Shadow. Something about the message had to have tipped them off to where he was. But, no matter how it happened, it's a magical word—rescue! Shadow is *alive*. But according to the reports, this happened hours ago. So much for Owen's promise to keep me informed.

Sabrina's cell chimes. She answers, raises an eyebrow, looks at me. "Yeah. Just a sec." She presses the phone into my hands.

It's Owen. *Duh.* Of course. The Army has my phone. He explains that it took a while to track down my housemate. "Sergeant Santos will be flown to a hospital in Germany," he tells me. "His injuries are not critical. In a few days, he will be returned stateside to the veterans' hospital in Seattle. That's the one closest to you, correct?"

"Uh...yes, I suppose so." I've never really thought about veterans facilities, but as Shadow's supposed fiancée, I probably would have.

"We'll keep you informed."

Then he thanks me for my help and tells me my phone will be delivered back to the zoo tomorrow. Good thing I'm working an extra shift there to make up for my days off last week.

Just as I'm punching in Marisela's number, she calls me to share the good news. We promise to meet up at the VA hospital whenever Emilio gets there.

The next day, when I get my cell phone back, both the protective case and the phone exterior have been polished until they're shiny. Which most people would consider a nice gesture, but which of course makes me uber-paranoid that the

Army cleaned them after dusting for fingerprints. Which of course makes me worry even more about my missing hairbrush.

I don't remember being fingerprinted or DNA-tested or microchipped as a little kid, and I have never been arrested, so the authorities wouldn't be able to match me to a record in any official system. But my prints and DNA were no doubt all over my house in Bellingham. When the ninja killers mopped up the day after the murders, did they collect that sort of stuff? Do they now know that I'm Amelia Robinson, and if so, what do they plan to do about it?

These thoughts make me feel like a schizophrenic. If only there was some sort of medicine I could take to make them go away. I'm glad that Sabrina is home with Bailey today, although it crosses my mind that means that they could both be killed in the same attack. These paranoid whisperings often turn into screaming matches in my head.

I remind myself that everything is not bad news; I actually have something to celebrate. Shadow's alive; he's coming back! The refrain runs through my brain throughout the workday. As I spend hours planting new grasses in a fenced-off corner of the Savanna habitat, I try to imagine what sort of shape my 'fiancé' will be in when he gets back.

On my lunch break, I hop the bus and take my laptop and tablet over to Dark Horse Networks. I've been afraid to use my computer since the home invasion. Inside the company's headquarters, I have to work to keep myself from pacing through the cubicle maze as Clark and Kent—yeah, they even call themselves The Supermen—run diagnostic programs on my computer.

The place really should be called Dark Cave Networks,

because they like to keep the shades drawn so they can see all the computer screens easier. The company does some sort of really highly paid security work. They like the idea that they are not part of the mainstream computing world, and I think that's why they wanted to sponsor an extreme racer like me instead of an athlete from a more popular sport. Bash, always the cynic, says it's a big tax break, too.

The atmosphere at Dark Horse reminds me, uncomfortably, of the days I spent underground last year. But the Nilsen brothers are always uber-nice to me, and they are my only sponsors for my race expenses, so I stifle my claustrophobia when I'm in their offices.

"I'm not seeing anything, Tana," Clark says now. "But this is a good idea." He points to the black velvet bindi I have pasted over the camera eye at the top of the screen.

Kent leans over the desk. He has reddish blond hair, invisible eyebrows, and a soul patch on his chin that looks like he missed that spot when he was shaving. He's a geek; he probably thinks it makes him look cool. "Why would you think someone installed a spy program?"

At first I think he's talking into the phone gizmo he has plugged into his ear, but then his eyes make contact with mine.

I don't want to get into the invasion, so I try to sound casual. "You can't be too careful, right? Can't people send those things in email?"

He folds his arms across his chest. "Speaking of email, what's up with all the Amy and Amelia questions from this P.A. Patterson in Africa?"

That's the one drawback to having these guys handle my website and racer email: no privacy.

"Are you sure they came from Africa?" I ask him. *Not from Bellingham?*

"Yeah, they did."

Hmmm. So maybe Pederson is not Patterson.

"But then, I suppose they could just be routed that way for some peculiar reason." Kent scratches the fuzz on his chin. "I didn't look at the entire trail."

Alrighty then. Pederson remains on the suspect list. Why can't I ever get a clue that points in only one direction, like a flashing neon arrow?

"We can block Patterson if you want."

"No," I respond, too quickly. Even though the messages are disturbing, they are links to my past. Plus, I want to see what P.A. Patterson is going to ask next. I explain to the Nilsens, "I don't want to upset even one fan anywhere. You never know who knows who out there."

"Excellent point," Kent says.

"As always, I appreciate your support, guys. And riding that bike was sweet. Thanks for the loan."

"You rocked it," Clark tells me. "But the bike wasn't on camera much, so we didn't get much of a bump from Ski to Sea. Maybe you should think about doing triathlons."

Kent chimes in, excited at the idea. "We could make you a Dark Horse Networks jacket for the bike and a Dark Horse Networks swim skin."

I snort. "Thanks for the vote of confidence," I tell them, although I suspect their suggestions are more about branding their company than about my athletic prowess. "But when it comes to swimming, I'm more of a manatee than a dolphin. It's not great advertising if Dark Horse comes in last, is it?"

Clark gives me back my laptop and tablet and then walks me to the door, where he stops to peer at me though his wire-rimmed glasses. "Next week we're finalizing the advertising for the Colorado Challenge. You're all set to do it, right?"

He's talking about a loop race through the Rocky Mountains in late June. The Colorado Challenge is not my favorite, because despite the name and the fact that the course winds through the mountains, it's not that much of a challenge for me. They advertise it as an ultramarathon, but it's only fifty kilometers, slightly more than thirty miles. Plus, the course is mostly on roads or trails, not a cross-country endurance race like I prefer. The terrain is actually not that rugged, so the race attracts a lot of weekend athletes. But for exactly that reason, it's a really big deal in Colorado. The local television stations always show the highlights. I've won the Colorado Challenge twice, so now The Supermen want me to do it every year because odds are good that their logos on my running clothes will see at least a few minutes of air time.

"Of course," I assure him.

But there's no way Colorado will satisfy my wanderlust and my thirst for genuine competition, so I ask, "And can I scout out a couple of overseas races, too?"

"Just let us know," Clark says, closing the door behind me. I blink in the bright sun like a tortoise that just pulled its head out of its shell, and head to the bus stop and back to my job at the zoo.

Three days later, I have my answer about the condition Shadow will be in when I see him next. The VA hospital in Seattle is—like all hospitals—a depressing place. As I walk down the hallway to Emilio's room, I pass an area where some sort of group therapy is going on. Each person seated in a circle of chairs is missing a limb or two. I quickly switch my gaze back to the gleaming vinyl floor tiles in front of my feet.

Marisela is already in Emilio's room, standing by his bed, holding his hand, which she drops as I enter, and then backs away so I can greet our returning soldier.

I walk forward, smiling. At least I hope it looks like a smile on my face. If I hadn't been told the man in the bed was Emilio Santos, I probably would not have recognized him. His head has huge shaved patches around gashes held together by black stitches. The right side of his face is black and lumpy, his chin is stubbled with whiskers, his lips are cracked, and his right eye is hidden beneath gauze and tape. His left arm is in a sling, and the size of his right foot's outline under the sheet tells me that foot is in a cast. Sergeant Emilio Santos is a wreck.

"Tana!" he croaks, holding out his free hand.

"Welcome back, Emilio." I grasp my fingers around the bed frame as I lean in uncertainly to kiss him. I aim for his left cheek, which is about the only uninjured spot available. There's even a red line across his neck, probably a souvenir from that machete in the ransom photo.

"I know," he groans. "I look like Frankenstein."

For a second, I think about correcting him, that he would be Dr. Frankenstein's monster, not the doctor, but then I decide that would be snarky. So I just say, "That's only temporary. I'm thrilled you're alive."

"Me too." He starts to grin, but winces instead because that obviously hurts his cracked lips, and he ends up licking them. I decide that his left eye looks reasonably happy.

Marisela picks up a glass by his bedside and aims a straw at him. He sips gratefully.

For a long moment, none of us can think of what to say. I have a million questions to ask about what happened over there and what his doctors say, but this is a family reunion. It doesn't seem the right place or time for an interrogation.

Marisela rescues us by pulling two construction-paper cards from her giant handbag. "From Kiki," she says, holding the rose-colored one out in front of Emilio.

The homemade card features a person with what looks like a walnut on his head—I suppose it's a helmet—with hands outstretched and a flying bird in each one. Beneath the image, WELCOME HOME!!!!! is printed in black magic marker. Maybe the birds are supposed to be carrying the soldier home? Kiki is not exactly an artist.

Kai is, though. His drawing is a detailed depiction of a soldier, seen from the back. He's wearing a heavy pack and has a rifle slung over one shoulder, and he is standing before a door that is just beginning to open. Over the door is a huge sign: WELCOME BACK, EMILIO! Somehow Kai made the letters look happy, and the flowers growing in abundance on both sides of the steps are a nice touch, too. It looks like the sort of house anyone would like to come home to.

"Tell the twins I think these are fantastic," Emilio says to Marisela.

"I will." She props them up on his bedside table, and then bends over her bag again. "I made for you *churros*." She extracts a small cardboard box dotted with grease stains, and places it next to the cards. "The nurses say they will heat them up when you want."

"Hah," he laughs. "They'll probably *eat* them up instead."

They switch to Spanish for a few minutes. I get about every twentieth word, just enough to decipher that Marisela is telling him about her job managing a migrant labor camp in Yakima right now and something about the twins. Then Emilio's expression goes dark and he rapid-fires off a bunch of staccato words that make Marisela clap her hand to her mouth and shake her head. The only words I get are *ejército*, which I know means *army*, and AWOL, which is military code for away without leave. Who is AWOL? But I don't ask, because clearly this is not a conversation that Emilio wants me to participate in.

After a tense few seconds of silence, they both remember that I am in the room and turn in my direction.

"*Y tú, cómo estás?*" Emilio says, carefully enunciating each syllable.

How am I? I tell them that my team came in third during my last race. At first they make sympathetic faces like *that's too bad*, and I have to remind them that there were *hundreds* of teams and third is a huge win.

Marisela says, "I see your one-foot partner on the news, but I don't see you."

"Jason was the hero of the day," I tell them.

Now Shadow's left eye looks as if it's glowering, so I quickly switch the subject to the happenings at the zoo. I tell them about how a vine snake escaped and nobody located it for several days until they found it snuggled around a hot water pipe in a utility closet. It's a good thing that species is not venomous. Naturally, the public never knew. There were two other vine snakes in the cage, and those skinny green reptiles blend right into the scenery.

Then a burly man in scrubs comes in, carrying a tray of bandages and other stuff I'd rather not think about. He tells us it's time to go. "Sergeant Santos needs his rest."

I lean over to kiss Emilio's cheek again. "I'm sorry I didn't bring anything for you, Shadow," I whisper.

"You brought the most important gift of all." He touches my lips with a gentle finger. "You."

We promise to come back the next day. On the way out of the hospital, Marisela pulls me to a stop by the nurses' station to ask about Emilio's condition.

A dark-skinned nurse looks up his records online. "He has a lot of injuries, but none are critical. It will take a while to adjust to living with only one eye, but he should be home in a few days. We can arrange for physical therapy and in-home nurse visits."

Only one eye? Marisela sobs all the way out to the parking lot, so I have to suck it up and drive us the nearly two hours back to my place in her old rattletrap Ford, all the while thinking Emilio will be home in a couple of days to learn how to live as a one-eyed man.

As if that weren't awful enough, I know that he doesn't really have a home. He usually sleeps on Marisela's couch when he's in country, but right now she and the twins are sharing a one-bedroom shack with minimal facilities.

"He can stay with you, yes?" Her face is red, her eyes are shiny with tears.

She knows that my house has three bedrooms. I borrowed a cot for her and set it up in the spare room, which usually holds all sorts of junk.

The idea of Emilio living at my house terrifies me. I lived with him at Marisela's for two years, but we were rarely alone. I was sixteen when he left for the Army. I haven't seen him in person for more than a few hours for the last two years. I am not ready for twenty-four/seven togetherness.

But I owe Marisela so much. She took me in when I was homeless; she taught me how to avoid the scrutiny of the authorities. She showed me where I could find work. She made me into a survivor. She never had much, but she shared it all with me.

I owe her nephew Emilio, too. He held me when I cried, without ever asking me the details of my past. He helped me dream about butterflies and happy days to come in the future. He encouraged me to train to be a racer. And he loves me, or at least what he knows of me.

I've never been a caretaker for a human being. I don't cook; I nuke. I am focused on my own problems. I consistently forget to even ask other people how they are.

I have to work, and half the time I have to commute there on my bike. At home, I have an elephant and four—no, five—goats and three cats to care for.

How will Sabrina take the news that an invalid is moving in with us? I can't ask her to pitch in to nurse my boyfriend, can I? That's not in the housemate contract.

And then there's the whole I'm-not-who-you-think-I-am-and-ninjas-could-break-in-at-any-moment-and-kill-us-all problem.

But here beside me, my hardworking foster mom is waiting for my answer, her face expectant and hopeful.

Emilio's parents are dead, victims of the cartel violence along the U.S./Mexico border. Marisela hasn't heard from her husband for nearly a decade, so he's probably dead, too. This family has suffered even more loss than I have.

It's time for me to grow up.

"Of course Emilio can stay with me," I promise.

Twenty-One

At first, having Shadow in the house is not such a trial. Marisela stayed long enough to get him settled. We got a proper bed for almost nothing from Craigslist, carted it home in Sabrina's pickup, and bought a lot of pillows on sale to prop up our wounded soldier.

Most of the time he can get around when he needs to, although he can't walk very fast, because the foot he was shot in is velcroed into this awkward boot thing. But sometimes his head injury makes the world spin, and he can't get out of bed, or even open his eye. That worries me. A lot. And then there are the nightmares, which I guess are to be expected after being tortured. I hear the moans from his room. I hear him get up, and I've watched him from my window when he limps outside in the middle of the night.

He doesn't go far. Just to the peeling Adirondack chair in the garden. He sits there and stares at the sky overhead. Bailey is used to him now, and sometimes he stretches his trunk over the garden fence toward Emilio, but he can't quite reach him. Sometimes Emilio holds out a hand and man and elephant touch each other in the dark.

Most of the time, I don't have a clue what sort of thoughts might be running through Emilio's brain. He sleeps almost all of the daylight hours.

In the beginning, I am afraid to touch him for fear of hurting him or waking him up. But he grabs onto me whenever I'm close, and his eye locks onto my gaze.

"Tee," he said the first time. "I know I'm a monster to look at. It's okay."

The guilt forced tears from my eyes as I leaned forward, putting my hands on his shoulders and kissing him. It wasn't okay that day, and it's not okay now. He's my friend. He's still Shadow. He's hurting. He needs me, just like I needed him and Marisela four years ago.

So I try to be the good nurse and homemaker I've never been, cooking—okay, mostly nuking—meals for him, making sure he takes his meds, doing his laundry, helping him get around. On the wall across from his bed I tack up a magazine picture of the monarch butterflies wintering in Michoacán, Mexico, so many thousands of them that the branches of the trees sag under their weight. The picture hangs above a battered secondhand dresser we picked up at a garage sale.

On the fifth day he is here, I am putting away some clean clothes in the top drawer of that dresser, trying to be silent because it's late and he's sleeping. Moonlight streams in from the window, illuminating the butterfly photo and giving me just enough light to see. I have just pushed the drawer shut when he says, "Those butterflies."

I turn. His good eye gleams in the dark. "Those butterflies kept me sane. They are all I thought about when they had me."

They. His kidnappers. Since the U.S. is not actually at war,

I guess we can't call them the enemy. I've heard Shadow call them ragheads and hajjis and sometimes, just "the bad guys."

"I knew I was going to see the monarchs in Michoacán. And I was going to see them with you." He peels down the sheet covering him and pats the mattress beside him.

I slide onto the mattress next to him, feeling awkward. He's wearing only sweatpants. His chest is bare and smooth. Despite the ever-growing whiskers on his cheeks and chin, Shadow never had much in the way of chest hair. I run my hand over his pectoral muscles, starting to go soft with no exercise, but still well-defined.

This is the boy I remember from the orchards, the boy who showed me how to pick like a robot and bag the apples without bruising them, the boy who could lift a hundred pounds of fruit without breaking a sweat. I lay my cheek against his neck and good shoulder.

He groans.

I quickly lift my head. "I didn't mean to hurt you."

"You're not." He curls his arm around my head, pressing me back against his body. I feel a wetness against my forehead. He's crying.

"I'm sorry I did this to you," he murmurs.

"You haven't done anything to me, Shadow," I tell him. "I'd give anything if this hadn't happened to you."

There's a long pause during which I simply listen to him breathe while he strokes my hair. This situation makes me squirm inside, because it reminds me of lying next to Bash during our Verde Island days, and that's the last thing I should be thinking about right now.

Then Shadow finally says, "I wasn't supposed to be off-base. But I couldn't take it anymore, being cooped up there, especially after CarJack ran over that little kid."

What? I don't know who CarJack is, but it doesn't really matter. "How horrible."

"It was an accident. The rear camera was trashed, but it probably wouldn't have mattered anyhow. You can't really see in back of those stupid APCs; they're not designed to back up."

I make an umm-hmm sound because I have no idea how else to respond.

"CarJack was driving, but I was there with him. It was only one thump. We didn't know what we hit."

Omigod.

"The kid was chasing a ball down the street. He couldn't have been more than four. Remember how hard it was to keep Kai and Kiki out of trouble when they were that age?"

"Yes." Although his twin cousins were five when I joined Marisela's family group.

And then, naturally, that poor dead kid makes me think about Aaron. Now I'm crying, too, getting Shadow's chest all wet, sniffling and trying not to sob out loud.

After a minute, he says, "Tee?"

"Yeah?"

"Why are *you* crying? You weren't even there."

I sniff and try to shut down the flood of my own tears. "I can imagine it too well, Shadow."

Emilio sighs heavily, his chest rising and falling beneath my cheek, his breath ruffling my hair. "So, after CarJack ate his gun that night, I just walked off into the desert."

Ate his gun? So CarJack was another suicide. As far as I

know, it's the second in their unit. I can't imagine what it's like to have your comrades kill themselves.

Shadow takes another deep breath and continues. "Then you and I talked."

And I didn't say *I love you.* I freeze, afraid to breathe, worried about what he's going to say next.

But he gives me a pass when he says, "After that, I just wanted to be alone for awhile, to have a chance to think."

I know that feeling too well.

"So I just snuck out. I didn't walk far, just to where I couldn't see the camp. I laid down and looked at the stars. They're so bright there. I thought about what our life would be like together, where we might live, about how we might have twins like Kai and Kiki."

I've been thinking about Bailey and Bash and Pederson and the drones; about everything except Emilio. And he's been dreaming about *our future. Our children.* I feel like I'm suffocating.

"So *I'm* sorry, Tee. And now..." He breathes in and out slowly for a few seconds before he finally adds, "They might charge me with desertion."

They wouldn't do that, would they? He only wanted to be alone for a few minutes. He didn't ask to be kidnapped and tortured.

"Thanks for letting me stay with you."

I rise up on my elbow to look at him. "You'd do the same for me."

His mouth goes tight, and his eye gazes up toward the ceiling. I guess that he's thinking about how there's no way he could do this for me right now. His gaze slides back to my face.

"I did this to myself. I did this to *us*. I'm supposed to be taking care of *you*."

I hate that he feels guilty about me on top of everything else he's going through.

"Shadow, you have nothing to be sorry for." I kiss his tear-stained cheek, at the corner of his good eye. "I can take care of myself."

His jaw clenches, his body goes stiff, and he turns his head to look at the wall. Somehow, that was exactly the wrong thing to say right now.

"Shadow?" I whisper.

He won't look at me. I push myself up off his bed and slink away to my own.

As the days mount up, I think Shadow must be bored to a stupor spending all his time in one place, so I try to entertain him with stories from the zoo. From the library, I bring him books on tape that I think he'll like. He was never much of a reader when he lived with Marisela and us kids, and I'm not sure how well he can focus now with one eye, but everyone likes good stories.

Sabrina seems okay with having him here. In fact, she seems to like it. She brought home a complicated puzzle of an old castle somewhere in Europe, and she and Emilio spread out the pieces across the dining room table and work on putting it together while I'm out running on my training course or seeing to the animals.

Emilio claims to like the strange concoctions Sabrina makes. While I nuke meals in the microwave, Sabrina mostly blends and purees—fruit and yogurt smoothies and soups that are odd mixes of vegetables and leftovers nearing the end of their edible lives in our fridge. I suspect that with her junkie mom as her only caregiver, Sabrina was one of those kids who grew up making tomato soup out of fast-food packets of catsup and coffee creamer.

Ten days after Emilio moves in, I am out at sunset, running my practice track around the property, leaping over rocks and doing chin-ups on tree branches, preparing for the Colorado Challenge. The western sky is a beautiful violet. It's quiet. Bailey is hanging out with Salt and Pepper near the pond. The other goats are near the barn. The cats are wherever they go to hunt in the evening. I have found no more footprints, and I have heard no more drones. Maybe Pederson/Patterson or whoever was checking me out has decided to leave me alone. But I still feel uneasy, because I am enjoying this brief period of freedom even more than the fresh air and exercise.

When I come back to the house, I find Emilio and Sabrina eating together at the kitchen table. As I walk in, they are laughing about something.

"Check it out, Tana! I made spaghetti." She twirls some long strands on a fork. "Emilio supervised."

"Yeah," he chuckles. "She now knows how to boil water and open cans of tomato paste."

Sabrina shoots him a look. "*And* add sausage and veggies."

I inhale the rich aroma of tomato sauce. "Smells good."

"Grab a plate."

"After I shower." As I walk out of the room, I have the uncomfortable feeling that I am an uninvited guest at their party.

Sabrina and I rearrange our work schedules so we only have to leave Emilio alone for three days out of the week. A nurse or physical therapist drops by for two of those. Marisela calls her nephew every day at noon. She'd call me immediately if Shadow didn't answer or if something weird was going on.

I'll have to change the gate code after he recovers and things get back to normal. But that's a worry, too; he needs more surgery on his foot and shoulder, and right now, even if the Army doesn't decide to court-martial him, it seems doubtful that they will want a one-eyed man back. What will he do if they don't?

Neither Emilio or Marisela ever told me, but I'd guess Emilio joined the Army to get his citizenship at the end of his service, which means the authorities know he's in the country illegally. President Garrison has mostly ignored immigration issues, but the contestants vying to replace him are practically frothing at the mouth about how they will close our borders and rid our country of foreign devils.

After sundown, if Shadow is still awake, he and Sabrina and I usually watch a movie or a couple of TV shows, and then the evening news. So now, two weeks into my stint of taking care of my soldier, I'm sitting on his left side on the couch, with Sabrina on his right, when my loon calls me to my bedroom, where I left my cell phone.

It's Bash. Hearing his voice makes me realize how much I miss him.

"I called you earlier," he says. "But you didn't answer."

"Sorry, I was out training. I leave for the Colorado Challenge tomorrow."

"Lucky girl. Anyhow, knowing you're a spook, I didn't leave a message."

"Wise choice," I agree. But I really should check my missed calls list more often.

"What's up?"

I tell him briefly about Emilio being kidnapped and wounded and now recovering at my house.

"And how's that going?" he asks.

I want to say so many things, but in my head they all sound like whining. "It's okay," I mumble. "What's going on in *your* life?"

"I have something for you." Muffled sounds on his end make me think he's rifling through papers or walking around as he searches for something. "Aha," he says, "Found it. My friend Geneva says both those scans you sent are DNA sequences."

I've been so distracted with all the drama at my house that I'd forgotten about the scans I sent him. The "clues" on the USB stick from my parents' past.

"She says they look like two strains of the same virus. Only certain portions of the sequence are altered. Does that make any sense?"

"Maybe. My mom worked on creating vaccines against viruses." I let those thoughts twist through my brain for a few seconds. Was one of those sequences the original Ebola virus? The exact sequence would probably be a big corporate secret for QTL, but the world knows they cracked the code and it's mutated so many times since then, so why would my Mom want to keep it secret? And what was the other strain? A sibling of the virus? I have no way of figuring out which is which. And I still don't understand why my mother would put them on the memory stick.

"You still there, Tarzan?"

I snap back to the conversation. "Yeah. Thanks for getting that info for me, Bash."

"Any time. Sorry it took so long. Geneva was out of town for most of June." There's a pause, and then he says, "You okay, Tana?"

I sigh. "Just tired."

"You know you can call me any time you want."

"Thanks, Bash. That means a lot." I tell him goodbye. I wish I could hug him instead.

When I slide back into my seat on the couch, Emilio glares at me with his one eye. "That was *him*, wasn't it?"

"It was Sebastian, yes." How could Emilio tell who I was talking to?

He answers my question, even though I didn't ask it aloud. "It's your tone of voice."

"Remember that I told you I wanted some chemistry advice?"

He shakes his head.

"Well, I did. It's been a few weeks, but Sebastian finally got the answers I was looking for."

Emilio turns away to aim his eye at Sabrina, who gives him a look I can't decipher. Then we all turn to watch the television again.

There's a familiar face on the screen. It takes me a second to figure out where I've seen the young woman before, but then the memory snaps into place: she's the courier gal I bumped into at QTL.

I turn up the volume.

"Elizabeth Abbott's body was found next to Marine Drive in Bellingham. It appears that the Western Washington University student was the victim of a hit-and-run driver. Elizabeth, known to her friends as Liz, grew up in the tiny town of Gold Bar. She loved life and travel. She often worked as a courier for Quarrel Tayson Laboratories, delivering vital vaccines to hot spots around the world. During one of her travels, she posted this photo on WhazHap."

The selfie on the screen shows the smiley student I met, her lips colored a plum purple and pursed as if she's about to kiss the camera she's holding above her head. On a shelf beside her at chest level is the little orange bag I saw her carrying at QTL, unzipped now. Liz holds an uncapped lipstick in her free hand. The caption beneath the photo reads *Is Passionflower from QTC my color?*

A solemn spokeswoman for QTL appears on the screen to say:

"Elizabeth was not an employee of Quarrel Tayson Labs, but we still considered her part of our QTL family. Our thoughts are with her relatives in this sad time. QTL is proud to establish a scholarship in her name at Western Washington University, where she was a student."

Then the newscaster segues smoothly into the next story:

"A new strain of Ebola has been identified as responsible for the outbreak that has taken two lives in Senegal."

I wonder if one of those dead people is Liz's friend she was going to visit in that country. That would be a nasty twist of fate, if both Liz and her friend died at the same time on different continents.

"Quarrel Tayson Laboratories reports that their rapid response team has already cultured the new strain of Ebola, and a new vaccine to prevent infection will be available in limited quantities within days."

QTL to the rescue again. I wish Mom could see what became of her discovery. It took her years to come up with the first vaccine; now it seems that QTL can manufacture new versions as soon as the need crops up. I didn't know they had a rapid response team, but it makes sense. Kind of like the hotshot teams that put out super dangerous fires in oil wells and on tankers. Superheroes.

"This deadly virus continues to mutate into new forms around the globe. If you're traveling through Third World countries, please consult your physician to make sure you're protected."

Then it's time for a commercial for teeth-whitening strips.

"I met Elizabeth Abbott," I tell Shadow and Sabrina.

Emilio reaches for my hand like I need comforting. "For real?"

"Where?" Sabrina wants to know.

Oops. I don't want to tell them I was snooping around QTL. "In a coffee shop in Bellingham, when I was there for the race." That's sort of close to the truth. I went to Starbucks right after I met Liz.

Most people would be shocked to discover that someone they'd talked to less than a month ago was now dead. I feel ashamed that I'm not more upset. Yes, it's sad. Liz seemed like a nice person. But the world is a dangerous place.

When I go outside to say good night to the stars, there aren't any. The sky is covered with clouds, like it's in mourning, and the wind gusts through the trees, giving the night a jittery feel.

Over by the bushes that used to be blueberries before the goats pruned them down to sticks, I spot a shape that doesn't belong. For a panicky second, I think it's a rifle barrel poking out of the shrubbery. When I investigate, it turns out to be my hairbrush, hung up between the bare stalks there.

The back of my neck goes all prickly, and I hold my breath as I scan the sky again. I don't hear the buzz of a drone. I don't see any movement other than clouds shifting around.

Bailey delicately pulls the hairbrush out of my hand, curious to know why it's important to me. I take the brush from his trunk and slip it into my pocket.

Is this a warning? A creepy physical reminder: *We can get you at any time.*

Maybe my hairbrush has been here for days. Maybe it never got on that helicopter. Nice thoughts. Somehow I don't think I'm that lucky.

I need a team of superheroes to zip in and help me figure things out. A rapid response team of my own. Tana's personal RRT. As soon as I visualize those letters, I know I've seen RRT somewhere before. Another few seconds pass as I rifle through my chaotic mental filing system, and then I have it—RTT was listed frequently on that spreadsheet scan my mother saved. So maybe that World Cargo West accounting data has to do with QTL, too.

Sensing my somber mood, Bailey moves close and drapes his trunk over my shoulder. This tells me that he senses no danger at the moment. I wish I could forget my worries as easily as my elephant can. Bash's mention of viruses, and then the news of Liz's death on the news, have spooked me all over again. I'm always waiting for the next awful event to happen.

But tomorrow will come soon enough, and I need to get some sleep before I leave for the airport to catch my plane to Boulder, Colorado. I look up toward the dark clouds. Tonight I'm grateful that I am healthy and prepared and ready to run the Colorado Challenge. I am thankful that my friends and my animals are alive, and that nobody I know is dying of Ebola right now.

Twenty-Two

The Colorado Challenge begins at seven a.m., which is six a.m. on my body clock. The sun feels too bright and too hot as I and ninety-six other competitors position ourselves at the starting line. My flight got into Boulder early enough yesterday, but I spent too much time at the hotel enjoying a three-course dinner and a pay-for-movie on Dark Horse's credit card. I got up before dawn to warm up with a swim in the hotel pool, and now I feel like I could use a nap instead of a cross-country run, but I know that will change the instant the starter pistol goes off.

As I do my stretches, a drone hovers a few feet above and in front of me. There are others buzzing around as well, but this silver flying spider seems way too close. Does this camera drone belong to a Colorado news station that is focused on me because I am the current champion to beat, or does it belong to SeaStone Security, who is trying to intimidate me?

Shake it off, Tana, I tell myself as the countdown begins. I focus my gaze on the terrain immediately ahead—a logging road cut through the national forest—and tune out the sound of the jovial competitors around me.

And we're off. I like to position myself close to the front so I can match the fastest pace but also observe if the runners ahead of me encounter obstacles that I can avoid. Then, after I have determined whether the lead runners will be real competition or not, I try to figure out the best way to get around them. In this fifty-kilometer race through the mountains, we are not allowed to deviate more than a hundred meters from the marked gravel roads and hiking trails, so the number of shortcuts is limited. Most runners stick to the cleared course, which of course is the most sensible strategy for avoiding injury, but that's marathon-runner thinking, stifling to an endurance racer like me. So there are only a few of us who crash through the underbrush, leaping over some logs and running atop others to make our own shortcuts. There are a pair of young racers—one male, one female—who glue themselves to my backside and follow my every move, which is understandable, but annoying. With every zig I make, I hear them zagging not far behind me.

The course is pretty tame and has been well prepared by the organizers, so there aren't a lot of surprises. I don't know any of the competitors here. As I vault over a stump, I wonder what Catie Cole is up to today. Jason's probably out biking. And X? No clue what he does in June in Ohio.

As I come down from my vault, I hear a warning buzz near my right ankle. I'm a few yards down the hillside when my brain identifies the source: rattlesnake! The yelp behind me confirms my analysis, and the ensuing crashing noises indicate that one way or another, the snake has slowed down my closest competition. I wonder if a drone caught that on film.

My mechanical minder sticks as close to me as a flying

machine can in thick woods, whipping around trees and zipping under branches, which means this drone has detailed avoidance programming or a pilot who is more skilled than most. At times, it flies within a couple of feet of my head. I feel like it's staring at my face.

At the first 20K checkpoint, I catch the gel pack and water packs that the volunteers toss as I trot through.

"You are second!" One of the men yells as I squeeze lime-flavored goop into my mouth.

"Fastest woman!" yells another.

Which means a man is in first place. I'm certain I was the first to deviate from the trail, so that means he's beating me so far by running on the cleared paths. I gulp down the water, toss the packs along the side of the trail, and pick up my speed to catch up to him.

My drone whirs into high drive mode, too. Sometimes it's a few yards behind me, sometimes a few yards ahead. I hate this relentless gargantuan mosquito that I can't swat. I can't escape its irritating high-pitched buzz and the blinding glints of sun that bounce off its metal skin when it flies in front of me.

I spy my competitor ahead as the route moves into the section that the map labels as The Squeeze. Here the logging road—abandoned long ago and partially eroded away—narrows to hug the side of a cliff. The remainder is about four feet wide, plenty of a space for a single competitor, but the drop-off to my right, if it didn't kill a careless runner outright, would definitely maim her as that runner bounced down the steep slope, careening off rocks and tree stumps.

So I although I speed up to close the gap between me and

the guy ahead—he looks like a marathoner, all long stringy legs and arms—I have no intention of attempting to pass him until we're out of The Squeeze. The path is filled with rocks that have tumbled off the unstable hillside to my left. Most are only pebble-sized, but they force me to focus on the ground in front of my feet so I don't sprain an ankle.

When I am about thirty meters behind the front-runner, a cascade of small rocks bounces down onto the trail, a miniature rockslide in progress. I leap to my right to avoid them, landing closer to the drop-off but still a good eighteen inches away from the edge. As I make my lateral move, I hear the damn drone shift, too.

It slams into my left shoulder, cutting my skin and knocking me toward the drop-off. I gasp as my right foot comes down only inches from the edge. I stumble, throwing my weight forward and to the left to keep from going over. It's only because I crash down onto my hands and knees that it doesn't hurt so much when the drone clocks me in the back of the head. Still, I see stars for a second while I'm down on all fours, gravel digging into my knees and hands.

I expect another impact but the whirring sound increases, and as I push myself to my feet, I see my minder drone rising overhead. Beyond it, higher and farther ahead, another drone hovers.

What the hell was *that?* Incompetent drone flying? SeaStone Security or the ninjas trying for a convenient "accident"? The front-runner tosses a look at me over his shoulder, but I am up and running again and gaining on him. His dark ponytail reminds me of Bash. I wish I had a partner in this race like I did on Verde Island with The President's Son.

Blood trickles down my arm and now I have a sore spot on my head and road rash on my knees and hands.

As we pass The Squeeze and the forest closes around us again, I am gnashing my teeth in fury.

Fortunately, I run fastest when I am angry, so I am only a few yards behind Mr. Ponytail when we pass through the next checkpoint. The volunteers note the blood running down my left arm and the dirt and scrapes on my knees and try to wave me over to the first aid tent, but the cut on my shoulder has almost stopped bleeding, so I'm not going to take time out for that. A couple of slurps of race gel—this time it tastes sort of coconutty—and gulps of water, and I'm off again.

Less than 15K to go. This guy ahead is good, but I can tell he's focused only on the zigzag road which makes up the remainder of the course, winding down to the finish line. In an open stretch, I check the course behind me, spying a clump of competitors—three men, one woman. But they are so far back that, barring an accident, they are no threat to the two of us in front.

Barring an accident. Like getting whacked by a drone. Is someone trying to make sure I don't win? I decide to risk leaving the road and jump off into the wooded hillside, crashing through the thick trees and leaping over obstacles to bypass the marathoner in front.

My drone sticks with me but is so busy avoiding trunks and branches that it doesn't seem as much of a threat here as in the open. I leap over a nurse log, crashing down next to a young buck that is so startled, it simply stares at me, wide-eyed and snorting, as I race past only a few feet away. I cross the road again further down the hillside but elect to keep to the woods. A pileated woodpecker takes flight overhead, nearly smashing into my drone, crying its wok-wok-wok alarm call.

The woodpecker leads me out of the forest, back onto the road, and ahead of me I see the banners of the finish line and the crowd behind them. The tape is tightly stretched across the road, so I must be the first racer. A cheer goes up, confirming my guess. The drone that has plagued me throughout the race vanishes into the sky as I dash toward the finish line, already envisioning cheeseburgers and fries and a banana split. Chocolate chip cookie dough ice cream. A beer, if I can find a place that will serve one to an eighteen-year-old.

Two drones rise from the ground as I near the finish line, flanking the crowd on both sides of the road and filming my finish. The roar of the bystanders abruptly doubles before I reach the tape, which tells me that Ponytail is now in sight behind me. But I finish a full thirty seconds before he does, which makes me proud. The next clump of competitors race in as he and I stagger around, getting our muscles and breathing under control. When I shake hands with Ponytail, I'm surprised to see that he is much older, at least in his thirties.

At First Aid, a paramedic insists on wiping down my scratched hands and knees and feeling the bump on the back of my head.

"I can't believe that drone whacked you like that." He shines a flashlight in my eyes to check for concussion. "You should sue that news station."

"Which station was the drone from?" I ask.

He shrugs. "No idea, but whoever was flying it should be fired."

I agree. He cleans the gash on the back of my shoulder

with stinging antiseptic and then bridges it with two butterfly bandages.

"Cool tats." He means my firefly tattoos, which I know must still be glowing, because although my exterior is cooling fast, inside I am still angry about the beating I took from the damned drone.

"Why do only two light up?" he asks about the tattoos, like everyone does.

I tell him the story that everyone who knows Tanzania Grey's history has heard: my parents died in a diving accident, so the two glowing ones represent Mom and Dad in heaven. The third, which doesn't glow, is me, because I'm still here.

"Sweet idea," he says, taping a gauze patch over the gash in my shoulder. "I'm sorry for your loss."

"It's been a long time now." I pull my shirt back on.

The third firefly is really for my brother. It doesn't glow because I don't know whether Aaron's in heaven or still on earth.

After I've sucked down a quart of water and combed my hair and put on a clean Dark Horse Networks tee shirt, Ponytail and I and another long, lean guy pose for photos with our ribbons. I accept my prize, an eight-hundred-dollar check that will help feed Bailey and my other four-legged dependents for a couple of months. I'm happy for me, but I'm even happier for Clark and Kent Nilsen, who will be thrilled that I have won the Colorado Challenge again.

A couple of drones hang in the sky to film the ceremony, but my attack drone vanished before I hit the finish line, and as soon as the ceremony is concluded, the rest are gone, too.

It would be nice to have friends to celebrate with, but the

crowd oozes away, families enclosing their racing relatives and friends, leaving me with only a reporter to talk to, and even she seems interested only in the drone bashing I received, not in my win. I miss JJ and X and Catie and all the other happy Ski to Sea finishers.

Back at the hotel, I chow down on a massive spread while sprawled across my bed, watching the news. From room service, I order a double bacon cheeseburger with bleu cheese and grilled onions and mushrooms. It's so good that it makes my eyes practically pop out of my head. I accompany the burger with a double order of fries and a chocolate shake and then order a strawberry sundae with extra whipped cream and nuts for dessert. I decide not to chance the beer, because if the management questioned my age about that, then they might question that an eighteen-year-old is renting this room, which might make them call on the credit card, and all of that would be uber-embarrassing, especially for the Colorado Challenge winner.

The local news shows the drone attack that nearly knocked me off the cliff, but instead of naming who owned the flying weapon, they characterize the incident as an accident, an example of how dangerous low-flying drones can be. The footage on the news looks like it was filmed from much higher up, not from the drone that harassed me throughout the race, which makes my mechanical flying monkey seem even more suspicious. It looks like the UAV4U, which makes me worry that SeaStone Security sent it. A scary thought passes through my brain: maybe my hairbrush wasn't enough; maybe that drone was collecting a blood sample?

Then, in my head, I hear an imaginary courtroom lawyer

protest, "Inconclusive! UAV4U has sold hundreds of thousands of drones. The pilot of that drone could be a fan trying to get a close-up of Ms. Grey to post on YouTube."

Although he's annoying, my pretend lawyer makes a good point.

On television, nobody even mentions investigating the drone, so apparently its pilot gets to remain anonymous and gets off scot-free. It's infuriating. My shoulder is throbbing and my head is sore. I want revenge, and I can't even face my attacker.

But I am proud of the way the newscast ends with a close-up of me and my first place ribbon:

"Racer Tanzania Grey did not let the frightening incident slow her down. She seems to be a lightning rod for danger. Last year, as our audience may recall, she was involved in an even more frightening event."

They retell the story of my kidnapping with Sebastian Callendro. Terrorists are mentioned, and our Verde Island victory is celebrated all over again. Next comes a couple of clips from Ski to Sea, one of me and JJ hauling the canoe from the river. And then finally the news story concludes with:

"So, while Grey obviously competes in dangerous sports, she always manages to come out on top. For the third time in a row, young Tanzania Grey is the winner of the Colorado Challenge."

The coverage makes me sound like a golden girl for a change. Take that, Catie! Too bad it also makes me feel like a freak. The celebration of me is all on TV, while the real me is alone in this hotel room.

But just when I start to feel sorry for myself, Clark and

Kent call to congratulate me. Their gushing makes me feel downright heroic for a few more minutes. Then I call Sabrina and Shadow to check on Bailey and tell them about my win, which leads to more attagirls, so after my sundae arrives and I conclude my phone call home, both my belly and my ego feel satisfied.

I trot down to the ice machine to get some cubes for my shoulder. Back in the room, I use a rubber band to seal them into the liner bag from the ice bucket, but my ice pack still leaks a little on my shirt. I stick a towel between me and the pillow and focus again on the television screen just as the reporter is introducing a new story.

"...the latest school violence, this time in New Mexico."

The screen shows the reporter standing outside a depressing one-story building, surrounded by a high chain link fence topped with loops of razor wire.

"Although he lives in a secure facility for troubled boys, thirteen-year-old Jaime Ramirez somehow obtained a knife and stabbed another student and a teacher's aide before he was shot by a brave custodian."

The reporter holds up a photo of a dark-skinned boy. When the camera zooms in on the picture, I nearly choke on a spoonful of whipped cream.

"The teacher's aide and the other student are in critical condition after being airlifted to Albuquerque General Hospital."

Jaime looks more African-American than Hispanic. And he has my mother's amber eyes.

I scrabble among the bed covers for the remote but when I find it, there's no pause button anyway, so I can't freeze the picture. On the screen, the photo flutters in the breeze as the camera zooms out to show the reporter and the school again.

"Authorities are unaware of the motive behind this attack, but it seems symptomatic of just how troubled many of our youth are across this country. This is Rick Santana, reporting from Los Cerros, New Mexico."

Am I losing my mind? I mute the next segment and boot up my tablet to search for more about that story. I find two text articles that repeat the facts from the TV news, but no photo or video of Jaime Ramirez, thirteen-year-old wannabe murderer.

I probably *am* losing my mind. My logical brain knows the odds are much better that he died four years ago in the attack on my family than that he's living under an assumed name in New Mexico.

Then again, look at my life. Anything is possible.

I would swear that young villain looked just like my brother Aaron.

Jaime's age is right. He and my brother—or at least my memory of my brother—look alike. But it seems crazy. How would Aaron end up in New Mexico? Could Jaime really be Aaron, or is he a doppelganger?

My imagination has never been able to let him go. My nightmares always begin with his screams. Sometimes he gets away from the ninjas and we escape together; sometimes I fight them and rescue him. Those are the good dreams. But on occasion, I get to watch a ninja slit his throat before the murderers notice me standing at the window and I have to run for my life. But no matter what happens in the dream, when I wake up I still don't have any answers about my brother.

After turning out the light, I can't sleep. It doesn't help

that my pillows are wet from the melting ice, but the main problem is that I'm desperate to talk to someone about everything that's going on. The only person I can truly share with is Sebastian Callendro. The President's Son is the only one on earth who knows my whole story. So a few minutes before midnight, I turn on my light, punch his number into my phone, pace to the window and stare out at the cloudy Colorado sky as I wait for the call to connect.

"Yeah?" a sleepy voice says.

"Sorry to wake you up, Bash, but I really need someone to talk to." I speak softly, because earlier I heard the folks in the room next door arguing about which restaurant to choose.

Bash yawns in reply.

I'm not sure where to dive into my craziness, so I begin with, "Thanks for that DNA analysis you gave me."

"*Ningún problema.*" Another yawn.

"Well, if it's no problem, I wonder if you could find out some other stuff for me?"

"Such as?"

"You know that kid who stabbed a couple of people in a school near Albuquerque? Jaime Ramirez?"

"Who doesn't? He's famous here right now. Lots of talk about violence in schools and troubled teens."

"Can you find out more about him? Do you have any connections at that school?"

He scoffs. "How would I have a connection there? It's a residential school for kids with psychiatric problems."

Psychiatric equals medical, which equals keeping information secret from anyone but family members. And 'residential' tells me the kids are not staying there voluntarily.

It's not a public facility. I sigh. "That explains why I can't find anything about his history on the internet."

"Yeah, probably. But why do you care?"

"Well, I ... maybe ... I think ..." I'm having a hard time saying it out loud. "I think he might be my brother."

"What?"

"Don't make me say it again."

"You're not kidding? How could that even be possible?"

"No idea. And maybe it's not him. But maybe it is. That's why I need to find out more. Is there any way to get into that school?"

"I think Ramirez is in a hospital now. He got shot by a janitor."

I wince at the reminder that Aaron is injured, although that's better than dead. Why is the world such a violent place?

Focus. I give myself a mental slap. "Is there any way you can help, Bash? Do you know any doctors or nurses at that hospital?"

"I don't think so." I hear him exhale heavily. "But there's a volunteer in my group who's a parole officer. Maybe he'd know something more. The construction crew is getting together tomorrow. I can ask him then."

"Thanks, Bash. Be subtle."

"You mean I shouldn't ask him if he thinks Jaime Ramirez is actually a missing boy from Washington State?"

His sarcastic tone makes me grimace. "Sorry. I should remember that you of all people know how to be diplomatic. Even if you rarely are."

"Thanks," he says. "Anything else going on with you?"

Oh, what the hell. It feels so good to talk to him. I tell him about winning the Colorado Challenge today, and then I can't stop the flood of news. He knows that Emilio was wounded and is now back, but not about the kidnapping and ransom attempt involving my phone. He doesn't know about the drones spying on my house, about Bailey slapping one to smithereens, about the drone that attacked me today.

When I finally pause, he says, "*Santa Maria!* I thought my life was a pain, but yours is a *telenovela.*"

That description makes me laugh. "Maybe, if I live, someone will make a movie about my life."

"Can I be in it?"

"You *are* in it." And then, finally, I am out of words. "Good night, Bash. Thanks for volunteering to find out what you can about that boy. Thanks for listening." I so wish he was here to put his arms around me.

"Stay safe, Tarzan."

"I'm trying." That seems to be the best I can do right now.

"Better yet," he suggests, "Come visit me; we'll put our heads together."

"Sounds painful," I joke.

But after I put the phone down, I think that truly, visiting Bash might be exactly what I need right now. Bash is three years older and probably a decade wiser than I am, and he has more resources than I do. Maybe between the two of us, we can solve some of the mystery around what happened to the Robinson family.

Emilio gets around well enough to convalesce without me. Sabrina will help him. Maybe Marisela can come to say for a few days.

What the heck. I fire off texts to my boss at the zoo and to Sabrina and Emilio and Marisela telling them that I won't be home for a few more days, and then I use my personal credit card to buy a ticket I can't afford to Albuquerque, New Mexico.

Twenty-Three

On my way through the mall area of the Boulder Airport, I pass a display of cosmetics under the banner *QTC Cuties*. I stop to check out the latest colors of lipstick: a very dark red called Black Rose, a sickly light pink called Candy Kiss, and that Passionflower shade that Elizabeth Abbott wore in her selfie. I would never be caught dead smearing any of those colors on my lips. But the lipstick tubes are actually very cool—sleek black plastic, with a ribbon of twisted silver up the side like a swirl of smoke. There's also a tiny mirror on the top. I guess if you are desperate, you can use the top to make sure you're putting your lipstick on straight.

I bet Specialty Containers makes those lipstick tubes. Having a sister company that specializes in packaging must give QTC quite the advantage. Why didn't my gift bag contain one of these slick lipsticks? My plain tube held only colorless lip gloss. *Gift*, I remind myself, and one aimed for an athlete, not a model. Plus, the bags distributed after Ski to Sea probably contained only unisex items for both male and female race winners.

"Can I help you?" A woman with painted-on eyebrows hovers near my elbow.

"I want to get my mom one of these cosmetic collections, but I'm not sure which she already has." I pull out my cell. "Can I snap a photo of this?"

"Knock yourself out." She turns away, already bored with me.

A sign advertises a free makeup bag with any $75 cosmetics purchase and an array of those clever see-through zippered bags in not only the white and aqua versions I've already seen, but also in yellow and green and pink, too. Their zipper pulls feature a row of three pearls.

If you don't buy $75 dollars worth of stuff, the see-through bag alone is $29.95. Yeesh.

Something about these cosmetics is chafing me, but I can't quite put my finger on it. Maybe it's seeing those bags again after knowing what happened to the last person I saw carrying them. But more likely, it's those outrageous price tags. I'll bet Catie Cole has all the free girly stuff she could ever want. Dark Horse Networks is great for sending me last year's hi-tech gizmos, but Clark and Kent would never send me cosmetics.

This morning Wordage served up *Begrudge—to envy or give reluctantly.* Even though I rarely wear makeup and I shun the spotlight, if I'm honest, I have to say that I *begrudge* Catie her beauty and media attention.

I choose a seat in the waiting area and pull out my aqua-colored cosmetics bag. Unlike the ones in the mall store, my bag has a crystal zipper pull instead of pearls. I can understand why someone would put a variety of stuff inside the bag, but why would the bag itself be different? Maybe mine is last year's model and the crystal pull was an experiment that didn't work out?

Suddenly I have a terrible suspicion about that zipper pull. This bag came with me on the train from Bellingham, a gift from the same company that bought my parents' house. My *murdered* parents' house. A gift from a company owned by Quarrel Tayson, the gigantic conglomerate that also owns QTL, which my mother supposedly wanted to ruin.

The bag has been sitting in my bedroom on my dresser, in my house that has been photographed by drones. My house that was invaded by strangers with tranquilizer darts and helicopters.

When I look closely, I see that my crystal zipper pull contains a gold wire or thread and what looks like a tiny gold bead inside. Audio transmitter? Camera? GPS?

I need a hammer. I scan the room. A few travelers—a couple talking to each other, a man with a toddler, and a woman reading a book—and their suitcases. No tools. Something heavy, then. My eyes finally light on one of those moveable black pillar things—I think they're called stanchions—that the TSA guards connect with ropes, creating mazes for us lab rats to crawl through. I take the cosmetic pouch with me, place it on the floor next to the stanchion, and tug the crystal zipper pull out to lie flat on the floor. Lifting the stanchion—yep, it's heavy, all right—I bash the crystal to dust.

The passenger holding the toddler stares at me like I just escaped from a mental hospital. I pick up the bag, scoot back to my seat, and return the cosmetic bag to my backpack.

"I always hated that crystal," I tell him.

"Uh-huh," he says, avoiding my eyes. He picks up his kid and moves to a chair several rows away.

Did the zipper pull on my gift bag contain a transmitter?

The little gold bead got smashed to dust along with the crystal, so I'll never know. It's entirely possible that my paranoia has now spilled over to include innocuous inanimate objects like these bags. But still, I feel better now that the crystal is gone.

When I hug Bash at the Albuquerque airport, it feels like I might be finally safe. I have second thoughts about that when we climb into his dented pickup and rattle our way out of the parking lot.

It's a long drive back to the rural community where Bash lives in a tiny apartment over an old lady's garage. It reminds me of the converted shed that was my first home after I passed the GED and got my job at the zoo. This is slightly bigger, with a separate bedroom. The main room holds a sagging couch, a small square table, two chairs and a TV. The kitchen is only big enough for one person to occupy at a time.

He points to the couch. "All yours, for as long as you want."

"Thanks." I sling my duffel onto the worn cushions, unzip it, and pull out my aqua cosmetic bag to find my lip gloss. The bag's shiny newness, so neat with all the matching aqua lids on the containers inside, makes my scuffed canvas duffel look like the piece of crap it is.

Bash notices the new bag. "You're color coordinated now?"

I hold it up. "It was a gift after Ski to Sea."

"From who?"

"Whom," I correct. "Specialty Containers Inc. Which is owned by Quarrel Tayson Corporation. Which owns half of Bellingham."

"Nice."

I can't tell if his comment means the bag is nice, or it's nice that the corp owns the town.

"How do you unzip it? Shouldn't it have a tab thing?" He makes an unzipping motion with his hands.

After my crystal-smashing activity in the Boulder airport, there's only a little nub left to grab onto. "It used to have this sparkly knob, but it seemed suspicious, so I smashed it off."

He quirks an eyebrow. "Do I want to know what *that* was really about?"

"Probably not." If it *was* a transmitter of some kind, at least I haven't led them directly to Bash. "If I'm right, I've been putting everyone I know at risk. If I'm just imagining things, you'll think I'm crazy."

"I already know you're crazy. But you've got good reason to be." Bash extracts a pan of homemade green chili and cheese tamales from his refrigerator. "My landlady makes these."

He makes a salad out of greens and tomatoes and cucumbers and then nukes the tamales. Plunking two open beers on the table along with a couple of forks, he announces, "Dinner is served."

We have so much to catch up on since we've last seen each other. We talk nonstop. Sebastian's stories involve his volunteer work here, building a recycling center and a water filtration system. I can tell that he's uber-important to this little community. That must be such a great feeling. Those of us who shovel dung for a living are not generally considered remarkable for our contributions.

I rack my brains to come up with an interesting story from the zoo, and finally share the tale of an escaped ostrich. Those big birds may look comical, but they are fast and dangerous. They can take out your eye with that neck-beak combo or disembowel you with those massive clawed feet. It took five of us and a gigantic tarp to get Bernice back into her cage. There's even an embarrassing YouTube video online, taken by a visitor that day.

Bash has seen the vids of the Ski to Sea race, so we chat about that for a minute, and I tell him all about Catie and JJ and X, and about surviving the strainer. He shows me a WhazHap photo of Catie and Jason that I didn't know existed. They are both holding up their hands in victory signs and grinning at the camera. The text says they are celebrating being signed for a series of television commercials, which makes me wish Xavier was here to have a drink or six with Bash and me.

We're on our second beer when I tell him Maxine's story about my mom, the news about World Cargo West and the cocaine, about the security guy Phineas Pederson, who lives next door to Maxine and makes my skin crawl and may have tried to kill me during the race, and about the helicopter and darting Bailey and searching my house and taking the hairbrush.

Bash's expression grows more and more shell-shocked as I pile on the details, but I feel more and more relaxed as I talk. It's such a relief to unload.

I finally wrap up with "So I'm really worried that now someone suspects who I am." I take a sip of the beer. "But I still don't know why they would care."

"Maybe start with the fact that they hoped you were *dead*?"

I shake my head. "Maxine said the whole family just

packed up and left."

"Tana, whoever is behind your parents' deaths is afraid you're going to find out the truth."

Were the ninjas sent from QTL because my mom was trash-talking the company's rep into the dirt? Were they hit men who used to work for cocaine dealers at World Cargo West? Did P.A. Patterson hire them? Phineas Pederson?

"But I still don't know anything," I wail.

"Since nothing drastic has happened for a while, maybe they've figured that out."

"How would *they* know that *I* don't know *anything*?" After two beers, the combination of those words seems so silly that we both laugh at the question. Meanwhile, my brain is screaming, *the zipper pull, the zipper pull has been transmitting everything*! Which seems so absurd that it makes me laugh even harder.

"Anyhow, *they*"—I put air quotes around the word—"seem to be leaving me alone for now."

"Wait a minute." He waves his beer in the air. "What about getting hit during the Colorado Challenge? Who did that drone belong to?"

Pederson's face flashes into my imagination and then flits right back out. I'm having a good time and I don't want to think about that right now. I shrug. "No clue. It took off at the end of the race. Probably just some incompetent amateur."

He gives me his *yeah, right* look.

I take another swallow of beer. "P.A. Patterson hasn't sent me any messages since the drones visited my house."

We look at each other for a long moment. The lack of messages might imply that now *they* are sure that I'm Amelia

Robinson, so they no longer have to test me with cryptic messages. But then again, maybe it's just another coincidence.

My poor brain can cope with only one mystery at a time, especially after two beers. So I ask Bash what he has learned about Jaime Ramirez, and then he and I hash out a plot to meet the young killer face to face in a couple of days.

In the morning, Bash and I go for a run just after dawn on a trail that winds through a nearby BLM area. The pinkish light makes the rocks and scruffy sage look almost pretty, and the air is so clear and dry that we can see the mountains to the north. Our running shoes make scratching sounds in the gravelly dirt, but we still surprise a hawk resting on a cactus. It takes flight abruptly, startling us with a loud cry, and we both pause to chuckle at the way we bolted sideways.

Bash pulls up his tee shirt, exposing his muscular chest and lean stomach as he wipes the sweat from his forehead. "I so miss this."

I don't know if he's talking about running in general, or about running with me.

"The guy ahead of me in the Colorado Challenge had a ponytail like you used to. The whole time, I wished you were running that race with me." It feels so good, so natural to do this with him again.

"Right, me and the Secret Service," he scoffs. "That race is such a cinch that they'd run alongside me, and so would half the press corps."

"Maybe you could run under an assumed name," I suggest.

He snorts. "Can I get an assumed face, too? You forget that when you needed to disappear, the world didn't know what you looked like."

He's right. Although he has exchanged his ponytail for a close crop and has disguised his face with a moustache and three-day beard, nobody who has ever seen T.L. Garrison's laser green eyes could look at Sebastian Callendro for very long and not recognize him as The President's Son.

He shrugs. "Next year. The Colorado race would make a good warm-up for something more challenging."

By the end of June next year, President Garrison will be an ex-president and out of the spotlight, so the paparazzi will have stopped dogging Sebastian.

I grin at him. "It's a date."

"And maybe by then, Emilio can run with us," Bash adds, trying to be generous.

"Shadow has never been a runner," I say, somber again. With one eye, Emilio Santos has no depth perception and with his brain injury, some days he has trouble even walking a straight line.

There's also the niggling worry that the Army may judge Emilio to be a deserter and sentence him to military prison or boot him out on his wounded ass with a dishonorable discharge.

Guilt weighs down my feet all the way back to Bash's apartment.

The heat and sweat make the cut on my shoulder sting and itch. I make it worse by getting the bandage wet in the shower. The first aid guy at the race gave me an extra bandage, but I have to ask Bash to put it on for me.

As he wipes down my wound and smoothes antiseptic cream on it, I struggle to keep my mind on Emilio and Jaime

Ramirez and the mysteries I'm investigating, anything to distract me from the tingling sensations Bash's fingers are causing all over my body.

After he pats the new bandage in place, he tweaks my ponytail. I turn, yearning to kiss him, but his expression is serious.

"Now," he says, "I have something to show you about Phineas Pederson."

We sit at the kitchen table as I read a printout. Phineas Arthur Pederson, 49, Director of Operations at SeaStone Security, used to be a partner in Tyrol Operations. I note that Pederson *is* a P.A., but the rest is lost on me. I glance at Bash. "So?"

"You've never heard of TOPS?"

"It sounds vaguely familiar."

"Troops for hire. Mercenaries."

Now I remember news stories about war crimes committed by TOPS. "So..."

"So your suspicions about Pederson are probably right. If he's not a killer himself, he knows where to hire them. Watch your back, Tana."

Shit. I'm so tired of watching my back. I'd rather be told, "You're paranoid, Tana. This is all coincidence; you're perfectly safe, and all is right with the world." But history has proven that's not likely to happen to me.

I tap a finger on the printout. "Where'd you get this?"

"If I told you, I'd have to kill you."

He means it as a joke, but I can't stop thinking that Pederson truly wants to kill me, and probably can whenever he wants. I'm going to have a hard time sleeping tonight.

Twenty-Four

The next day, Bash drives me to the small rural hospital where Jaime Ramirez is convalescing. It's a nondescript place, beige adobe and glass on the outside, one story, set in among rocks and cactus and dirt in what Bash tells me is called xeriscaping. For someone from the uber-green Pacific Northwest, all that desert brown and gray looks like it should be called *zero*-scaping. But it's always wise to follow Mother Nature's lead, and she seems to want rough and stickery scenery in New Mexico. I suppose I could get used to it in time.

As I nervously push open the back door of the facility into a brightly lit tiled hallway, I am already sweating through the blue scrubs we bought yesterday at a thrift store. The pants are a little short for me, but maybe nobody will notice that my ankles hang out. It's a good thing that most medical staff wear athletic shoes now, too, since that's all I brought with me.

The older woman approaching in the hall glances at me uncertainly. I nod, smile, and chirp, "Hi, how are *you* today?"

Her brow wrinkles in confusion and she passes me without a word, probably wondering where she met me before.

I'm dressed like I could work here, but I need a prop, so I duck into the first supply closet I see. I wouldn't know what to do with the needles and bandages, and I'm not going anywhere near the stack of bedpans. There's only one item I see that might work for my purposes. I grab a sterile catheter kit from a shelf, stifling the gag reaction I have to the idea of its use.

When I emerge from the supply closet, the hall is vacant. I lift my chin and try to walk like I own the place, checking rooms as I pass. No, not him. Definitely not her. Then I see a likely looking patient under the sheets in a bed and sure enough, the chart in the holder on the door says Jaime Ramirez.

I'm dismayed to find a security guard sitting in a chair in the corner, reading a paper. He glances up as I enter. I take hold of the top bed sheet like I'm going to uncover the kid, and then I pause and wave the catheter kit at him. "Some privacy, please."

He glances at the kit. His cheeks get pink. He stands up. "I'll go get a cup of coffee. You'll stay till I get back?"

"Sure thing," I tell him.

As soon as he leaves, I bend over the boy and peel the sheet back from his neck and shoulders so I can get a good look. His eyes are shut. He's either asleep or unconscious. His head is wrapped with a cloth bandage that holds a big gauze pad in place over his left ear. On that side of his face, his cheek is bruised and swollen and his left eye is underscored with a dark shadow. The news said he was shot, but I don't remember them saying he was shot in the *head*.

His black hair is braided into tiny rows, a style that my nine-year-old brother would never have allowed. But the skin color is exactly as I remember it, café au lait, slightly darker and redder than my bronzy skin. His face seems more angular than my memory of Aaron's, and this kid has an earring, too. My brother didn't have a pierced ear.

It's been four years. I'm just not sure. And I'm ashamed of that. Shouldn't I recognize my brother on sight? Shouldn't we have a spiritual link?

I shake the kid's shoulder. He groans and murmurs something that sounds shockingly like "Fuck off."

"Wake up." I shake his shoulder again.

"Dammit." He rolls over onto his back. There's a metallic clank as he jerks the handcuff attached to his right wrist against the bed rail it's wrapped around. "Lemme alone, bitch."

Now I can see his whole face. Definitely more mature than I expected. He has the beginning of a moustache on his upper lip and a scar beneath one eyebrow. Neither are familiar to me. There are acne, or maybe chicken pox scars dotted across his forehead.

But then I see the dark patch on his neck and the large mole beneath his right ear. My heart does a backflip, and my breath catches in my chest.

When we were little, whenever I wanted to aggravate Aaron, I called him Spot.

"Aaron," I murmur. My heart starts a joyous chorus: my brother, my brother, my brother is alive!

He opens his eyes to stare at me. Hazel eyes, like my mom's. Like *my* eyes. His pupils are gigantic and his lids sag to half-mast. He's drugged, or maybe it's a brain injury. I wonder if he's able to understand me.

"It's me," I whisper. "Amelia." It feels so strange to say my real name.

"Get away from me."

"You're Aaron Robinson." It sounds like a wish when I say it.

"No," he groans. "I'm Jaime Ramirez."

"Our family used to live in Bellingham."

His eyes widen. A mask of terror slides onto his face. "You're in the wrong room, psycho. Get outa here!"

Why is he so frightened? Is it because he thinks our parents' killers are after him, too? I persist, trying to change my tone to casual and sisterly. "We had a dog named Joker."

"Nunh-uh. No way." He tugs anxiously at the neck of his hospital gown, staring at me with eyes rounded in fright, like any second I might pull out a knife and stab him.

I swallow. "Joker, our black Lab. I saw him on the boardwalk in Bellingham about a month ago. Can you believe that?"

His knees come up and he tries to push himself to a sitting position, but he can't because of the handcuff. "That never happened. What are you trying to make me do? You're not real."

Maybe he thinks he's dreaming; I get that. I've had so many dreams where Mom and Dad and Aaron were with me, only to wake and find that I was alone.

"I am real, Aaron," I assure him. "And I am really here. I'm your sister, Amelia."

"My sister was Anna. She's dead; she died in a car crash." It sounds like he's quoting from a script. "My name is Jaime Ramirez."

I understand how scared he is. *I* still don't comprehend what happened four years ago, and I was fourteen then. Aaron was only nine. How can I reassure him?

"I used to call you Spot, remember?" I flick a finger at the mole beneath his ear as I smile in what I hope is an encouraging and non-threatening way. "I'm your big sister. Our mother was Amy. Our father was Alex."

"That was a nightmare," he whispers. His gaze bounces around the room. "You're not real."

When he starts to turn his head toward the wall, I cup his chin in my hand to bring him back. "Alex, Amy, Amelia, Aaron. We were the Straight A's, remember?"

Now his eyes look more confused than scared. He puts his free hand on my wrist and grips it hard, like he's trying to decide if I'm solid. I move my hand from his chin and clutch his shoulder firmly to convince him.

"What do you want?" he whispers in a hoarse voice.

Outside the door, we hear laughter. "Yeah, you always say that!"

The security guard is back.

I hurriedly stomp my foot on the waste bin pedal and toss the catheter kit inside, and then pull the sheets up around the boy's shoulders. As the door opens, I bend over my brother and whisper in his ear. "Say nothing, Aaron. I'll be back."

I pivot to face the guard. "All done."

Then I turn back to Aaron. "That wasn't so bad, was it, Jaime?"

"Bitch," he growls.

I give the guard a shrug and a what-can-you-do look and stroll out of the room. I can't believe it. My brother is alive! And I finally know where he is.

I lift his chart from the slot on the outside of the door and explore the hallways, walking beside a man pushing a tall cart of lunch trays to hide myself as I pass the nurses' station. Finally, I spy a doorway marked *Insurance*. Through the half-door partition, I see four people in front of computers. The walls are lined floor to ceiling with thick folders. Whoever thought computers might reduce paperwork was clearly deluded.

I hand the chart to a girl with turquoise hair. "Doc wants a copy of this."

She frowns at the thick file. "The whole thing?"

"Yeah," I tell her. "Needs to send it overseas for a consultation."

"Where do you want to send the scans?" she asks.

Damn. I should have thought about that; she's not going to hand me a paper copy. I can't give her my email address. "Darn it!" I say. "Doc said to put it on a USB drive. Then he forgot to give me one."

She sighs. "They always do. That's why we keep extras. I'll be back in a few minutes."

"Me too." I zip off to the closest restroom. I figure I'm a lot less likely to get into trouble in a toilet stall than loitering in the hallway.

When my watch says ten minutes have passed, I go back to the insurance office.

Turquoise Hair thrusts out the memory stick. "Here you go, uh..." She stares pointedly at my left shoulder.

I dip my chin to look at the bare blue fabric there, too. "Damn it, I lost my nametag somewhere. Again. The pin is bent and the damn thing keeps coming undone."

I sigh heavily and rub my forehead. "It's been that kind of day, you know? Well, that's just great. Now I have to go look for it." I meet her eyes. "I'm Lindsey, by the way. The service sent me." Three cheers for outsourcing; nobody thinks it's weird for strangers to show up in any workplace these days.

"Nice to meet you." She waves the chart. "Want me to file this?"

"No, I need to return it to the patient's room."

She leans on the partition that separates us. "Isn't Ramirez a really scary dude?"

I shrug. "Still a kid. There's hope."

"If you say so."

I slide the USB drive into my pocket and walk back toward Aaron's room. A large muscular man in scrubs dashes past me in the hallway, carrying a syringe. As I round the corner, I see a cluster of personnel at Aaron's doorway, and I hear shouting inside. It's mostly an exchange of obscenities and a man's voice pleading, "Calm down! You need to calm down now."

A woman in scrubs printed with flowers turns as I approach.

"What's going on?" I slide the chart back into the slot on the door.

"Total freak-out." She rolls her eyes and then adds, "Again. Ramirez asked the guard for a drink of water and then punched him in the face when he was close enough."

A bearded man beside her says, "The kid's an animal."

"Schizo," the first woman says matter-of-factly. "The brain injury probably makes it worse. Can't wait until they transport him to the jail."

Over their shoulders I see Jaime/Aaron, his free arm clamped down by the syringe-carrying guy, slumping into unconsciousness on the bed. The guard, his right cheek bleeding and swollen and already turning purple, holds down my brother's shoulder above his handcuffed arm.

"When will he be transported?" I ask.

She shakes her head. "Whenever the docs say he's well enough, I guess. He keeps reopening his wounds."

Now that she has mentioned it, I see a wet patch of bright red on the side of my brother's hospital gown. I feel a twinge of sympathy pain in my own ribs.

The bearded guy turns back to me and sort of squints, creasing his forehead with lines. "Who're you?"

"Lindsey. Temp," I explain hurriedly. I take a hasty glance at my watch. "Better get back before I get into trouble. My shift's almost over, and I gotta wrap up my notes."

I feel his eyes on my back as I stroll back the way I came. My breathing doesn't slow down until I'm around the corner and headed for the back door. I'm tempted to jog, but instead, I pull out my cell phone and act like I'm talking on it. A nurse's aide carrying a tray of instruments passes me as I say, "Yes, I understand, I'm on my way." I hope I sound like I've been summoned somewhere outside.

When the door closes behind me, I finally allow my shoulders to relax. But my nerves are still jangling and my head is pounding by the time I make it to the back of the lot. Bash's pickup is parked under the shade of the lone tree there, and I slide onto the seat beside him.

He puts down the magazine he's been reading. "Well?"

"It's him, Bash."

"Wow." He stares at me for a long minute with the President's famous laser eyes.

I nod.

Then he turns away, starts the engine, checks the rear view mirror as he backs out of the parking space, wheels the truck around, and focuses on the road ahead as he repeats, "Wow."

"Yeah. I can't believe it, either." I wish I could read Bash's mind right now. Does he suspect I'm imagining all this? Is he worried that I'll involve him further in the huge mess that is my life?

Well, I'm worried, too. "He's Aaron," I say. "But I'm not sure *he* knows that." I massage my throbbing temple with my right hand.

"What happened? How'd he end up here?"

I sigh. "No idea." I rub my fingers along the thighs of my scrub pants, feel the hard outline of the USB drive in my pocket, and pull it out.

"Evidence?" Bash asks.

"I hope so. This contains Jaime Ramirez's medical records." I turn it over in my fingers, remembering the hidden USB drive I found after my parents were murdered. My former life has been reduced to a few digital files. It would be so nice to have a living person to help me for a change.

"What are you going to do, Tana?" the living person beside me asks. He shoots a quick sideways glance at me.

"Not a freakin' clue." Unfortunately, that's the truth. There are all sorts of ideas bouncing around my skull right now, but a coherent plan for the future is not one of them.

What will my brother remember when he wakes up? Did he understand who I was? Does he remember our family? Why did he stab those two people? I have so many questions I'm afraid my head might explode.

"I'm sorry for letting my lunacy invade your life, Bash."

He snorts, and stretches his right hand out to pat my

thigh. "That's okay, Tarzan. It's your turn."

That makes us both laugh. He's right; our times together have been more than a little, well … abnormal. It makes me feel better to know that he understands; that I have one person I can talk to. I reach down and intertwine my fingers with his. After a moment, he squeezes my hand and pulls his away and puts it back on the steering wheel. I sigh and turn to the window.

My eyes are not accustomed to the sun-bleached pastels of the desert. We pass a rocky pasture with a few goats in it. Do they eat cactus? Probably. Poor things. There are bits of paper and plastic caught on the barbed wire strands of the fence. Everything here looks so bleak to me.

My little brother is alive. I am no longer alone.

I thought I'd be so happy if I found Aaron.

I thought we'd be a team.

But I'm almost sorry I came. I still don't know who to trust. I can't tell anyone who *I* am, so how can I tell anyone who my brother is?

Instead of feeling relief, I'm seconds away from having a panic attack. The desert scenery rushing past the window is as blurry as my brain. I can't find anything to focus on.

This version of Aaron is a thirteen-year-old would-be murderer known as Jaime Ramirez. What the hell happened to him in the last four years? And how am I going to get him out of there before he ends up in prison?

Twenty-Five

Jaime Ramirez's medical records are not the wealth of clues I'd hoped for. They begin four years ago, with a checkup at Todos Santos, which turns out to be that residential school for troubled boys that was mentioned on the newscast.

Jaime Ramirez is listed as an orphan after the death of his parents and sister Anna (*sparse records, probably illegals*, a note explains) in a car crash. At age nine, Jaime is diagnosed with juvenile schizophrenia, a rare condition, and placed on heavy anti-psychotic meds. Another notation reads *Often hears voices telling him he is someone else.*

Someone named Aaron Robinson. It breaks my heart.

Phobia of tattoos.

Like those V-shapes I spied on the neck of one of the ninjas who killed our parents.

Can become violent.

Understandable, when a boy is fighting for his life.

Many different drugs are listed. *Psychotherapy. Hospitalization for delusions. Electroshock treatment.* Jeez, I thought they stopped that decades ago. Tears run down my face as I scan the pages. No wonder Aaron is scared stiff.

Bash is frying burgers on the stove, but he pauses to pat my shoulder.

"How am I going to rescue him?" I wail.

"I don't see how you can. At least not now."

I close the file on my tablet screen. "I got in once. Maybe we could kidnap him."

Sebastian sets a plate with a hamburger and a big pile of coleslaw in front of me, and slides into his chair. "Let's think about this, Tarzan.

He takes a bite of his burger and chews for a few seconds. "He's wounded, he's in the hands of the law, and he'll be on trial as soon as he's able to appear in court."

I bite into my burger. Bash is right. Even if I could get out the door with Aaron, my brother would be considered an escaped and dangerous criminal. The authorities would be hot on his trail. I exhale a frustrated breath. "I have to be able to prove who he is and what happened."

"A DNA test would prove you're siblings. But how close are you to proving what happened to him?" He pulls a pickle out of the bun and chomps on it.

"About as close as Earth is to the sun."

"Nothing in the records?" He nods toward the tablet.

"The only things that might help are the year when Jaime Ramirez appeared at the school, which is the same as when Aaron Robinson vanished, and the fact that his guardian is M.C. Smith from White Rock, British Columbia, Canada."

"Do you know an M.C. Smith?"

I am chewing a mouthful of coleslaw, so I just shake my head. I was expecting P.A. Patterson or Phineas Pederson or maybe even SeaStone Security to be listed as Jaime Ramirez's guardian, but this M.C. Smith is a total mystery to me. Still, I'll bet there's a connection. I swallow and say, "White Rock is just across the border, north of Bellingham."

"So maybe that's a place to start."

"There are only a couple of phone numbers listed, but maybe we could find an address." I don't know who this *we* is, but I'm pretty sure I can't do it alone. The thought of going to Canada by myself to confront this Smith, who might be one of the ninja killers, is terrifying.

"Could Emilio go with you?" Bash picks up his beer.

I shake my head again. "Even if he could get around that well, which he can't right now, I don't think they'd let him leave the country before his hearing. Plus, he'd want to know what I was doing."

After swallowing, Bash sets his beer bottle back on the table with a thump. "Well, crap."

That about sums up the situation.

"Do you think Jaime—I mean Aaron—understood what you told him?"

"I couldn't really tell."

"Do you think he remembers you?"

"I don't know." A disturbing thought leaps into my brain. If my brother *does* remember who I am, then he will remember how I abandoned him on that horrible night. How I left him there, alone with my parents' murderers.

And bam—I'm standing there in front of my front door. One of the ninjas turns toward me. I can't see his features because of the ski mask, but his eyes look straight at me. And then I take off running.

"Earth to Tanzania Grey."

I snap back to the present, my heart hammering like a woodpecker on a dead tree. The remaining half of my burger is in my hand, paused midway to my mouth. Bash is standing beside the table, holding out my cell toward me.

Sabrina is on the phone. "Karrie and Dave and I have been covering for you, but the boss says he's replacing you if you don't get back pronto. Nathan can't save you if you keep disappearing like this."

Crapola. "Tell the boss I'll be back at work day after tomorrow. I'll fix my flight in a minute. How's everything going?"

"Bailey and the goats and cats and Emilio and I are fine."

I have an itchy feeling that there's an unspoken *no thanks to you* at the end of her sentence. I end the call and turn to back to Bash.

"Gotta go?" he guesses.

I nod and pick up my burger again.

"I have to get back to work tomorrow, too," he says. "We have equipment deliveries coming that we've been waiting months for."

I have a vision of the "oh-Stan-the-man" babe with the tool belt tapping her toe waiting for Bash to show up.

He adds, "I'll have to drop you off at the airport super early."

"That's hours out of your way. I'll take the bus. You've already helped me so much, Bash."

"Anytime, Tarzan." We clink beer bottles and do our best to enjoy the rest of our evening together.

Before we go to bed, we both go outside. The sky is

cloudless, and the heavens are spangled with diamond lights out here in the high desert, arranged in slightly different patterns than I see at home. The moon is not full, but the constellations are bright enough that our bodies cast blurry shadows on the ground.

Tonight, I am grateful that I have a friend as good as Bash, someone who knows all my secrets, someone who understands and accepts me for who I really am.

"Nobody else I know does this." He throws out his arms as he stares at the stars above. Then he wraps an arm around my shoulders and pulls me close. "I've really missed it."

Me, too.

It takes me fourteen hours of patched-together transportation to get from Bash's apartment in New Mexico to my house in Washington State. Wordage teaches me *Goad—1) to provoke a reaction* or *2) a pointed stick*. Geographastic informs me that the Mariana Trench is the deepest part of the oceans, at approximately 10,994 meters (36,070 feet) below sea level. I wonder if anyone has ever seen what lives down there. I even study some chemistry, learning all about the periodic table of the elements. How did all this stuff ever get discovered, let alone measured and organized? It's mind-boggling, but I'm up for any distraction to get my mind off my brother. I am returning home with more secrets than I had when I left. More questions, too. It's a heavy load.

After flying into Sea-Tac Airport, I head for the light rail station that will take me to downtown Seattle. Like the Robert Frost poem, I have miles to go before I sleep, and it's going to take me a couple of hours to travel them. From the end of the rail line, I'll have to take three buses and then walk almost a mile to get back home.

When I finally trudge up my own driveway, Bailey greets me just inside the security gate. Is he a psychic elephant, or has he been waiting there every day since I left? The first scenario is sort of awesome; the second is just plain sad.

Inside the house, I find Sabrina and Emilio bent over the puzzle at the dining room table. Beneath their fingers, the image of the castle is nearly complete. When Emilio turns toward me, I nearly jump backward. The bandage over his eye has been replaced by an eye patch, which features a huge appliquéd blue eye on a black background, quite the contrast with Emilio's own remaining eye, which is a deep brown.

I stare, open-mouthed.

He grins. "Like it?"

The strap slips off my shoulder and my duffel bag lands with a plop on the floor. "It's memorable," I hedge. "Not your typical pirate look."

Sabrina jumps up and disappears into his room. She's back in a flash, and tosses three more eye patches onto the table. One is the plain black I was expecting, one features a lightning bolt, and one is a camouflage pattern, like Emilio's Army fatigues.

"Where did you get these?" I pick up the lightning design. The bolt is appliquéd over a plain black eye patch.

Sabrina beams at me. "I made 'em. I used the machine at work. Well, I bought the three black ones and stuck other stuff on them, but I made the camouflage one totally from scratch."

The zoo has an old sewing machine in the workshop, but I had no idea that Sabrina knew how to use it.

"The drone came back," she tells me.

Shit. "When? What did it do? Is Bailey okay?"

Emilio gives me an odd look. "Why is your first question about *Bailey*?"

"To be fair, that wasn't my *first* question, and—" I abruptly remember that neither of them people know that Bailey was attacked by intruders before. "...and I can see that the two of you are okay," I finish lamely.

I also saw Bailey outside, but it's dark and I didn't exactly inspect him.

Sabrina checks the calendar on her cell phone. "It dropped by four days ago. It flew around the house, checking all the windows, and then it was gone."

She swipes the screen and shows me a shot of the mechanical beast outside of the living room window. I'm not a drone expert, but it looks like it could be the same one that took photos the first time.

"That's creepy," I say. Even creepier is the fact that the date matches up to the evening after I smashed the crystal off my cosmetic bag. Were *they* trying to find me after the transmitter went dead?

"I talked to Dreck." Sabrina grimaces to show that it wasn't a pleasant experience. "He said he doesn't know what I'm talking about."

She looks angry, but she also looks worried. "Then," she adds, "he offered to sleep here to protect us."

"Of course he did."

Emilio is still staring at me, and I realize he's expecting something more. "I'm so glad you're both safe."

I walk to him, lean down, and give him a peck on the lips.

When I look up, Sabrina pretends to be entranced by searching for a puzzle piece.

"Well, how is His Royal Highness?" Emilio demands.

How does Shadow know I went to see Bash? I didn't tell anyone where Bash was or what I was going to do with my time off. I suppose there's no use in denying it now.

"Sebastian's fine," I tell him. "I was so close, I just had to go. And on my sponsors' credit card, too," I lie.

"He's working on some cool recycling projects, which is what he's always wanted to do." I make a face. "I'm not so keen on the southwest in the summer, though. We had to go running at six a.m. so we wouldn't die of heat exhaustion."

"Gotta do what you gotta do," Emilio replies.

I have no idea what he means by that, but his tone is bitter. I sling my bag over my shoulder again. "Guess I'll unpack and shower."

Emilio reaches across the table and clasps his fingers around Sabrina's hand. She raises her chin, surprised, but when he smiles at her, she smiles right back.

Shouldering my duffel, I head for my room. I don't know what Shadow is up to. Is he trying to *goad* me? I'd like to get an uber-pointy *goad* and poke *him* with it.

Even though it's nearly dark, I strap on a headlamp and go for a run around the track, trying to wear myself out and sort through my feelings. I am relieved when my explorations turn up no new evidence of intruders or drones or elephant attackers, although I keep a wary eye on the trees as I do my laps. After I am tired and sweaty, I sit on a stump under the stars while I cool off both physically and emotionally. My elephant insists on hoovering me all over, sniffing for heaven knows what. Is he trying to determine where I've been? Does he fear I've been consorting with other elephants? Finally, he relaxes and is content to stand in front of me and lay his heavy trunk across my lap. It's nice to feel like *someone* missed me.

I understand why my boyfriend is jealous of Sebastian. I have lied to Emilio Santos from the day I met him about who I am, so I couldn't tell him about seeing my brother on the news. To Shadow, it must seem like I was sneaking off for a romantic rendezvous with my former race partner.

Bash is my only true confidant, and maybe on some subconscious level, Emilio grasps that. Plus, with his lean, muscular frame, dark hair, laser green eyes and strong jaw, Bash has always been a hunk. In the past, Emilio Santos radiated a similar dark smoldering attractiveness, but now the nickname I gave him out of affection seems like an ugly reminder that he is currently only a shadow of his former self.

The thought of how circumstances change people brings me back to the problem of my brother. Can I find a private way to communicate with Aaron? I wonder if he even wants me to. He's been Jaime Ramirez for four years, and I am now Tanzania Grey. I know how *I* got to this place, but what the hell happened to Aaron to turn him from a geeky African American kid into a psychotic Hispanic juvenile delinquent? I have to think of a way to get information out of that M.C. Smith in White Rock. Something else I must hide from Emilio and Sabrina.

I understand why my soldier boyfriend might be attracted to my housemate. Sabrina didn't know him from before, so maybe it's easier for her to accept him the way he is now. And maybe it's easier for him to be with someone who doesn't share any part of his past.

Will Emilio take her to see the monarchs? Although I am not prepared to marry him, if he leaves me, I'll have nobody to truly care whether I live or die. And, wounded warrior or not, I'll never forgive Shadow if he breaks Sabrina's heart.

Twenty-Six

I dream about drones all night and wake up feeling more tired than when I went to bed. In my nightmares, first Emilio and then my brother turn out to be piloting the machines that attack me. As I ride my bike to work the next morning, a van passes too close, nearly sideswiping me with its passenger-side mirror. In a moment of startling clarity, I realize that *they* don't have to kill me by drone. If Pederson and his people really want to get me, they can do it at any time. I don't understand why they're waiting. It would be so easy to arrange a casual accident, like forcing me off the road.

Shades of Elizabeth Abbott, the courier gal found dead at the side of Marine Drive in Bellingham. I know Marine Drive. There's a nice sidewalk that stretches the whole length of it. Why would Liz be walking in the street where she could get hit by a car?

But she was working *for* Pederson and QTL; it's not like she knew some deep dark secret they didn't want revealed. I can't think of any reason SeaStone Security would want to kill *her*.

I, on the other hand, might be a danger to them. I feel like someone is poking me with a sharp stick to see if I will turn on them and reveal their deep dark secret. I have a feeling my mother knew that secret. Maybe my father did, too. But I don't seem to be getting closer to discovering anything worth killing for.

As I scrub the windows of the chimp exhibit, my imagination comes up with all sorts of daring scenarios of me breaking Aaron out of the hospital and then working together with my brother as a dynamic duo to solve the mystery of our parents' murders. But the truth is, I'm not even sure that Aaron remembers his past. And when my brain chooses to consider all the things that might take place between his escape and our big revelation to the world, it seems likely that those events will include a lot of police and interrogations and maybe even flying bullets.

I can hardly go on the run with an elephant.

But could I find a way to spring Aaron and hide him? In the movies, they might use a fake ambulance service. I ponder that for a while. Even if could enlist the help of my friends—JJ and X would probably be up for it—to play the roles, they'd want an explanation. I'd be risking their lives. And where could I take Aaron that the police couldn't find him?

I text Bash the fake ambulance idea, as ridiculous as it is. I get no response. He's probably hunkered down with Miss Tool Belt, building something that will save the world.

I keep wondering whether Pederson tracked me from Bellingham to my house via that zipper pull on my cosmetic bag. If he did that, he could have also tracked me to the race in Colorado and then sicced the drone on me there. Maybe planting transmitters is a routine thing that SeaStone Security does so its clients can keep watch on certain people.

The first time I saw those bags was when I met Elizabeth

Abbott. It seems possible that QTL would want to put a transmitter on Liz's bag. She was a courier they'd want to track. If she followed through on what she told me, she took an unplanned trip to Senegal to see her friend. If she was carrying a transmitter, they'd know she'd deviated from their plan. Would they have killed her for that?

On my break, I bring up the selfie of Elizabeth Abbott to check out her bag. Inconclusive; I can't see a zipper pull in the photo. And while she didn't end up with the plain plastic tube I received, the Passionflower lipstick Elizabeth is holding up in the photo is in a silver tube. The top, lying beside her on top of the cool orange bag, is plain silver, too.

Why didn't she get those cool smoke-swirly-mirror tubes like I saw in the airport store? Did QTC give her another trial version that didn't work out?

I snort at my own thought. *Didn't work out*. She's dead. *Something* sure as hell didn't work out for Liz. I hope she died instantly when that car hit her, and didn't suffer for hours, lying alone at the side of the road.

I peer more closely at her photo, enlarging it so I can see more detail. The half of the silver tube that she's holding up has lines near the top. They look like they might be screw threads. "Were they trying to keep the lipstick from escaping?"

"What?" Karrie asks. She's working at the counter, chopping up veggies for the wallabies.

"Nothing," I assure her, waving my phone in the air like that's an explanation. Maybe that's the next cool thing, lipstick tubes that screw together instead of slide.

Something nags at me about that photo, but I can't zero in on it. Does Liz fit in with the scans on my memory stick? She was transporting vaccines for viruses to Casablanca. She stopped in Senegal, where an outbreak of Ebola triggered QTL's rapid response team. But Liz came home just fine, and died in a traffic accident over a week later.

A series of memories flit through my brain.

Charlie's mom chirping, "We bought the house from SCI—you know, Specialty Containers Incorporated, one of the Quarrel Tayson companies."

Maxine Newsome snarling, "Amy wanted to take down QTL."

Bash, talking about the scans on the memory stick. "My friend Geneva says both are DNA sequences. She says they look like two strains of the same virus. Only certain portions of the sequence are altered. Does that make any sense?"

RRT in the QTL spreadsheet on the memory stick.

Pederson, with a mercenary background, working for QTL.

Liz Abbott, a courier for QTL.

QTL is the connection.

I lick my lips and then take a deep breath. This is the company my mother helped to build. Can QTL really be my enemy? I don't want to believe it. How could anyone fight a giant corporation?

It's probably just my paranoia kicking in. I tend to see conspiracies all over the place. Why would QTL want to kill anyone? They are in the business of *saving* lives; that's how they make their money.

Sometimes a lipstick is just a lipstick. And sometimes college girls go out walking in dangerous places where they shouldn't be after dark. Who knows, maybe Liz drank a lot when she wasn't couriering drugs to exotic locales.

Bash texts back that a fake ambulance won't work, because the authorities would still track Aaron and where would we hide him? At least he's kind enough not to say my idea was totally lame.

I can't just drop the idea, though. I've got to find a way to help my brother. I need to find out more about how he ended up with this "guardian" in Canada.

Since I'm on my bike today and won't have Sabrina to answer to, I stop on the way home to buy a burner phone. That act alone feels dangerous.

After dinner, I go out to run around my track. It's been so long since the invasion now that I've almost quit searching for intruders on the property. My end, if it happens at all, will probably come in a bullet from the sky.

After two circuits, I stop and pull out the burner phone. When my breathing is normal, I call the hospital in New Mexico and ask about Jaime Ramirez.

"Who's calling? Are you a relative?"

"I'm his guardian," I say. "M.C. Smith."

I have no idea whether M.C. Smith is male or female, and I hope the gal on the other end doesn't, either. I hold my breath while she looks for information.

"Ramirez is resting comfortably, recovering from his wounds."

"Is he scheduled to be released soon?"

Her tone turns exasperated. "Jaime Ramirez cannot be *released* any time soon, but his doctors say he should be ready for *transport* in about a week."

Snippy bitch. Then I remember that I am M.C. Smith, who no doubt knows all about the justice system, because he or she is probably a criminal, too. "I see. Thank you."

I turn off the phone. Should I have asked to speak to my brother? Even if they gave me the number for Aaron's room, I can't imagine that someone else wouldn't have listened to our conversation. My brother is a prisoner as well as a patient.

I pace for several minutes, screwing up my courage. Then I punch in the first number listed for M.C. Smith in White Rock. My anxiety level is so high, it's giving me a headache.

A man answers. "Hello?"

"May I speak to M.C.?"

"Clementine hasn't lived here for quite some time. What is this about?"

Clementine? Did I hear that right? I tell him I'm calling from the hospital that is caring for Jaime Ramirez.

"That means nothing to me, dear. Let me give you her cell number." And he rattles off the second number on the medical records.

I hang up. So M.C. Smith is a female named Clementine, who no longer lives at that address in White Rock. Who names their kid *Clementine?* Makes me wonder what the M stands for.

I punch in the cell number. After what seems like an eternity, a woman answers.

"M.C. Smith?"

After a brief hesitation, she says, "Yes?" She draws out the question like she might be worried about answering.

"I'm Winnie Sanders, calling from the hospital in New Mexico. As I'm sure you know, Jaime Ramirez will soon be transported to an incarceration facility. I need to clarify a few items in his records."

There's a quick intake of breath, and then she says in an icy tone, "You already have everything you need."

"Well, ma'am, perhaps I don't have all the original records. I see that you are listed as Jaime's guardian."

"Yes." Again, the word is hesitant and drawn out.

"Are you a relative? How did you come to be Jaime's guardian?"

For a long minute, I hear only her soft breaths, but then she snarls, "Who the hell is this?"

The muscles in my neck clench. *Steady, Tana.* "The hospital, ma'am."

"Give me the number of the administrator right now so I can verify this call."

I frantically punch the End button and drop the phone on the ground. My heart is pounding. When the underbrush behind me rustles, I whirl around, expecting an attack.

The tan goat blinks at me, a blackberry vine dangling from his mouth as he chews. A leaf is caught above his right eye, which makes him look ridiculous. A few yards away are two other goats, and in the distance I hear a big crack as a branch is ripped down. That gray trunk snaking up into a tree is all I can see of Bailey, but the sound is familiar and unmistakable.

On the ground, the face of the phone lights up. It begins to buzz, the vibrations making it dance a slow crawl through the dirt. I take a step back and stare as if it was a rattlesnake. *Shit.* M.C. Smith has star-69'd me.

I can hear my heartbeat in my ears. Clearly, my nerves are not steely enough to be a spy. Burner phone, I remind myself. No way to trace it to me. At least I did *that* right.

After the phone goes silent, I pick it up, brush the dirt off on my shorts, and put it back into my pocket. There's no message, but I still feel uneasy.

I'm pretty sure I've heard M.C. Smith's voice before.

Twenty-Seven

Every wacko escape scenario that I envision for my brother ends with the police or SeaStone Security chasing us down. For days, I come up with dozens of new ridiculous plans. Days in which Wordage teaches me *Equinoctial—happening near the time of an equinox, Contingency—a possible future event that cannot be predicted with certainty, Subterfuge—deceit used to achieve a goal,* and *Ironic—happening the opposite way of expected; usually amusing.* Days in which Jaime Rodriguez is judged and convicted and scheduled to be locked up till his twenty-first birthday in a secure facility for juvenile offenders. Days in which M.C. Smith calls my burner phone twice.

The first time she leaves a voice message: "Who are you?"

The second time, it's a text: *What do you want?*

I can't stand to keep the burner in the house with me. It's hidden in the barn between bales of hay. I pull it out each evening, afraid the next message will be *We're coming to get you.* But the messages simply stop. It feels like M.C. Smith and I are both holding our breath.

God only knows what Phineas Pederson is doing. If he's

the one behind the drones, he probably fears that I know about SeaStone Security, since the last photos sent from the drone that Bailey destroyed were of me and my elephant at WildRun. But he has no way to know whether or not I tracked down the drone's owner, unless he has a contact at UAV4U. This feels like a game of *I Know That You Know That I Know*, but without much actual knowledge on my part. It would be sadly *ironic* but not at all amusing if I get killed because Pederson thinks I know something I don't.

At home, Emilio continues to heal physically, but he still has nightmares, and he continues to act more affectionate toward Sabrina than he does toward me, which may be understandable, but still hurts.

I work long hours at the zoo to make up for my time in Colorado and New Mexico. I'm glad for the physical labor, because my mind is lost in a mental fogbank, trying to think of what I can possibly do to rescue Aaron, about whether he's criminally insane, and about whether I can live with myself if I simply leave my brother where he is. Every scenario seems hopeless.

Then it finally occurs to me that the whole problem is that Aaron and I are alive when *they* don't want us to be.

Aaron needs to fake his own death, I text to Bash.

Hours later, I'm in the aviary, raking up the husks and feathers that accumulate around the feeders, and scrubbing the icky bird drippings off the seed and water basins, when Bash calls.

The zoo is closed. I'm alone except for my feathered friends, and it's not like a leopard could jump me in an aviary when I'm not paying attention, so I pull out my cell.

"It could work." That's the first thing Bash says to me.

"Care to elaborate?"

"Your suicide idea. I've been asking questions, and it's really all about the paperwork, the record-keeping. You of all people should know this. I think that's how we can move your brother."

I glance around the aviary to be sure nobody is listening. An arm's length away sits a scarlet macaw, staring at my hand. I know that bird is plotting to grab either my phone or my ring, so I turn my back to him. Never trust a parrot; they are worse than dogs when it comes to stealing things they want to play with.

"I'm listening," I murmur softly.

"Jaime will be transported and checked into the juvie jail tomorrow as scheduled. It's Esperanza Juvenile Correctional Facility outside of Albuquerque."

I groan. "How does *that* help?"

"Esperanza, despite the hopeful name, is famous for suspicious deaths among its inmates. It's the perfect place for your brother to commit suicide."

"*What?*" I yelp. Behind me, one of the parrots echoes my exclamation. "I said *fake* his death."

"It will be suicide only on paper, Tarzan."

"There's one big problem, Bash. Aaron thinks he's Jaime; he's not going to cooperate."

"I get that. We'll have to drug him and take his body away. And then we'll have Jaime immediately cremated in yet another bureaucratic slip-up."

Bash and I are on the same wavelength now. If Jaime Ramirez is dead, the authorities are finished with him. His guardian Clementine Smith would be, too. "How can we fake his death?"

He chuckles. "Never underestimate how many managers want to please the Prez. I might have let Bio-Pop's name slip once or twice."

A spark of hope ignites in my chest. "Aren't you putting yourself at risk?"

His voice drops into a lower register. "Agent Willerbee, Secret Service, requests your assistance on behalf of President T.L. Garrison."

Ah, *subterfuge*—that is a vocabulary word I truly identify with. "Very clever. Everyone thinks Jaime Ramirez offed himself in juvie. How do we get him here? How long do you think it'll take for the drugs to wear off?"

It's scary to think I will be taking care of a violent thirteen-year-old along with my injured soldier used-to-be boyfriend. I don't know when I'm going to work. Or sleep.

A tiny purple hummingbird zips past my shoulder to the nectar feeder in the corner, where it gets into a hover-match with a green one who wants total ownership of the sugar water there.

"Ever heard of the Bayview Institute for Healing?" he asks.

"No."

"It's about eighteen miles from your house."

"Good to know. So what?"

"It's a super-secret place where celebrities and politicians go to get un-drug-addicted and de-programmed and such."

My heart lifts. Bayview sounds like exactly the sort of place Aaron needs. If he's off the drugs and not zombied into some alternate universe, he might get back to reality. Then, at the thought of reality, I slam back down to earth. "This super-secret place is probably super-expensive, too, isn't it?"

"*Naturalmente*. But no worries, T.L. Garrison is paying the bill, via an offshore bank account."

I'm quiet for a minute, thinking about how much I owe Sebastian Callendro and how risky this all is and trying not to speculate about why our president has an offshore bank account. A flutter of wings overhead alerts me to the small flock of bee eaters gathering in their favorite tree for the night. It's growing dark and I need to finish up and get on my way home.

"Hey, there have to be *some* benefits to being The President's Bastard Son," he says into the conversation void.

"What do I need to do?"

"Absolutely nothing."

My vision of leading a heroic rescue evaporates. "But—"

"It would be too dangerous for both you and Aaron. Don't try to contact your brother in any way. You can't afford to be connected with Jaime Ramirez. He can't be connected to you or your part of the country, either."

He's right, of course. If *they* learn I've found Aaron, it could be a death sentence for both of us. Disappointment and relief wrestle with each other in my head, and somehow emerge as gratitude. This gift is too big to grasp. "I can never thank you enough, Bash."

"It would be too suspicious to make it happen right away, and you already have thanked me. How else could a homely guy like me break into a *telenovela*?"

We laugh. He says he'll call me when it's time, probably in three to four weeks. Such a long, long time to wait. I'll have to run extra laps around my track to wear myself out enough to sleep at night. I slide my phone back into my pocket.

Then it's just me and the birds. They're quiet, settled in for the night. The singing is all inside my heart.

Twenty-Eight

I feel like a mouse forced to play a waiting game with all the neighborhood cats. During the day, I wait for news about Aaron. When I commute by bike, I wait to be hit by a car. At night, I sleep lightly, waiting for another drone attack. I have a terrible fear that I will wake up in the middle of the night to find a helicopter in the front yard, a dead elephant in the back, and armed invaders inside the house.

I'm not the only one waiting in this house, though. Emilio's on edge, too, getting more and more anxious as his hearing approaches. He's still plagued by nightmares; I hear the growls and whimpers that come from his room after he goes to bed. I've seen him wander out into the yard more than once in the middle of the night.

Poor Sabrina doesn't know how to act around either of us these days.

The night before Emilio's hearing, a noise wakes me up at three a.m. As I sit up in bed, I hear the sound of a man's low, threatening voice. "...kill you."

A woman whimpers in response.

I'm up in a flash, grabbing the baseball bat I keep under

my bed. All is quiet in the living room. Was I dreaming?

"No! Stop!"

Sabrina.

I dash to her room, pausing just outside to sneak a quick look around the doorway.

A man is on top of her in her bed, his hands around her neck. At first, I think it's one of the ninjas from my past, but then I recognize the battered face, even though his lips are curled in a sneer I've never seen before.

"Emilio!" I rush toward him.

I'm standing on his blind side, so he has to twist his head around to see me. His expression is flat, as if he doesn't know me. "I'll have to kill you, too," he snarls, then tightens his hands around my housemate's throat.

"Emilio!" I slap him hard on the shoulder. "Emilio!"

He laughs and squeezes harder. Sabrina shoves her hands against his chest, trying to push him away, but he's sitting on top of her. Even in the dim light from her bedroom window, I can see that her face is turning dark.

"Emilio!" I slap him again, this time on the back of his head. He makes a growling sound, but doesn't let up. "Emilio!"

Swatting him with the bat might kill him. For a second, I wonder if I can get to the tranquilizer gun, load it, and dart him before he kills Sabrina. No way, I decide. She might be dying right now.

I thrust the bat beneath Emilio's chin, climb onto the bed behind him, reach around and grab the end of the bat on the other side of his head, and pull back with all my might, pressing the solid wood against his throat.

He grunts and rears up, tossing us both to the floor. The

impact knocks the breath out of me, but I manage to stay conscious. Now he's lying on top of me. I can't let go of the bat.

"Emilio!" I yell in his ear. "Shadow! You're home! You're in the U.S.!"

He struggles against me, kicking, his hands on the bat next to mine as he tries to pull it out of my hands.

"Shadow! You're home! It's Tana!"

Emilio may still be recuperating, but he's been lifting weights and he's stronger than I am. My palms are getting sweaty, his weight is pressing me down so I can hardly breathe, and I wonder how long I can hang on. He pulls his head forward, and then abruptly snaps it back, whacking my nose with his skull and thumping my head into the plank floor. My vision goes white.

"Emilio! Marisela! Kiki! Kai!" I yell, racking my brains for anything that bring him back to reality. "Emilio! Michoacán! The monarchs!" My face is throbbing; my hands are slipping. I'm running out of strength, words, and breath. "Shadow!"

Abruptly, his body goes slack on top of mine. "Shadow?" When I relax my grip, I hear him groan. I let go of the bat, and it falls to the floor with a clunk and rolls a few feet away. He quickly rolls off me and scuttles to the wall, where he crouches on the floor, hunched over, his face in his hands.

Sabrina sits up against the wall behind her bed, rubbing her throat, her eyes wide with shock.

"You okay?" I ask.

She nods slowly, staring at Emilio in horror.

"He wasn't himself. It's PTSD," I tell her. "It's like sleepwalking, only worse."

She doesn't respond. I don't blame her. No matter the

cause, it's terrifying to see someone suddenly become violent. It must be horrific to wake from sleep with a friend's hands around your throat.

I stand up, walk over to Emilio, and tug on his arm. "Shadow. Let's go."

He looks up. Even in the dim light, I can see the tracks of tears on both his cheeks. He's not wearing an eye patch. His right eye socket contains an ugly implant thing while he waits for his matching artificial eye to be completed, but his tear ducts still work on that side. When I hold out my hand, he takes it, and slowly rises from the floor. I lead him to the living room. We both collapse onto the sofa.

Despite my wish for a regular gun that might take down a drone, it's a damn good thing we don't have one in this house. Tonight, one or more of us would probably be dead.

"I thought..." he begins. "They had me. And they'd already killed that other guy. And I had the chance to escape." He shakes his head and then runs his fingers through his hair. It's long enough now that this makes it stand on end. "Oh God, Tana. I am as bad as they are."

I wrap my arms around him. He crumples into my embrace, his face against my neck. "It's post traumatic stress, Shadow. It's not your fault."

"Oh God. I could have killed Sabrina. I could have killed you."

"You didn't."

"I should be locked up. I'm a monster." He sobs into my neck for a minute.

It's a weird feeling for me. I was the one who cried on his shoulder so many times when we lived together at Marisela's. "Remember all the bad dreams I used to have? Remember how

I'd wake up screaming?"

He sits back and rubs his hands over his face.

"That's PTSD," I tell him. "I'm sure you know other soldiers who have it. I know all about it, too. Sudden flashback nightmares. Daymares, too."

"Because of what happened to your parents," he murmurs quietly.

"Yes." He doesn't know the full story, but he knows they both died. "You've lived through horrible things, too."

"Over there, you see bombs and guns everywhere," he tells me. "Bodies lying in the streets. You have to study everyone, all the time, even the kids, to try and figure out if they need your help or if they're going to try to kill you. Here, moms study cereal boxes in the stores, trying to figure out if gluten is dangerous. Sometimes I don't know what's real anymore."

I know exactly what he means. "It's an insane world."

"What am I going to do?" he moans.

"Talk to someone who can help you deal with it?"

"Oh, God." He hides his face in his hands for a minute, and then he takes a deep breath, stands up, and limps to Sabrina's room. I hear him apologizing in a low voice, asking for forgiveness. I don't hear what she replies, if anything.

This makes me think about my brother. His PTSD must be even worse than mine. I need to apologize to Aaron for leaving him with the ninjas, for everything that's happened to him since. I don't see how I can ever make things up to him, but I have to try.

Outside the window, I see a flash of movement. When I look out, I see only dark sky, the garden fence, the barn and the silhouettes of trees in the distance. Did I only imagine a drone? Did I see an owl flying past? I stretch out on the couch to keep an eye on the window.

Shadow comes back, and climbs onto the couch, slipping behind me to share my pillow. "Tana," he murmurs in my ear. "I might not come back from my hearing tomorrow."

"What? Why?"

"If they decide to court-martial me, I'll end up in prison. Or maybe in Mexico."

Marisela and Emilio probably assumed everyone was safer if I didn't know they were illegal. I totally get that. Now Emilio is telling me for sure that he's not a U.S. citizen.

"You'll come back." How could the military look at Emilio and the evidence of his capture and torture and still find him guilty of a crime? I wish I could be there to support him, but no civilians are allowed.

"If I don't, explain to Sabrina for me, okay?"

"I won't have to," I tell him. "You'll be back."

He persists, "But if the worst happens?"

"I'll tell her. And I'll come visit you wherever you end up." I feel like maybe I should promise to bring Sabrina, too, but I don't.

Throwing an arm over me, he pulls me to him, spooning. "I don't deserve you, Tana," he murmurs in my ear.

He's right. He doesn't deserve to be saddled with my problems on top of his.

Soon I hear gentle snoring. I close my eyes, too, and dream of butterflies dripping from trees in a place where the skies are filled with drones.

Twenty-Nine

The next day, I am distracted by the thought of Emilio's hearing, but I dutifully troll the internet for news on Jaime Ramirez like I've done every day since I found my brother. Still, it still comes as a shock when I read about his suicide in the juvenile facility where he was locked up. The story doesn't make the television news or a nationwide newspaper. Juvenile psychos are apparently too common to be newsworthy these days unless they're spraying bullets into a crowd.

The online article includes a picture of my brother: a booking photo, with height measurements behind him and an ID card in front. He looks stunned, and maybe slightly sleepy and scared. You can see the little boy behind the criminal get-up. I have to tell myself over and over again that the suicide is a fake, that Bash planned and arranged it, that Aaron Robinson is alive, that I'm only looking at the last photo of Jaime Ramirez, who was never real to begin with. Still, it makes me cry to read about the young boy who took his own life and then was cremated without even a memorial service to commemorate him.

On the day of Jaime's "suicide," my burner phone records a text message from M.C. Smith: *What kind of game are you playing?*

I almost fainted when I read that. I presume the juvie jail called her after Jaime's "death." But there's no way to tell if she sent that text before or after she found out about her ward dying in New Mexico.

It takes all my willpower not to call Bash, but he's right, we shouldn't have any contact at the time of Ramirez's death in case *they* are listening.

I wonder if M.C. Smith *believes* that Jaime Ramirez is dead. I wonder if she feels relieved that he's gone. If she's involved in the cover-up of my parents' deaths, it seems like she'd be glad to have that complication removed from her life.

Emilio comes home from his hearing, subdued but relieved. He's been demoted to Private First Class for leaving the base without permission, but at least the military has decided that he will be allowed to complete his term of service. His new orders, along with his artificial eye, will arrive in a few days. He says he doesn't want a celebration, but Sabrina and I splurge for pizza anyway, and he smiles as he shares a long telephone conversation in Spanish with Marisela and Kai and Kiki. It's a big load off Emilio's shoulders, and mine, too. I'm not sure what Sabrina thinks about any of this.

Two days later, I get a text message telling me that Ford Ryan will arrive at three p.m. on Tuesday at the Bayview Institute. It's addressed to Gigi Ryan. The message vanishes as soon as I close it on my phone.

I fake a dentist appointment to get off work early, so I'm there when a white van pulls up and two men march Aaron into the Institute. He stumbles between them; they have to hold him up. Clearly, he's drugged into a stupor.

The Bayview coordinator tells me that I won't be allowed to see or communicate with Ford in any way for thirty days, during which he will be weaned off all drugs and undergoing intense therapy to learn how to remain drug-free. The strange tone they use as they say *Ford* and *Mizz Ryan* makes me aware that they understand that these are cover names, for discretion's sake. I wonder what they will call Aaron while he's here and if he'll ever be able to work out who he really is. He has been drugged and brainwashed for nearly a third of his life.

Before they lead him away, I put my arms around my brother and rest my cheek against his forehead. He feels thin. His whole body is quivering. He lost his earring somewhere along the way, and his whiskers are gone, too, making him look and feel younger. He sways slightly in my embrace, and judging by his smell, he hasn't bathed for days.

This could have been me, drugged, brainwashed and imprisoned, had I not escaped my parents' killers.

"Aaron," I breathe in his ear. "I'm your sister, Amelia. I love you, Aaron. I will be back. Get well. I am Amelia, and I will be back."

He says nothing, just stares at me, his gaze glassy and unfocused. As they escort him away, he glances over his shoulder at me with a confused and heartbreakingly familiar expression. Then heavy sliding glass doors glide shut between us, locking him away from me again.

As the doors close behind him, I realize that today my brother's eyes look exactly like those of Joker, our Labrador

Retriever, as he was dragged away from me on the boardwalk in Bellingham.

Thirty days is a long time to wait. At the zoo, the female tiger gives birth to three adorable cubs. Babies are always a mixed blessing there, because although the public loves them, all the workers know that as soon as they are grown, they will be sold or traded to other zoos.

Emilio helps me build some hurdles and a climbing obstacle for my training course. If he has more PTSD attacks, he somehow manages to keep them to himself, or maybe he shares them with this local group of vets the VA put him in touch with. His artificial eye finally arrives, and it's a perfect match, so close that you'd never guess unless you pay close attention to how it doesn't move quite like a real eye would. He still limps, but the military doctors haven't scheduled him for foot surgery yet. The Army makes him go through a battery of aptitude tests, and then he gets his orders to report to California for training as a helicopter maintenance technician.

When the docs at Bayview Institute finally let me see Aaron, they tell me that he was so full of drugs, it's a miracle that he's still alive. I sense that they are curious about where and how he got this odd mix of medications, but they are paid for discretion and don't ask. I certainly don't volunteer the few clues I have.

To my dismay, I discover that although he's now drug-free, Aaron is hardly back to normal. Some days I wonder if I really rescued him. At first, my brother acts totally lost. He rages at me, calling me Bitch and insisting that his name is Jaime and that his sister died in a car wreck, sticking to the script that has been drilled into his head.

But I stick to mine, too, although it scares me to say the truth out loud to an unstable boy, even if our conversations take place behind closed doors. I tell him over and over again about Joker and Mrs. Talston and Mom and Dad and the house with the woven fence in Bellingham. I remind him about being the Straight A's and the way I called him Spot and he called me Stick when we were mad at each other. I recall a lot of silly pranks we pulled as kids.

My guilt is so deep that some days it feels like I'm down in that Mariana Trench. Although mine has been a hard life, I've been growing up the last four years, learning to be hardworking, resourceful, and independent. My brother has been locked up and brainwashed into psychosis. He alternates between swaggering like a street thug and wanting to be comforted like a small child. And the docs tell me that he is, emotionally and intellectually, around nine or ten, stuck at the age his mind was lost to drugs. The situation is complicated by the fact that his thirteen-year-old body is flooded with the hormones of puberty.

This all terrifies me. I can't be a mother to Aaron; I can't raise a nine-year-old or even a thirteen-year-old. What was I thinking? I still want my own mother. The only person I can truly share my fears with is Sebastian. I run up my cell bill by calling him almost every day.

Sabrina and Emilio are naturally curious about where I go on my bike after work. I finally decide to tell them a partial truth: my recently orphaned cousin Aaron is a recovering addict in this facility. Sabrina is sympathetic. Shadow seems suspicious about this cousin I've never mentioned before. But then he has to report for his new job in California, so he doesn't get the chance to meet Aaron. On the day he flies out, he gives roses to both me and Sabrina and kisses us both, although he does let his lips linger on mine while he only kisses her cheek. I'm not sure if that means he's keeping his options open or dismissing both me and my housemate.

I grab his sleeve before he turns to go. "Videochat soon?"

"Of course." He flashes a smile first at me, and then winks at Sabrina before he walks out to the taxi that's waiting for him.

Sabrina and I are awkward with each other for a couple of days before we find our friendship rhythm again. The house seems a bit empty without our soldier, but the atmosphere seems lighter, too.

The day after Shadow leaves, instead of calling me Bitch, Aaron leans close and murmurs, "I know you are real, Amelia."

I throw my arms around him. "Welcome back, Aaron."

He pulls away. "I thought my name was Ford now."

At first I think he's kidding, but I see in his eyes that he's genuinely confused. He's been told he was Jaime Ramirez for the last four years in New Mexico, and then presto, he's Ford Ryan here in the Institute, and now I'm working hard to convince him he's still Aaron Robinson.

"We are pretending, Aaron. It's like we're undercover. Your new code name is Ford Ryan, and for here, mine is Gigi Ryan, but outside of here, everyone thinks I'm Tanzania Grey." I hug him. "Only you know the truth, that I'm Amelia and you're Aaron."

"How'd we end up like this?"

Tears stream down my face, and I can only shake my head. "We'll figure it out together."

A shadow of horror clouds his eyes. "Mom? Dad?"

Jeez, this hurts. "Dead."

"That was real?"

I nod sadly.

He leans forward, his face anguished. "Did you *see* them? Did you *touch* them? Are you sure?"

Suddenly I'm *not* so sure, and I have to struggle to stay present in this room with my brother. The dark pools on the carpet surrounding their bodies. So much blood. They weren't moving. If they survived, why haven't they ever looked for us? No, they have to be dead.

I tell him, "I saw them, Aaron. They're dead."

"I remember...ninjas." His eyes search mine, daring me to tell him he's crazy.

I nod my head. "Me, too. That's why we have to use our fake names. We are hiding from the ninjas. Do you know who they were?"

"Everyone said I dreamed them."

"Do you know M.C. Smith from Canada? Clementine Smith? She was listed as your guardian."

A shadow passes over his face, but he shakes his head. "I just woke up there, at Todos Santos. Nobody ever came to visit."

That makes my heart hurt. I press my lips together and swallow hard to dislodge the constriction that threatens to close off my throat. I found Marisela and her family; Aaron had nobody who cared about him. He stares at the slippers on his feet as he reaches up to rub his neck. The gesture reminds me of the dark marks I saw on the attacker's neck the night of the murders and makes me think he may be repressing an ugly memory.

"I'm so sorry, Aaron." I put my hand on his arm, but he flinches, so I lay it back in my lap again. "I hope you found some friends there."

He snorts. "Isaiah and Trex were all right; the others..." His voice trails off and he shrugs and sighs and shakes his head again.

"Why did you stab those people?"

Aaron looks up at me, a slight frown crinkling his brow. "I had to."

He sounds as though the reason should be self-evident, as though stabbing people is normal behavior for a thirteen-year-old boy. I'm talking to Jaime again. I'm not sure I should quiz my brother about his life during the last four years any more right now.

I probably should find a trained psychologist to help him. But for that to truly help, we'd both have to reveal the truth about where we came from. Where would that lead? I don't know any psychiatrist who would believe us and protect our secrets. They could easily send Aaron into the foster care system, or lock him away again. Bash and the others who helped fake Aaron's death could be charged with all sorts of crimes. I could, too.

I have an uninvited and unsettling vision of Bailey rocking from side to side as he waits for me outside the gates of a prison.

Aaron is still staring at me as if trying to penetrate my brain. "Where have you been?"

A wave of guilt washes over me. I remind myself that I didn't know what happened to my brother. He's with me now only because I was lucky enough to see a few seconds of a newscast. I take a deep breath. "I've been looking for you, Aaron. We have a lot to talk about, a lot to catch up on. But it's dangerous. Don't talk to anyone else about all this, okay?"

He squints his eyes and scrutinizes me intently. I worry that he's trying to decide if I'm real, or if I'm just a new liar sent to brainwash him yet again.

"I'm going to take you home with me," I tell him.

He looks as if he's afraid to believe me. "When?"

"Soon." I have to make sure his current state of mind is going to stick.

Thirty

y cousin, Aaron Grey. That's how I introduce my brother to everyone. I think he needs to be called by his real first name, but Aaron Robinson still seems too risky.

So now Aaron lives in what used to be Emilio's room. Telling Sabrina that my cousin attempted suicide in the past, I hide the tranquilizer gun and my baseball bat. Following Marisela's guidance, I enrolled my brother in the school down the road, telling the principal there that he's recovering from a brain injury.

Aaron was mortified that his test scores qualified him only for fifth grade. He reverted to Jaime Ramirez when he found out.

"I'm not stupid!" he snarled. Cursing, he stamped around the house, slamming drawers, looking for a weapon. I was glad I'd locked up the kitchen knives. Finally he banged open the front door and ran outside, picked up a fallen branch and whacked the maple over and over again until the branch shattered into pieces. Sabrina was at work; I'm glad she didn't witness that temper tantrum.

Aaron was always a geek as a little boy. I remind him that he's still smart and just needs to catch up. Now he's so determined to be a straight A again that he spends hours each day reading and working through online education programs on my computer. He also runs on my track, and vows that one day he'll be able not only to keep up with me, but to beat me.

Next month will bring Aaron's fourteenth birthday. With Clark and Kent's help, I've set up a tablet computer. I know my brother will love the night sky app that identifies all the stars and planets. I wanted some games for him, too. "Nothing violent," I told the Nilsen brothers. "Nothing with shooting or killing of any kind."

When I said that, Kent looked at Clark, and they both frowned. Apparently my request limited the game choice substantially. But the Nilsens finally came up with a world building game and a treasure-seeking quest, and an uber-fun flying simulation where the user can pilot anything from a glider to a spaceship.

Aaron helps take care of the cats, the goats, and Bailey, although I have to nag him to shovel out the barn. We are getting to know each other again, and I hope that in time he'll be able to contribute a few clues to help solve our mutual mystery. When he's strong enough, I'll show him those photos that Mom and Dad left behind and see what happens. Right now, I'm afraid he'd shatter.

One evening, Sabrina comes to me in the kitchen as I explore the refrigerator, trying to come up with something relatively nutritious to nuke. Aaron's out in the barn.

"Tana?"

I pull my head of the fridge. "Yeah?"

Her expression is sober. She twists her hands together nervously. "About our living situation here."

Uh-oh. My heart sinks. Sabrina wants to leave and I don't blame her, but I so don't want her to go and—

"Do you want me to move out?" Her gaze darts away from my face, and then back.

It takes me a second to process the words. "What?"

"Well, first there was me and Emilio, and I'm sorry about that, whatever that was..."

"Nothing to be sorry about," I say. I don't know what that was, either.

"...and now you have Aaron."

I'm speechless for a couple of seconds.

Tears glint in her eyes. "Did I ever tell you I had a younger sister?"

"No." I brush a finger across my lip, afraid of what's coming. "What happened?"

She looks at the floor. "My mom always said she wandered off. They found her out in a field in January. She was frozen. She was three years old."

Omigod. I shut the refrigerator door and wrap my arms around my housemate.

I feel my friend's breath on my ear as she murmurs, "So I know how important family is. I understand if you want me to go."

I pull away so I can look her in the eye. "Never, Sabrina. You *are* family to me."

"Oh, thank God." She smiles through her tears.

That's when I know I have to tell her. I owe her the truth.

So I explain the whole sordid tale of the Robinsons. It's terrifying to tell my story, but it's also a relief. Now two people know who I really am. When I'm through explaining the last four years of my life and how everyone in this house could be in danger of dying at any second, I know she's going to tell me that now she's definitely moving out.

Instead, she simply says, "I get it, Tana."

Then she takes my hand for a minute and grips it hard in sister solidarity. "I have a favor to ask," she says.

"Yes?"

"You know how you told me that those college girls in Bellingham used a lot of red cushions to disguise their cheapo furniture?"

"Yeah?"

"Can I make a bunch of blue pillows for our place?"

I am so relieved. "That would be wonderful, Sabrina." I give her another hug.

Aaron comes in at that moment. We decide we can make homemade pizza out of leftover flatbread and cheese and veggies in the fridge.

My brother often comes with me when I venture out under the stars, amazed that he is allowed to wander around the property even after dark. It's sad to think that like Bailey, Aaron lived in strict confinement before coming to WildRun.

My elephant immediately accepted my brother. When Bailey drapes his trunk over Aaron's shoulder tonight, I see my brother's smile in the dark as he says, "This is so weird."

Yes, it is. I look up at the soft night sky, a mix of high thin clouds and stars. Tonight I am grateful that I found Aaron. I am thankful to Sebastian Callendro for giving me back my brother.

"I want to be up there." My brother's voice is wistful as he studies the heavens. "Flying."

"I know what you mean." I copied the flying simulator app I got for Aaron onto my computer, too. Maybe when we're both expert pilots, we'll get a drone of our own. I'd like to see Pederson's face when he notices a drone hovering outside *his* window. But that would mean going back to Bellingham, and that might start the cat and mouse game all over again.

No drones have appeared for six weeks now. I've received no more emails from P.A. Patterson and no more messages from M.C. Smith. I choose to believe these are good omens. Just having Aaron with me is enough for the moment.

When I turn to go back in, my brother hesitates. "Can I stay out here for a little while?"

"Sure," I say, although I'm always worried that he might run off when left on his own. Or that a stray bullet from the woods or from a drone flying overhead might strike him down. I'd like to prepare for every *contingency*, but I know that's impossible. These things could happen at any time, and staying together won't stop them. I might be my brother's keeper now, but I won't be his captor.

When I go inside the house, everything's quiet. The lights are turned out and Sabrina's already asleep, her bedroom door closed. I stand behind the dark living room window and watch the boy and elephant side by side under the stars. The scene causes a mix of confusing emotions in my chest that is physically painful.

I am glad that Aaron can see stars again instead of an institutional ceiling over his head. Having my brother back brings me happiness, but also *trepidation—a fear that something might happen*. When I was alone, I had nothing to lose. Now I have Bailey *and* Aaron.

My cell chirps and buzzes in my back pocket. It will be Bash adding something he forgot to say when we talked this afternoon, or maybe Shadow answering the voicemail I left him earlier. But both my guesses are wrong: it's a message forwarded to Tanzania Grey from Dark Horse Networks. I don't think Clark and Kent ever sleep.

There's no text, just a picture. It's a photo, taken about five years ago at the annual QTL Family Picnic in Bellingham. I'm holding out an egg on a spoon to Aaron. I am totally focused on the egg; Aaron is grinning at the camera. I remember this. Mom and Dad insisted I participate in what I thought was a stupid pass-the-egg relay race with the other kids.

What the hell? There's no sender ID.

I quickly text the guys at Dark Horse: *Who sent this?*

The response from Kent seems to take forever to come back: *Arrived via dark net. Untraceable. From an old friend? Stalker?*

Don't know, I text back.

U OK?

Don't worry. I save the message even though I really don't want to, and shove my phone back into my pocket.

Although it's a warm evening, chills radiate down my backbone. My brain replays the vision of Pederson taking my photo at Maxine's house, then the moment during our river rescue when his face morphs from homicidal to helpful only after he notices the drone filming overhead.

I try to imagine all sorts of innocuous meanings behind that photo, but my brain keeps circling back to the only message that makes sense: *We know who you are.*

I want to run screaming into the night, but no place seems safe any longer, and I need to guard Aaron and Bailey, still outside in the moonlight playfully taking turns shoving each other. By the time my brother comes back inside, I've managed to control my shivers enough that he doesn't notice.

Aaron is wearing a cat draped over his shoulder. He's in the habit of taking the tabby to bed with him. Spying me at the window, he walks to my side, padding quietly through the dark house. Then he surprises me by taking my hand like he's still a little boy instead of nearly as tall as I am.

His expression is troubled. He and the cat gaze earnestly at my face as he asks, "We're going to get them, aren't we, Amelia?"

It would be easier to be the big sister and tell Aaron, "No. It's too dangerous. They're like rattlesnakes. If we leave *them* alone, odds are they'll leave *us* alone."

But I don't believe that. I started this by going back to Bellingham for Ski to Sea. Now that I've opened that door, I don't know how to shut it. Revealing what really happened is the only way Aaron and I can live the lives we were meant to have. I owe it to my parents to discover the truth.

I still have no idea who *they* all are or what they might do, but whatever is coming, we Robinsons will face it together.

"Yes, Aaron," I promise my brother. "We will find a way."

If you've enjoyed RACE TO TRUTH,
please consider writing a review on
Amazon, Goodreads, and/or any other online book site.
Reviews help authors sell books!

On the next page is a preview of
RACE FOR JUSTICE,
the exciting conclusion of the *Run for Your Life* Trilogy.

Preview of
RACE FOR JUSTICE
Chapter 1

Just when I thought that the mysterious P.A. Patterson was gone for good, Dark Horse Networks forwards a message from him to me. It's an invitation to a multi-day endurance race that is being held for the very first time.

Brand new races are often disasters, with a lack of food or sleeping accommodations. I agree with my sponsors at Dark Horse Networks that it's best to avoid them until the second or third year, after the kinks have been worked out. But this time, Clark and Kent Nilsen seem eager for me to participate. *Africa is a huge untapped market for our services*, they write. And the race does sound exciting.

Extreme Africa Endurance

Challenge - Zimbabwe

An exciting 100 kilometer loop race that crosses rivers, canyons, and winds through hills, forests, and grasslands. All efforts will be made to keep racers safe, but wild animals such as hippos, lions, and leopards may be encountered.

Not to mention bandits and thugs who may lie in wait along the way. I've always wanted to participate in a race in Africa, but I heard such tales of violence from my parents that I'm reluctant to go there, even though Zimbabwe is my mother's birthplace.

But supposedly all the violence is over, and the country is on a new path to peace and prosperity, and the government is eager to attract tourists. There's a link to a website. When I go there, I am bombarded with advertising about how wonderful the accommodations for racers and media and fans will be— exotic game lodges and luxury hotels. There's even a video. I click the play button, and it flashes some views of the race course. Some lean dark-skinned runners gallop along the course to show how it will go. As the runners pass, the camera zooms in on enthusiastic fans clapping in the background, clustered together behind a barrier tape. In the crowd, one woman with curly chestnut hair pulled up into a ponytail has her eye pressed to the camera as she turns with the crowd to track the racers as they vanish into the distance. The crowd then disperses, leaving the photographer looking down at her camera. Then she raises her head and looks directly at me.

My heart nearly stops. My whole body throbs with the sudden ache of longing to throw myself into that woman's arms. I run the vid over and over again, stopping it every few frames to stare at her straight nose, her curly brown hair. When she looks up, she's smiling, just a little, like my mother did so often when she had a secret.

Could it be? I found my brother. Is it possible that my mother is alive?

Then the woman turns away, following the crowd, and I'm not sure. Her hair is longer and looks several shades lighter than my mom's. She's wearing some sort of khaki colored uniform that implies she's working there.

Mom?

I know it's too much to hope for. Videos can be altered. If *they* know I'm Amelia Robinson, then they know I have a personal connection to Africa. I could be eaten by a lion or ambushed by an armed mugger there, and die an easily explained, convenient death. This might be a setup by the ninja invaders I saw in my house four years ago. I know this might be a trap designed especially for me.

But I also know that my next race will be in Zimbabwe.

~ END OF PREVIEW ~

To be notified when *Race for Justice* is available,
sign up for Pam's mailing list at http://pamelabeason.com.

Books by Pamela Beason

The Neema Mysteries
THE ONLY WITNESS
THE ONLY CLUE
BOOK 3 – COMING SOON

The Summer "Sam" Westin Mysteries
ENDANGERED
BEAR BAIT
UNDERCURRENTS
BOOK 4 – COMING SOON

The Langston Green Romantic Suspense Series
SHAKEN
BOOK 2 – COMING SOON

The Run for Your Life Young Adult Suspense Trilogy
RACE WITH DANGER
RACE TO TRUTH
RACE FOR JUSTICE (coming 2017)

Nonfiction E-books
SO YOU WANT TO BE A PI?
SAVE YOUR MONEY, YOUR SANITY, AND OUR PLANET
TRADITIONAL VS INDIE PUBLISHING: WHAT TO EXPECT

Keep up with Pam on http://pamelabeason.com

About the Author

Pamela Beason is the author of the Summer "Sam" Westin Mysteries, the Neema Mysteries, and the Run for Your Life Young Adult Trilogy, as well as several romances and nonfiction books. She has received the Daphne du Maurier Award and two Chanticleer Book Reviews Grand Prizes for her writing, as well as an award from Library Journal and other romance and mystery awards. Pam lives in the Pacific Northwest, where she escapes into the wilderness to hike and kayak as often as she can.

http://pamelabeason.com

Acknowledgements

No writer can produce a good book alone. I owe a big THANK YOU to the following people, who read the drafts of this book and helped to improve the story: Jeff Angus, all-around genius and author of *Management by Baseball*; Sara Stamey, college writing instructor, freelance editor, and author of *The Ariadne Connection*; Robert L. Slater, teacher and author of *The Deserted Lands* novels and stories; Christine Myers, who I hope will soon publish the amazing stories she has written; and most of all, I owe my gratitude to Jeanine Clifford, who read and re-read my drafts with infinite patience and made many suggestions that helped shape *Race to Truth* into the book it is today.

www.ingramcontent.com/pod-product-compliance
Lightning Source LLC
Chambersburg PA
CBHW061018120726
47910CB00006B/1996